Readers love
ELLE BROWNLEE

Force Play

"If you are a fan of baseball you will LOVE, LOVE, LOVE this!"
—Open Skye Book Reviews

"This was a good story—I enjoyed the characters and loved cheering for the underdogs."
—Inked Rainbow Reviews

Emergency Contact

"The two together make a great couple. In fact, they are the perfect formula for a nice story that will have you rooting for their HEA all the way to the end."
—Hearts on Fire Reviews

"I did not want to leave these two. Even through their sometimes prickly, sometimes quiet stubbornness I felt an inexorable warmth and rightness radiating from them."
—It's About The Book

By ELLE BROWNLEE

Drawn
Emergency Contact
Force Play
One Holiday Ever After (Multi-Author Anthology)
One Night Ever After (Multi-Author Anthology)

Published by DREAMSPINNER PRESS
www.dreamspinnerpress.com

Drawn

ELLE BROWNLEE

DREAMSPINNER PRESS

Published by
DREAMSPINNER PRESS

5032 Capital Circle SW, Suite 2, PMB# 279, Tallahassee, FL 32305-7886 USA
www.dreamspinnerpress.com

Drawn
© 2016 Elle Brownlee.

Cover Art
© 2016 Brooke Albrecht.
http://brookalbrechtstudio.com
Cover content is for illustrative purposes only and any person depicted on the cover is a model.

ISBN: 978-1-63477-703-2
Digital ISBN: 978-1-63477-704-9
Library of Congress Control Number: 2016907091
Published October 2016
v. 1.0

Printed in the United States of America

This paper meets the requirements of
ANSI/NISO Z39.48-1992 (Permanence of Paper).

CHAPTER ONE

SEN WIPED away the funky sweat only New Orleans conjured—even in early spring—and studied the corkboard of his guiding signposts hung next to the door. Vintage postcards, a rumpled napkin, and two paw prints marked *Mardi* and *Gras* stamped on a paper truck-stop placemat.

"You brought me here," he said to them. His annoyance over the murky heat couldn't undo his fondness or conviction in them. He tapped the orange ball-tipped straight pin that secured the postcard depicting a famous corner in the French Quarter, and he sighed.

In two years no new signs had arrived to lead him elsewhere, though he waited for them. Two years represented an eternity in his life, and the lack of signs made him nervous, but he tried to be patient during the silence.

Sen made quick work of putting away the groceries he'd forced himself to get. He stuffed everything in the fridge, reusable bags and all, and then drank his requisite two glasses of water.

His mother had instilled the water ritual in Sen's family. She advocated hydration as the key to clarity and overall good health. Hungry? Start with water. Bored? Quench your thirst and focus returned. Headache? Always a dose of H2O before any meds. Since just running a quick errand in New Orleans stripped its fair share of everything from the body even on a cooler day, he had picked the habit back up.

Sen set the alarm on his phone and left it on the deep window sash overlooking the tangle of green vines obscuring any view, and shuffled to bed. With the deadline looming for a commissioned piece, he'd had a short nap some days before and then pushed around the clock to finish the painting. His eyes burned and his limbs were heavy, but the ache had its rewards—job done, deadline met, and a pleased customer—very satisfying things. Even better were getting paid and his plan to sleep past dinner the next day. Best of all he didn't hate the painting and cover it over with gesso halfway through. Every artist had their phases and struggles, but his creative block, as high and long as the Great Wall, made him wonder whether the universe knew his fate to be that of an artist-turned-barista, instead of the other way around.

Sen yawned. "At least I make good coffee."

Pulling multiple all-nighters wasn't too different from his norm, of late. He hadn't slept well the past several weeks, and work provided a welcome distraction from fatigue and remnants of strange dreams. If he couldn't sleep, he could get stuff done.

Sen kicked off his shoes, stepped on the cuff of his jeans, wriggled just so, and slipped them past his lean hips to slide to the floor. He stood teetering on his feet awhile, stop-started, and lurched forward again. The world pitched as he stumbled toward the bed. He could practically feel its cushy embrace. He had his T-shirt half-stripped and caught around his arms when the phone rang.

Sen closed his eyes and sighed. Then he shucked his arms free and crossed back into the kitchen area.

"What is it, Adriane?" he answered, voice thickening around a yawn.

"Oh my gosh, Sebastian! It's the middle of the day already. You should be up and moving," Adriane scolded, but sounded amused.

Sen scowled and read the clock over the faux fireplace opposite the kitchen. Twenty after ten.

"Adri, hello and good morning. And I am up and moving, unfortunately. But I'm about to remedy that by diving under the covers, so make it quick." He looked with longing at the cocoon of blankets waiting on his amazingly comfortable bed—the one true splurge he'd made in life—and batted aside any guilt the mundane, workaday world insisted he should feel.

It wasn't as though he stayed awake binge watching junk TV and was about to waste a whole day sleeping. The nature of the beast he fought had him keeping odd hours and odd jobs, and in between, with whatever stolen minutes he could cobble together, he painted. He was on the long end of a few all-nighters as he clawed ever closer to success as an artist who could actually make a living from painting alone.

"Hopefully that's negotiable." Adriane laughed. "Don't fall asleep yet."

"Hmph," Sen grumped. Adri calling instead of texting was a bad enough sign. She wanted something, and he probably wouldn't like it.

Adriane and Sen had been buddies almost since he arrived in New Orleans. They met through mutual friends who had since drifted away, but they'd stuck to each other like glue. Adriane liked to tease that they were a picture in ironic contrasts. Sen was a neat and tidy artist, while Adriane was a powderpuff explosion who happened to run a successful cleaning service. They made up for that contrast with his devotion to instinct and following his gut—he even chose donuts based on what serendipity and fate seemed to present—and her pragmatic, methodical approach to everything—including always getting the same donut, despite having thirty flavors to choose from, because she knew it was what she liked, so why mess with success.

"Sorry for interrupting your decline, sweetie, but this does work in my favor."

Sen scrubbed his eyes and yawned again. "Why does that not reassure me in any way?"

"It shouldn't. Your defenses are totally down, and I'm totally taking advantage." Adriane paused for effect. "I need a huge favor. Please."

"On a scale of one to Everest, how huge are we talking?"

"I'd say it's an eight. Think Mount Saint Helens. No, wait—Pompeii— because that's a disaster mountain."

"Those are volcanoes, not mountains." Sen leaned against the refrigerator and closed his eyes.

"Sure, whatever. Disaster mountain is my point." Adriane clucked her tongue. "One of my fairies has completely flaked. I haven't seen or heard from her in a few weeks, and I'm on the verge of losing all the clients she looks after. The best is today's and I literally can't afford to let it go. The gig is weekly, a full four hours, and the client is easy. I just need you to fill in today. A house— and not even too far away from you," she said as her drawl rose in pitch.

Adriane called her employees fairies, short for the name of her business. The Fairymaid Brigade made cleaning happen by magic. The name also sexed things up a bit. Everyone liked magic, and few people got excited about life's mundanities. Her business plan worked, her fairies were sought after, and the Brigade took off.

"What's the catch?" Sen dumped the grounds from a reusable coffee pod and started a fresh mug brewing. The urge to hang up on Adriane and crawl into bed was strong, but he'd do the job, and they both knew it.

"No catch. Promise. Well, maybe Ballard, but that's another matter entirely." Adriane snickered.

"Wait. What or who is a Ballard?" Even with his brain running full speed Sen wouldn't know what that meant.

"Never you mind—for now." Adri cleared her throat. "Aaaanyway, please, can you, Sen? Normally I'd just go do the job myself, but I'm swamped here, and I can't go into why, but you know. Dan can't even stand up yet, and Phoebe kept me up until two this morning, and I'm still manning the office like usual. I'm at my wit's end."

"I think you just went into it. And I'm feeling guiltier by the second, although I haven't done anything." Sen rubbed his forehead. "Didn't Dan start physical therapy and it was going well? And only last week, you were crowing about Phoebe sleeping through the night."

Adri grunted, and Phoebe's baby noises filled Sen's ear and then retreated.

"Sorry. Changed arms. Who knew newborns weighed a ton? And the doctors and nurses assured me you were only seven pounds, four ounces, sweetie." Adri made nonsense sounds at Phoebe and sighed. "Her being a good sleeper was last week. Each week is a whole new ballgame. Hell, each day is. And Dan threw his back out again—more or worse or something—when I went into labor and he had to heft me to the car. So he's back to square one on the injury rehab."

"Ah." Sen stifled a yawn. "I'm getting the picture."

"I haven't even gone into all the people I called before you to sub this house cleaning today. It's a difficult gig to staff, because it's midday Wednesdays, and most of my fairies take the evening work as a second job to make a little money on the side. But I know with your flexible schedule you can swing it." She lowered her voice as though to impart a great secret, and Sen could just see her eyes, all sweetly rounded but ready to shine with triumph. "You'll do such a good job, and I can just send you over without having to worry about a thing. I can trust you to save my butt and this gig. Please?"

"And that *please* makes three. Plus the guilt. And imagining Phoebe going hungry and Dan never being able to walk again. I'm sunk," he groaned. "And hold those dulcet tones for a real emergency, like asking me to watch Lucy and Desi Cockatiel when you're out of town again. I'll do it." Sen gulped down most of the coffee, set the maker to brew another cup, and went in search of clothes.

Adriane cheered. "You're a hero. Thank you, thank you. I so owe you after this one. But you're already late. Job starts at ten sharp."

"Already late?" Sen made outraged noises. "You're the one who called me at twenty after, lady." As he passed the dining table—a huge old oak door he rescued and put on reclaimed pipe fittings—he considered curling up on it and falling asleep while she listened, just to spite her. "You should be giving me a bonus, not demerits."

"I know, but I'm trying to keep you motivated. And I had to be sure my other fairy had definitely flaked for sure before I bothered you. Just get there fast as you can, work the rest of the four hours, and we'll call it even for today."

"Call it even. Nice." Sen stood in his studio/living room/dining room, thinking about the job, getting dressed, and wanting sleep all at once. "It's a good thing I like you, Adri, and that I'm doing this for the higher calling and pure motivation of protecting your baby's security. No wonder your worker went AWOL," he muttered. "Is there a uniform? Like deely boppers? A wand? Gauzy wings?"

Adriane snort-laughed. "Nah. Wear what you won't mind cleaning in without looking like you need to be tidied up yourself. You know. Do you still have that lapel pin I gave you? Do wear that."

Sen got back into the old blue jeans and a clean T-shirt and then poked through a shoebox in the bottom drawer of his dresser for the pin.

"Right, got it." The small square pin had the Fairymaid logo etched in pink on an iridescent background. Glittery cutout wings were attached to the top corners.

"Anything I need to know for being there? Dogs, cats, free-ranging lizards? Does this person have any quirks I should worry about—say, rooms not to go in or things they don't like touched?" Sen tried to drag his sandy hair into a ponytail one-handed, but the fine strands defied his attempts. He gave up, got socks and comfy sneakers, and then sagged onto the edge of his bed.

Since they met he had substituted for Adriane on occasion. It wasn't something either of them wanted to become full time and get in the way of Sen's painting or their friendship, but Adriane appreciated the reliable last-minute help, and Sen couldn't argue the extra money.

Too late he realized the mistake of making contact with the bed. The mattress called to him and dragged him down until he lay, phone tucked under his chin, so he could stretch both lanky arms wide and grip the hardwood floor with his toes. Adriane rustled some papers importantly. Probably a blank notebook, but it sounded good.

"No. I don't see anything in my write-up that'll jump out and bite you. There's a key code for all the doors, a note to clean out the fridge once a month and the bed linens once a week, but no special instructions."

"Mmm-hmm," Sen breathed as sleep beckoned.

"Hey," Adriane yelled. "Wake up, loser. You can't save my bacon if you fall asleep."

"Mmm, bacon." Sen lay another minute, let out an aggrieved sound, straightened to sit, and slapped his thighs. "Yeah, yeah. I'm up." He shook his head, put on his socks, and then willed himself to start moving. "This sounds easy enough. I can do this."

"Of course you can. I have every faith in your remarkable abilities. Don't even worry about deep cleaning. Showing up and sprinkling your particular magic will be enough."

He laughed. "Butter me up all you want, babe. I'm really fine with that." He stood, twisted back and forth until his spine cracked, and then went to pack a snack and a travel mug of coffee.

"If you can stay awake for it, I'll buy you dinner later, as an extra thanks. We can meet at Casa Burrito and have too many cheap and delicious margaritas. By then Phoebe should be down for the night, and Dan isn't going anywhere. And you can tell me about the renovations done to the house. Deal?"

"Deal. Provided that after I face-plant in my tamale platter, you don't take any pictures and post them to social media."

Sen packed essentials into his messenger bag and stuffed in a book and sketchpad on a whim. "Tell me the key codes and where I'm going, and I'll be on my way."

"I could just text them."

"I like pencil and paper. As you're aware."

Adriane read the info out twice as he scribbled in a notebook. He jammed it into the bag, grabbed his keys, and pushed outside. He kept his bike locked to the rickety landing outside his apartment door, and he fiddled with the lock to get the just-so twist until it surrendered and opened. Sen trotted down the stairs and wove around the trees and overgrowth to the alley that backed onto the listing carriage house he rented.

"If you don't show to Burrito tonight, I'll send out a rescue party. In case you've passed out in a swamp or something."

Sen straddled the bike and hitched his bag to rest on the small of his back. "I'm a better friend than you deserve, Adri."

"You really, really are. Thank you, peaches. Phoebe sends spit-bubble kisses, and if Dan weren't stoned on painkillers, he'd totally send spit-bubble kisses too. Or maybe since he is stoned he sends extra. Anyway, it should go fine, but let me know if it doesn't or if you have questions or—"

"I'll text when I'm there and inside. Okay?" Sen waited and then made a prompting noise.

She agreed, and he hung up and got moving.

He left the blocks with some houses still bearing Katrina-inflicted damage behind, and crossed into a better neighborhood of tony streets lined with mansions nestled among live oaks and huge lawns. Sen turned down a cross street and banked a sharp left, then a right, and slowed as he ticked off address numbers. Well into the neighborhood, he pulled in front of the house set back from the others at the end of a cul-de-sac.

Sen shivered. The stately and imposing house, cloaked in low-hanging tree branches, presented a dramatic picture. He wasn't intimidated, but reverberations of déjà vu rattled his mind and breath. He shivered again.

He biked down the winding driveway to find the side door he'd been told to use, and admired the place—all stately, imposing, and gorgeous. Sen had never lived in a real house and liked that fine, but he could imagine making a home there. The style and setting made it too modern to be an original plantation house, but old enough to have lots of character. Sen preferred worn edges and imperfect lines, and he hated plantation houses—too much bad history, too much patched-over sorrow, too many shadows powerful enough to creep in and steal the light.

Places steeped in terrible history had ghosts—impressions and energy if not poltergeists. He'd known that his whole life.

As if reading his thoughts, a rush of wind cleared the clouds from the sun, and warm pools of yellow dappled across the house and the live oaks with their shawls of Spanish moss.

The house was really a mansion, and New Orleans to its roots—a layer cake of Greek revival pillars and ornate wrought iron. The wraparound porch and balcony were verdigris and white. Along the front, windows big enough to walk through were aproned by charcoal-gray shutters, and a third floor had dormers and boxy eaves. Over the double main door was a terra-cotta frieze of fruit, acorns, and leaping stags, along with the name Greycote.

The side entrance was almost as grand as the rest of the house, serviced by a circle drive protected by a portico that ran around the turreted gable at the corner of the house. A three-tiered fountain bubbled at the foot of the gable, and a path led into a narrow garden bordering the drive. Sen stashed his bike, found the keypad, and opened the door. He ran his fingers over the carved side panels as he went, delighted at the continuation of the fruit and acorn theme—a doe and her yearlings posed in readiness to leap among the ivy, and a serene rabbit crouched in the bottom corner.

Sen had never been impressed by wealth, had no urge to pursue it, and considered showplaces boasting an obviously high price tag ostentatious and unwelcoming. But a quality imbued this house, and he couldn't quite pin it down—in the bigger yard, the considered details that sparked his imagination and tactile sensibilities, and an indefinable feeling of familiarity.

The door opened on silent hinges to an equally silent hallway. He hesitated before crossing the threshold, suddenly reluctant and awkward about just going in. A foolish thing to feel, all considered, but he did.

"Hello?" he called into the darkened house and waited a long moment. When no answer came, he took in a long breath and went inside. Prickles danced across his skin when both feet made contact with the floor, and he shook with a full-body tremor as the door closed behind him.

"Silly," he said to dismiss the strange feeling. It almost worked. He focused on the tangible reasons why he was there and began to explore.

A narrow hall ran the length of the house, split at the center by a curving double staircase that met upstairs at a balcony. He circuited the whole first floor to get his bearings. Each room he glanced into was well-appointed and gave the impression of being untouched. The only room that seemed lived-in was the study at the back of the house just off the side door, dominated by a teak desk parked in front of a fireplace and loaded with the latest and greatest in computers and gadgets.

The house kept going and going, from the two-story foyer and enormous cinnabar-colored sitting room on one side to the Wedgewood-blue parlor on the other. Of course there were more fireplaces, but the rooms were empty of anything soft or enlivening, like throw pillows, scattered rugs, art, or knickknacks. As he poked around, he found a full bathroom, a powder room, several closets, and then a mudroom and utility space complete with a third bathroom. The huge and rambling kitchen had vintage appeal and modern conveniences. Sen would bet his meager savings account the stainless steel industrial oven had never been used.

He pursed his lips, disappointed. The house, although beautiful, had no warmth or welcome, no art or personal pictures and objects. Someone had nodded at arrangements in a showroom and forgot about it all once they were delivered, including most of the vast rooms. The study offered a glimmer of hope, with crammed bookshelves and patterned parquet flooring that creaked underfoot, but there were still no pictures or softening details.

Sen wandered into the foyer, planted his feet, and wondered why he was there. He figured he could give the whole downstairs a white-glove test without cleaning anything, and it would pass with flying colors. How he would find four hours' worth of work was anyone's guess—unless he wasn't supposed to be there. Was it accidentally the wrong day? Or house?

"The key code worked," he said aloud to tamp down growing anxiety. "And this is definitely the correct address, and the house matches Adri's description. So." Sen sighed. "So it's fine, and I'll just find something to do and no big deal."

He jumped when his phone chose that moment to chirp, and answered Adri's text to say that yes, he'd found the place and gotten in without a problem. He didn't mention there was nothing to do or that he both loved the house and was super uncomfortable there. He didn't text to ask if he could just leave, because she'd freak and call, and he had no explanation beyond a feeling. She sent back a thumbs-up emoji.

"Okay, then, how about that fridge?" Sen pocketed his phone, left his bag on the island, and opened it.

He took in the bag of gourmet coffee beans, the partial case of craft beer, and the pathetic white Chinese takeout box with a wry huff.

"How very inspiring." He checked the freezer and shook his head at the neat stack of low-calorie frozen dinners, but the huge box of off-brand ice cream sandwiches made him smile.

At the back of the house, a narrow service staircase adjoined the kitchen and the utility room. He climbed the boxy spiral to the second floor's long hallway, line of doors, and light from the balcony that overlooked the foyer. All but two rooms were bare. One was obviously the owner's and the other a guest room—and Sen's imagination ran wild speculating.

The third floor wasn't just empty, it was unfinished. Drywall was up, and the walls were crisp, primer white, but there was no crown molding, no trim, and the fixtures were plain. Sen spun on his heel to trot back downstairs when something glittering caught his eye. He couldn't resist investigating. At the far end of the house, where the gable peaked, he found a beautiful space and breathed out an enchanted whistle. Windows wrapped the curved room, which was glazed with the morning sun, and looked down over gardens and green oak boughs and swaying moss.

Sen knew the room was why the house had been built and why Ballard had decided to buy it. It added to the mystery of the house and its owner. Ballard paid to have a pristine house cleaned, set up the downstairs like a magazine spread, and slept in an indifferent bedroom, but had brought a single deep chaise to this room. Maybe without fully understanding the draw to be up there.

Just the chair—plush and wide, and covered in a charming and unfashionable 70s-throwback plaid. There wasn't even a side table or a lamp, only the chaise plunked in the middle of the room and situated to have a good view out the windows. Sen sank into the chair and itched to sketch in the wonderful light and ambiance, so different from the indirect, watery light that made it into his apartment. It would be somewhere to concentrate and get lost in full absorption without being disturbed—rather than the bustle of a park or a coffee shop.

Something rustled when he crossed his feet and tucked them under the chaise. He dropped to a knee and investigated.

"Finally," Sen said, relieved to find a trace of imperfection. He reached for the object and pulled out a balled-up sock, soft and misshapen from being worn.

Sen's fingers itched, and his palm burned. Heat swept up his arms—through his veins—and circled his heart. The room darkened as if shutters had closed, and he jerked upright and stumbled to the windows. Quick-moving black clouds roiled across the sky and spread to obscure the sun and envelop everything in their path.

He choked on air so heavy it suffocated him and fumbled with opening a window. Thunder clapped, and a torrent of rain unleashed, pummeling the ground. Fast-running rivulets and deep puddles formed in the grass. Dizziness lurched Sen sideways. He clamped his eyes shut and shook his head. When he looked outside again, the storm continued to rage.

Indistinct yelling forced his attention to a circle of trees and the cluster of people gathered within them. A figure ran toward them in the downpour. Sen watched in horror as the gathering turned on one among them, felling the person with blows from fists and weighty, blunt sticks. Lightning flashed and glinted off a sharp line of metal. Sen recognized it as a long, thin dagger, and he grimaced in anticipation of the stroke.

He gasped as searing pain twisted in his guts. Instinctively he pushed a hand against his side, and it came away wet and sticky with blood. He grunted and fell backward as the figures he'd seen from afar loomed over him. His swollen tongue filled his mouth and disorienting blurs of color and light filled his mind, preventing his answer to the continued calls of his name. Sen's lungs ached and he coughed. It rattled around in his chest. Cold water seeped into his clothes, and he curled onto his side. Sen held out his hand, expecting it to be taken, but grasped only emptiness.

Someone shouted his name, and he searched and met an anguished, piercing gaze. Recognition hit him like a bolt, and a tumult of emotions stronger than the storm shot through him, ricocheting down his limbs and echoing in his mind. The storm clouds pushed through the windows and boiled to fill the house, stealing him into blackness.

Sen startled awake and fell off the chaise.

He groaned and used the windowsill to help him stand. His head pounded, his throat was dry, and his heart beat too fast. The sun shone bright and merry, and he squinted out into the yard. No menacing figures, no trace of an attack or rain. Spanish moss swayed peacefully, and birds flitted between the trees and the dry ground. Sen patted his side and found it whole.

His breath sped as he remembered the storm clouds, churning and angry like a living thing, and the familiar gaze and splinter of emotions it left behind in him. Thick shadows began to gather like fog in the corners of the room, and he didn't wait to see if they were real.

Sen scrabbled into the hall, skidded down two flights of stairs, grabbed his backpack from the kitchen, and careened out the side door. Sand and gravel churned as he ran, and he got halfway down the cul-de-sac before he slowed.

"My bike," he groaned as he stood and sucked wind.

Sen watched the house for a long while. Nothing about it changed, nor did the sky behind it. Despite his sharp and wary reluctance, he trudged back to the side door.

"It's fine. It'll be fine. I need the bike. I'll get the bike, and…." He licked his lips. Then he could go. Given the benign neglect Ballard treated the house with, his not cleaning probably wouldn't be noticed.

He grabbed his bike but didn't move. Gusts of wind scudded the clouds clear, brightening the sun. The carvings on the door swirled, and the figures danced. Sen closed his eyes and rocked on his feet. A full-body yawn overtook him, followed by another. That had to be it—extreme fatigue plus buzzing on too much caffeine had him seeing things.

Sen propped his bike back against a pillar and walked to the door. He ran his fingers over the carvings, which were hard and unforgiving and definitely not dancing, and stilled his touch on the rabbit. Exhaustion had seeped into him, taken over, created the illusion from dissatisfying days trying to paint and fitful sleep filled with bad dreams.

He should leave. Sen curled his hand into a fist. He could stay and clean, and it would be fine.

Sen squared his shoulders, opened the door with purpose, and retraced his route all the way back to the turret room. The mellow, sunny day offered no threat, but Sen stayed on the lookout for shadows. He kicked over the forgotten sock and hesitated to pick it up, but no burning or stabbing or storm cloud dramatics assaulted him. Grabbing the sock used up the last of his bravado, and he flopped onto the chaise and let out a long, long sigh.

"Holy shit. Holy shit," he said and scrubbed his face.

Sen lay listening to the breeze. But he couldn't stay there, so he gathered his reserves and trudged downstairs to the kitchen, taking the lonely sock with him.

He chased snatches of the brief, intense vision, but couldn't pin anything down. Sen dug a sketchbook from his bag and filled a page with rapid doodles and impressions of what he'd seen, and the angry voices raised in threat whispered behind his ears and in his mind. The rabbit appeared, as did circle motifs and interlocking jagged lines that felt sharp as he drew. He stopped himself from further deepening the groove on the paper as he retraced a pair of piercing eyes over and over. He pushed away from the counter and stood, hands on hips.

Adri counted on him, and the house hadn't turned black again, so he devised a plan. He'd clean the high-traffic spaces and then reorganize something, because reorganizing always calmed him.

"Okay, then. See? It's cool," he told himself and went to find the pantry.

There were bottles and wipes and sprays of every type imaginable, and no food—not even a forgotten, desultory pack of ramen noodles. The barrenness made the fridge seem glutted. There was more craft beer, a wine cooler, and some protein-shake mix. His phone chirped. He squawked, dropped everything, and rolled his eyes.

Sen read a text from his mom.

Just checking on things. Dad says hi. How's the persistent ennui?

His dad hated cell phones, and his mom was a technophile. She was in the "technology will eventually make the world a better place" camp. His dad just wanted to be left alone, but more in a pioneer spirit than survivalist paranoia, thankfully. It had shaped a lot of how Sen was raised—separate from the mainstream but not radical or isolationist.

He wondered whether hallucinating was a step past ennui or a step toward curing it, and he replied. *Things fine. Doing stopgap cleaning for A & still pushing to paint. Ennui is... is.*

Sen wasn't prone to funks, but that didn't mean they couldn't happen. Once he had a breakthrough with painting or collaging, he'd be fine. Then the upcoming group show would happen, his pieces in it would be great, and he could move on from New Orleans. Maybe without guiding signs, as long as his internal compass cooperated and told him a general direction to go.

Rooting for you. Add ginger and honey to some green tea for balance. And try some freeform writing!

Sen smiled. *Will do. Thanks, Mom.*

His mother believed tea cured all ails and brainstorming resolved most problems. She had been right about it many times, but he doubted even tea could stop the skull-splitting action currently happening behind his face.

Sen located a glass, drank water, and then, a refill down, mindful of and deliberate with each step of the process—the sound of the flowing tap, the solidity of the glass, the lukewarm water not at all like cold rainwater—grounded himself back in the here and now. Curiosity prodded him to check the other cabinets. The one next to the sink had table settings for four. One drawer had some towels, another held silverware, and all the rest were empty. How depressing—or he read too much into the signs of a bachelor who preferred going out.

He retrieved the scattered bottles and wipes. Cleaning might not take him four hours, but he'd do a good job, and then put the day and the house behind him.

The master bedroom seemed a good place to start, as impersonal as everywhere else, but at least it was obviously used. The walls were restful gray, setting off the earth tones in the heavy brocade comforter and dark mahogany furniture. Expensive cologne lingered in the air, expensive suits hung in the closet, and an expensive king-size bed was angled to make the most of the view into the back garden.

Despite the zillion-dollar mattress, covered with zillion-count linens, the bed and its thrown-back blanket and two squashed pillows didn't inspire any desire to crawl in and get comfy. Sen shrugged and stripped it bare, hoped he wouldn't find any nasty surprises lost in the sheets, and then found a nearly empty hamper in a closet. He stuffed the bedding, along with a T-shirt discovered rumpled in a corner of the bathroom, into the hamper and ran it downstairs. The T-shirt didn't summon any storms but, like the sock, it showed a hint of normalcy and someone actually living there. Sen dumped everything in the washer, punched the digital readout to what seemed a good setting, and stood there until water began to flow.

He tramped back upstairs and donned the frilly pink cleaning gloves left by a previous Fairy and scrubbed and polished the master bathroom from the ceiling down. Then he organized the spare toiletries in the shower and on the sink into neat lines, all labels turned to the front, blotted the sink dry, and called it done.

Sen roamed the hall, found the linen closet, and grimaced at the actual horrors it revealed. Blankets and sheets and pillowcases were wadded and shoved onto two middle shelves. The upper shelves were bare, and a pile of pillows sat on the floor. He decided to be cheerful about the second hint of personality, and yanked everything out to spill onto the floor.

Sorting didn't take long, because he'd have to refold it all, so he tossed everything into three piles—sheets, blankets, and small stuff. Then he decided on a dark blue sheet set and went to make the bed.

When Sen finished, he stepped back to admire his work. He'd layered a crisp white blanket under the brocade comforter and turned back all three layers so they folded over in striking lines of color. He unwrapped pillows from their store packaging, put shams that matched the comforter on them, and propped them against the curved headboard. Then he pounded the two remaining pillows back into shape, stuffed them into blue cases, and leaned them against the new pillows. On a whim he stuck a pewter-colored bolster pillow in front of those four and flicked its tassels into wide fans.

"Might as well, right?" he reasoned.

Sen decided there was no more to be done in the bedroom and tackled the linen closet. He found true joy in bringing order to chaos and got great satisfaction from folding everything into crisp squares and laying them in very organized piles. He stashed an extra duvet on the top shelf, used another for blankets, and then matched sheet sets and pillowcases on the remaining two shelves.

After that he trailed back downstairs and washed the lonely coffee cup tucked into the corner of the farm sink. Then he was at a loss. He paced the length of the house twice, peered around with an avid eye for fierce inspection, but didn't see anything out of place—no dust on the mantles, no lint balls under the sofas, not even any recycling to take out.

With about an hour remaining of the promised four, he had done a good job cleaning, and that had cleared his mind. Ghost sensations of the cold rain and knife in his belly lingered, and if he closed his eyes, he could still hear that voice calling for him in an English accent—a name he didn't recognize but knew meant him. But their strength continued to fade along with his headache. Sen considered texting Adri to ask if he could cut out, but the contrary desire to see the turret room tempted him, so he brought his sketchbook and snacks upstairs.

The shadows had lengthened as the sun dropped and cooled, but diffuse light warmed the room with a gentle glow. Wide-eyed, Sen perched on the chaise and waited. Nothing happened. No beastie leapt out at him, no cold spot formed around his shoulders, and there wasn't an orphaned sock in sight.

He thought about the house and its owner and their histories. The ice cream sandwiches and disorganized closets might reveal chinks in the pristine façade, but the turret room represented something more. It spoke of sentimentality and appreciation, and the single chaise bought for comfort indicated someone unafraid of being alone.

Sen didn't want to contemplate whether something else compelled Ballard to be up there.

As he glanced around the room, an unexpected detail caught his attention. Above the top left corner of the doorframe sat a carving no bigger than his palm—a small rabbit perched upon an acorn. It matched the rabbits carved into the main entry doors.

"And what are you doing, little fella?" he asked and got up to stroke its long ears.

It gave no answer, of course, but he wouldn't have been surprised if it had.

"I'll confess, I'm glad I found you. It's nice to have some company." He regarded the rabbit. "Have you seen anything here? Know about any ghosts?" he asked, because it felt good to say it aloud, but its sphinxlike expression gave nothing away.

His thoughts slid into daydreams, and his daydreams into dozing. He saw the flash of a knife and that familiar, burning gaze. Then rain washed everything away and condensed into an impenetrable fog. The alarm he'd set buzzed, and as he lurched upright, he swore he saw the last of the fog slink from the room in sinuous, blue-white tendrils.

Sen pushed from the chair, the room, and then the house, and back to his bike. He turned and gazed at the house from the street.

"Thank God I'm not coming back here," he said. The sun was shrouded in clouds, save for a slant of light, like a beacon leading to the turret, as if to contradict his words.

CHAPTER TWO

WHEN HE got home, Sen showered and then prepped a canvas to give his itchy fingers and restless mind something to do. His fatigue had given over to warm lassitude, and his brain wouldn't quit on remembered snatches of the strange sock-inspired vision at the mansion and the mansion itself. Maybe in that mood, he'd get further than some rough-sketched lines he'd cover over again. But if not, at least he was painting. Even in a creative rut, he believed he should make stuff relentlessly, and pushed to do so.

His goal was twofold. If he kept painting, eventually he had to stumble into a good idea, and he needed work to present to the gallery owners he'd met through a client. He'd invited the owners to his apartment to look at his work, and both Lars and Bharti said it showed talent and promise, but wasn't quite there yet. They liked his style and aesthetic and believed in his ability to discover that something more by giving him a space in their upcoming local artists' spotlight.

So he tried to find that elusive *something* that everyone crowed about. When he set his goal, the show was months away, and he had plenty of time to prepare, paint, and get choosy about his best work. But time slipped away faster and faster, and the pressure to perform had given way to the apprehension that nothing he painted would be good enough. The flare of wanderlust that distracted his hand and imagination didn't help. The show anchored Sen to New Orleans through its opening, at least, but he was ready to move on. It made having to focus on cranking out great work even harder and more stressful.

Sen gravitated to oils and mixed media, and over the years, he had dabbled in several styles and expressions. Being good at reading people translated to being gifted in portraiture, and while he could evoke the feeling of a place in a realistic landscape, he wanted more. Portraits and landscapes were reliable trade but didn't scratch the surface of everything his mind's eye could see, and he had to share.

That was part of the problem. His work hadn't told him what it wanted to be. He had several great paintings to his credit, but he lacked cohesive vision. Nothing had to be matchy-matchy, but it did all have to belong together, and so far his work didn't reflect that. Art with an eclectic, experimental voice wasn't a problem, but eclectic and experimental still needed an interconnecting thread to mount a show. What he produced had spark but no fire, and he wanted it to catch.

He needed to do more than set himself apart and present paintings that were fresh and intriguing without seeming forced. Whatever he painted had to come from the heart or the end result would be flat. In the past year, he hadn't managed to paint one heartfelt thing.

Sen closed his eyes and pulled in a centering breath to quiet the noise of his unanswerable questions and worries. He dunked a paintbrush in the solvent mix of turps and walnut oil he preferred, daubed several mounds of paint smears on his palette to wet life, and didn't allow hesitation or any more worry to stay his hand.

Anger, fear, and frustration surged through him. Sen tasted cold rain and bile, then blood, and heard someone yelling. The emotions—including his confusion and anxiety from the day—spilled onto the canvas in bold, messy strokes. He painted feverishly and without pause, as if possessed and driven by what he experienced in the turret room. He loaded a gob of paint on the brush and streaked a bright white arc across the canvas. Then the flow abruptly stopped.

Sen stood and stumbled back from the easel. He didn't know what to make of the painting, abstract and raw and so unlike anything else he'd done. It fascinated and frightened him, and he stared at it and tried to divine its secrets.

Bulbous, gunpowder green clouds crowded the upper left corner, sinuous and complex as a mythical beast. From the bottom a spire rose out of mists to where the leading edge of the clouds descended into the center, lighter green and convulsing with movement created by numerous overlapping brushstrokes. The white streak emanated from the clouds, left to right, and cut between two murky shapes. But the longer Sen looked, the more cohesion and form they took. Cold fire rippled through him, and he covered his mouth with a hand. The shapes were eyes, the same penetrating gaze from before—and they gave nothing away.

Sen huffed and grabbed a palette knife to scrape the canvas down, but then the certainty that he needed the painting stilled him. He carried it around the apartment, tried it on various nails in various walls, and then hung it in the corner between the kitchen and the bed—not readily visible but very present. A tangible release loosened the tightness in his chest and shoulders once he let go of the canvas and stepped away. Relief and anticipation swept through him like a cleansing wind, taking with it much of the darkness and tension that had crept inside him while he was at Greycote.

Energized, Sen nodded a parting acknowledgment at the messy storm of paint, hurried back to the studio area, and grabbed another prepared canvas.

He scraped his palette clean, and the blank canvas beckoned his brush and color choices in a way he hadn't experienced in too long. As the paint began to flow and shapes and lines appeared, he relaxed into the work and floated in the satisfying zone where he knew exactly where to highlight or shade, build layers, and add definition.

"Sen? Sen!"

He looked up to see Adriane standing in the door, Phoebe's car seat at her feet. Aside from the clip light he'd absently snapped on a while ago, his apartment was dim, and the sun had set. Sen flopped an oilcloth over his canvas and hurried over.

"Adri. Hi. Come in, come in. Is something wrong?" He took one of the plastic bags from her and grinned at Phoebe as he picked up the car seat. He flipped on the main lights and then kissed Adri's cheek. His stomach rumbled as the aromas of Casa Burrito registered, and he propped Phoebe on the table and found his phone where he'd left it by the coffeemaker. He'd missed five messages from Adri. "Oh. Umm. Sorry," he said and waggled the phone at his easel by way of explanation. "Totally lost track."

"I figured you'd passed out. But I wanted an enchilada the size of my head, and Phoebe is following the cliché of falling asleep without protest if we go for a drive. Plus I still owe you for today, including that tamale platter." Adriane set a second bag on the table, added a six-pack of Coronas, and started divvying up food. "I don't see any bruises or road rash on you, so I'll assume you made it home from the job okay."

Adriane was petite and sparkling, and Sen admired her dark brown coloring and darker brown eyes. If she hadn't been married when they met, he might have asked her on a date. During their introduction he said something awful and sarcastic, and she hadn't missed a beat. She gave it right back. They'd been close ever since.

"'M fine, and did," Sen answered around a mouthful of avocado and tomato as he grabbed mismatched plates and forks. "And starving."

"Convenient, then, that I handed them the takeout menu and said yes." Adriane grinned. To go with their enchilada and tamales there were carnitas, a pile of tacos, rice and beans, sweet plantains, and the avocado salad.

They set to eating, and after the initial rush of sating appetites and moaning over the glorious food, they slowed to pick at the leavings. Adriane tapped her bottled water and studied Sen with a mix of speculation and glee.

"What?"

"What do you mean what?" Adriane shook her head. "That's what I want to ask you."

Sen fanned his hands and nibbled a tortilla. "I'm exhausted. I inhaled cleaning products and solvents today, and I've had three beers. If you don't tell me what you want to ask, I can't help you."

Adriane huffed. "Fine. Mr. Ballard himself called me today when he got home."

"Who?" Sen frowned. Then it connected. "Oh. The dude with a Stepford-clean mansion who pays to have it cleaned on a weekly basis." The blood drained from Sen's face.

He couldn't think what he'd done to cause trouble or any complaint. Was there something he hadn't done? Maybe he'd missed a room that desperately needed cleaning, like a secret passage or storage shed, or something Adriane had forgotten to tell him about.

"Did I forget to set the house alarm? Given I was sleepwalking by the time I left, it's possible." His brow creased as he tried to think about what had gone wrong.

"Sen, sweetie. You're not in trouble, and neither am I." Adriane poked at him. "Ballard called to tell me you weren't to be replaced. He's never called me before, not to compliment or complain. So tell me, what did you do?" She folded her hands in front of her and leaned closer.

"No wonder you brought dinner. Curiosity was killing the cat." Sen rolled his eyes. "I didn't do anything, really. I cleaned his bathroom and bedroom, made the bed, redid the linen closet, and then I sat in a chair for the rest of the day."

The storm vision and passing out afterward flitted through his mind, but he banished it.

"Duh." Adriane's perky little nose twitched. "That's it?"

"That's it! I swear." He laughed. "Maybe he's never seen nicely organized bedding sets before?" They chuckled, and then the rest of what Adriane had said hit him. "But what did he mean, I wasn't to be replaced? Adri, I can't keep this job indefinitely. Not at all, but especially with the group show coming up."

"Yes, you can." Adriane looked determined, and when Adriane looked determined, it usually meant things were going to go her way. Sen groaned in complaint, but she waved a hand. "Hear me out, at least. And have a beignet."

She produced a paper bag she'd kept hidden and set it in front of Sen.

"You run a cleaning service and play so dirty. It's terrible and awful, and I hate you." Sen took the bag, rolled the beignets onto a napkin, and inhaled several instead of breathing.

"It's true." Adriane beamed. She checked on Phoebe, who was still sawing logs, and then she laced her hands together and got serious. "Look. I have an unconventional compromise to offer."

Sen had another beignet and made a go-on motion.

"You keep going to this job every week, clean whatever parts of the house he deigns to use, and then you have my permission to sit somewhere for the remaining time to sketch or moon about thinking of your paintings, or whatever artistic thing it is you do to get ready for the show. See? It'll work out perfectly."

That sounded inviting and very unlike Adri.

"I don't want to take advantage of your client. Or you." He shivered like he had when he stepped into the mansion. "You'll have to put someone else on the job sooner rather than later. And warn Ballard it's temporary. I won't stay indefinitely."

"I know, and I'm already on it. But for a 'desperate times, desperate measures' stopgap, it'll do." Adriane ate the last of the yellow rice instead of a beignet, which showed her commitment to convincing him. "My hands are so full right now I can't take over. I mean, if I could, problem solved before I'd even called you today."

Sen glanced at Phoebe and pictured Dan prone on the floor, hating life, and guilt at the idea of quitting on her twinged in his belly.

Adri seemed to follow his thoughts. "Yeah. So. I know you'll do a great job, and everything that needs it will be cleaned spotless. I trust you to do that, and Mr. Ballard should have taken my advice when he hired me that he didn't need four hours weekly, but either he or his assistant didn't care to listen, so he'll get a slightly overpaid job well done, and you'll get some extra cash. I'm okay with that. I kinda have no other choice too, but still, okay with it."

"What if he comes home early?" Sen hedged. There was nothing saying they'd get caught, but no guarantees they wouldn't. Hardly high crime, but it was still wrong. Not so wrong he hadn't already cataloged the art materials he'd bring next week or how quickly he could clean and get to sketching. But still.

Adriane raised an eyebrow. "Oh, please. From the dirt I managed to dig up, he's a bachelor workaholic who's barely home to sleep. He won't walk in on you in the middle of his all-important workday. You can always just keep an ear out for the door, with a rag and a spray bottle handy. So the minute you think you hear something, hide your pencils and start cleaning the windows." She blushed and grinned sheepishly and then giggled. "Sen, I'm terrible. I'm going to rot in hell. Tell no one else this is what I'm plotting."

"This is not the least of what'll banish you to the brimstone, my dear." Sen smirked. He couldn't ignore the pull to go back to that house. He wanted to know what had happened there, in the home's history and to him, and he wanted to help. "Okay. I'll agree."

"Hooray! I knew you would." Adriane raised both arms in triumph.

"I'll agree," Sen stressed and then finished. "So long as you keep looking for my replacement and you promise not to get mad if Mr. Ballard ever does find out and cans us both." He raised a counter eyebrow to hers and waited.

"Pinkie swear." Adriane offered her hooked pinkie, and Sen took it with his. Her eyes twinkled. "Oooh. I know! The day he actually comes home, he'll fall in love with you at first sight, in all your cleaning glory, with your gorgeousness and cleverness rising above your dirty jeans and tee. And he'll be so charmed he won't get angry at all. Then I won't have to fire you to save face, and he won't ever complain."

Sen blinked very slowly. "Adri, you are one-thousand-proof ridiculous."

"It happened for me, didn't it?" She tipped one shoulder and danced her left hand around, weighted by the boulders of her engagement, wedding, and recent anniversary rings. A mother's ring with Phoebe's birthstone graced her middle finger.

"Marriage happened *to* you. With your high school sweetheart." Sen smiled.

Adriane was convinced it could be that easy for everyone, and equally convinced she'd get him set up and happily married one day.

"Just because you're love 'em and leave 'em, with broody dry spells in between, doesn't mean you're immune." Adriane started to clear up the carnage from dinner.

"No. I'm a serial monogamist, and very attentive while in said monogamy, which is completely different." Before she could argue, he added, "I know yours is a fairy-tale romance, but there's nothing fanciful or pretend about it. Unlike this would-be situation. Or any others you've tried to cook up."

"Bah. For an artist, you sure lack imagination," Adriane accused, and threw a wadded-up napkin at him. "I'll find the right boy for you. It's my mission, which means it's gonna happen."

Sen caught the napkin as he stood up to take the dishes to the sink. "What if you should be finding me the right girl instead?"

Adriane scoffed. "Pul-eeze. If—no, when—you find your forever person, it'll be a dude. You've always been pickier about the men you date, and you take the breakups harder. Or I should say, actually hard at all." She nodded decisively. "So, yup. It'll be a boy who bowls you completely over and then lassos you in."

"That's so mixed I don't even think it's a metaphor any longer." Sen ran water on the dishes and left them for later. Much, much later. There was nothing he could correct in Adri's assertion. He was picky. "Maybe I'll end up with a hot, rich couple who want to patron a poor artist. You never know."

"What kind of patronage are you talking about?" Adriane mugged suggestively. "If the couple is hot, is all I'm saying."

Sen's mouth pulled down in consideration. "Well, hunh. If they're hot, and we had chemistry, and they paid all my bills, I'm not against some other mutual benefits. All I'm saying is you never know."

"Hmm. Sure. Never know," Adriane said with utter lack of conviction. "And for something completely different—I love this table."

"Not so completely different. You tell me that every time you're here." Sen laughed and then added, "Take it. You can have it."

"It's just with Phoebe and us moved to the bigger house, I'm going crazy nesting. I'd say you know what I mean, but you don't." Adriane narrowed her gaze. "Wait. You're actually serious. Is your locale expiration date coming up soon?"

Sen shrugged. He wasn't sure. In his twenty-five years, he'd never stayed anywhere longer than a year, and he had an ingrained tendency to roam. He considered staying in New Orleans pushing two years an accomplishment. But he also had no attachment to things—belongings, keepsakes, holdovers—so if she loved and wanted the table, he could easily find something else.

Uprooting and rambling on had been his whole life—a life he was content with, and saw no reason to stop. People knew that about him, because he was always up-front about it, especially when he got close to someone, which limited the people he chose to get close to. Over the years he'd learned that was for the best—too long in one place or with one person and things got strange. Not quite sour but never, ever, exactly right.

He *was* on the verge of his expiration date, and he had been suppressing his wanderlust to stay a resident of New Orleans and be in the New Orleans up-and-coming artists show. But he wasn't going to outright tell Adri that.

"I dunno. I haven't really given it much thought. But I am actually serious about the table." He yawned. "Glad for you to have it."

"When I can talk the hubs into coming over in his he-man truck, and he can talk his buddies into hauling it around for us, maybe I just will." She pointed across the room at his studio area. "Did you start something new? Can I see?"

"I did, and no you can't. It's not ready… I'm not sure about it yet." Sen handed Adri her purse and steered her toward the door, and then he went back and snagged Phoebe. "She's just starting to wake up. Good timing." He grinned at Adri's groan. "Thank you for dinner. Please go. I'm so tired my eyes are burning pits, and I can't feel my teeth."

Adriane's expression softened as she glanced back to the covered canvas. "Still having trouble? You'll find your way again. You're an amazing artist with a true gift to share, and never despair otherwise." She tucked her purse under an arm and gave Sen a hug. Then she shoved money into his back pocket, squeezed his butt, and stepped back.

"I'm so glad you ruined the sincere moment," Sen said. "Good night. Get home safe." He tickled under Phoebe's chin. "Night, sweet pea. Give your momma lots of trouble."

He opened the door and watched until they were down the stairs and out of sight around the front of the house.

Sen killed the lights, detoured to the bathroom, and used the last of his energy to brush his teeth. Then he stripped to his briefs and crawled into bed.

He watched shadows from the streetlamps shining through the trees as they sculpted hollows and reliefs on the ceiling, and he took in several meditative breaths. Once he had that first strange painting out of his system, the second flowed like water. More like a dam bursting. It created a convergence of the aesthetics and ideas he'd been playing with all along but never thought to combine. Already he understood the interplay of the two would elevate his work.

But he wasn't ready to share it. He didn't want to talk about it, even to a sympathetic and interested audience like Adri, and he had no explanation for the storm-vision thing that brought it about. For the time being, the paintings and inspiration, and where they might lead, had to be only his.

CHAPTER THREE

SEN STEPPED from his bike onto the sidewalk and scanned the yard. Greycote, sun-drenched and quiet, greeted him. He lowered his head and biked to the side door—the carvings didn't react to his presence, and the gentle breeze didn't change—and got to the pantry without incident. Cleaning took about an hour, and then he invented tasks for another hour and some. He readied the trash to go out and then went upstairs, inexorably drawn to the turret room.

He paused in the hall, but crossing the threshold produced no response other than bathing him in serene light. The backyard and sky remained unchanged, and disappointment tempered his relief, because everything appeared normal.

Sen checked on the rabbit—he hadn't imagined it—and then he settled on the chaise and started to draw. He penciled in sweeping, abstract shapes, and repeated the ones that most satisfied his hand. A pair of eyes distilled from the fray of loops and lines, and recognition tickled his brain. He drew them again, without abstraction, but their meaning and identity stayed just out of reach, like a place once visited and remembered in detail but whose name you can't recall.

Sen changed directions and began to sketch fanciful rabbit couples in period costumes, somehow knowing every stitch and fit of their clothes. He got into a groove and filled the page with rapid gestural lines. He moved on to a second and a third page as the rabbits multiplied like, well, rabbits.

"Augh." Sen barked in frustration as his hand jerked a skidding line off the page when something broke his concentration.

A car door slammed, and he shot to his feet to look outside. The angle wasn't great, but he saw enough to realize someone had arrived.

He clapped his sketchbook shut, stuffed it and an everywhere mess of colored pencils into his bag, and then ran downstairs as the side door to the house closed.

Sen raced down the hall on tiptoe to the master bathroom and crouched by the double sink cabinet as the footsteps sounded up the back stairs. Quick grabs and hasty shoves had everything removed from the cabinet, and he appeared for all the world as though he'd been absorbed in reorganizing for goodness knew how long.

"Hello?"

"Yes? I'm in here," Sen answered and poked his head above the open cabinet door to smile at whoever approached. Blood pounded just under his skin. Good thing he'd taken Adri's sly advice and left the spray bottle and rag in there before he retreated to the turret room.

Only his second week, and the first of their grand scheme, and he was already busted. Hoisted with his own petard, he supposed.

"Hi there. I'm sorry to interrupt without forewarning—I didn't mean to take you off guard by showing up. It's unusual for me to be home, but today has been crazy, and it was unavoidable. On the bright side, I'll be out of your way again momentarily."

Sen noticed two things about the likely Mr. Ballard. First, the careful phrasing that it was unusual for him to be home without an added qualifier like "during the week" or "on a workday," which might be an unconscious giveaway that he spent very little time there at all.

The second he almost didn't catch but did see. A shadow crept around Ballard's shoulders, clinging to follow Ballard as he moved. It expanded, billowing out like storm clouds, and then Sen blinked and they were gone.

Sen swallowed. He decided it must be an illusion from looking up at Ballard and into the bathroom light that reflected from the mirror.

Ballard held out a hand. Sen couldn't resist the magnetic compulsion to stand, walk over, and take it. He jolted when they made contact and, inexplicably, the vivid portrait of a young man he didn't recognize flashed in his mind.

"Morgan Ballard. Good to meet you," he said and glanced at his hand. He made a fist and let it out again, and his stance relaxed.

"Sen—Sebastian. Good to meet you," he echoed. "Have we"—*met before*, he thought, but didn't say—"been meeting with your approval? The Fairies, that is." His voice shook, and he cleared his throat. He hated how flustered he sounded.

It could be chalked up to surprise, but there was more happening he didn't get. Sure, Morgan was hella attractive and smelled amazing, with palpable body heat, and that always got Sen's attention. But Sen was usually easygoing and confident and never tongue-tied.

"Tongue-tied" made him think about his actual tongue, then Morgan's, then them tied together, and he skidded his feverish thoughts to a halt. Sen had experienced immediate attraction, always physical and fleeting. His reaction to Morgan was different. It thrummed deep inside him, anchored by a sense of affinity and belonging. If he got hooked up to a lie detector and asked whether they were longtime friends, he would answer yes and pass with flying colors.

Sen stepped back and crossed his arms to fight the growing, powerful urge to kiss Morgan.

"Yes. Thank you, Sebastian."

Morgan lingered on his name, and Sen's mouth went dry.

"My compliments on the linen closet." Morgan nodded. "Adriane informed me the new cleaner she was sending was the very best, and she didn't exaggerate. I'm pleased to hear you're staying on."

"Hey, we're pleased you're pleased with my work," Sen managed to say in a light tone.

Not as if he'd ask, but he still didn't know what he did cleaning-wise so different from anyone else. He should make a joke about the job being easy, considering there wasn't much to clean, or compliment the house, or do anything other than stand there. He wanted to make small talk. He couldn't do more than stare.

Morgan's suit enhanced rather than diminished his tall, powerful frame. He was taller than Sen—and Sen was no pipsqueak at a lean six feet—with chiseled features, stormy slate eyes, large square hands, and dark honey-gold hair trimmed on the sides and just long enough to dust his brow. Not at all Sen's type and everything he wanted to grab at and climb like a tree.

"What I need is in my study, but I didn't want to be rude or set a bad tone by coming and going without introducing myself. That'd be weird." Morgan peered at the assembly of things on the floor. "I hope you're finding everything you need okay."

"Yep, no problem. Thanks. Cleaning supplies, detergent, helping myself to a few beers." Sen cracked a grin and scrabbled back onto more solid ground.

Morgan chuckled. "Glad to hear it." He glanced around and then checked his watch. "Well, I won't keep you, as I already need to be going. Have a good rest of your day."

"Thanks. You too. And I *won't* see you next week." Sen's laugh was flat but passable.

"Right, right," Morgan agreed after a hitched pause. He pivoted from the bathroom, and as he passed the bed, he remarked, "You know, I forgot I even owned that weird little pillow. I think it came in the bed-in-a-bag set."

All Sen could muster in answer was "Huh. It probably did."

Morgan's deep, gravelly voice wreaked havoc with Sen's equilibrium, and talking about anything related to bed made Sen's gut tighten. Also, a bed-in-a-bag—how depressing.

He followed Morgan downstairs without meaning to.

"Dryer quit," he said, as though Morgan had asked for a reason why he followed and that excused him. He walked half the length of the hall and stopped in the foyer.

Morgan stopped too, reluctant to leave, unless Sen was mistaken.

"I'm in the middle of a meeting." Morgan tilted his head. "Literally. I was just starting my part of the talk when the thumb drive with my entire presentation got corrupted."

"No backup?" Sen frowned. Given all his observations and limited info, that seemed unlikely.

"Not there. At least, not assembled and ready to go. Parts-pieces deal." Morgan pulled a thumb in the direction of his study. "I finalized it last night."

"Got it. Did you at least throw coffee and donuts at the attendees before cutting out? Otherwise things could get restless and then turn ugly." Sen shook his head. "I've heard about meetings, and nothing good."

Deep laugh lines bracketed Morgan's eyes and mouth when he smiled. Sen wondered what it'd feel like to trace them with his tongue.

"I had catering bring lunch in—because naturally this happened on the one day I didn't feel like dragging my laptop into work." Morgan shifted but didn't move away. "So here I am."

"Here you are," Sen echoed. He licked his lips and did a funny half shrug when Morgan's stare became intent. "Always the way, isn't it?"

"Lesson learned." Something flickered in Morgan's gaze, and he pressed a hand in the air between them. "Please, don't worry about me being here. I'm half out the door as it is. You don't have to wait around to get back to work or show me out or anything."

Sen wasn't being dismissed and had no reason to be disappointed, but he batted aside shades of both.

"Good luck with finishing—and starting—the presentation. I'm sure it'll go great," Sen enthused and did a nodding-waving thing. Morgan smiled an acknowledgment and turned around.

Sen didn't have to peek over his shoulder to know Morgan watched him all the way into the kitchen and until he disappeared around the corner into the utility room. He sensed that bright, pewter gaze on his nape, but he couldn't tell why Morgan was doing it.

He collapsed onto the floor in front of the washing machine the moment he heard the side door shut and a car engine crank. Morgan's arrival had been a near miss. He could have found him lazing in the turret room, but even if Sen had been discovered, the house was clean and two kitchen drawers were reorganized. There was no reason for Sen's insides to still be fluttering—not from being caught off guard—and their encounter hadn't been explosive or even interesting. But there he sat, damp with flop sweat and every nerve abuzz.

Sen put his phone on his sternum, hit speaker, and dropped his arms out wide. The cool travertine soothed him, and he closed his eyes as the phone dialed.

"Talk to me," Adriane answered without preamble.

"Oh my God—what the what even—he showed up," Sen enunciated from behind clenched teeth.

Adriane squeaked. "Nooo," she whispered. "I can't believe it. That's almost creepy. Oh, man. I'd have died! Are you okay?"

Sen's answer was a pitiful moan. Then he heard her tight noises and said, "And I can't believe you're laughing. You're heartless."

"I asked if you're okay," she said when she regained her composure. "All right. Maybe a little heartless. But you have that special élan to get out of sticky situations, and I'm sure the place looks well-scrubbed. I wouldn't have suggested the little plan without knowing you could handle both. Plus there was no angry call from him or threatening e-mails, and you're calling me, still there in one piece, which I assume means he's gone and you survived."

"Barely." Sen pouted. "I devised a good cover and remembered how to talk and everything. You'd be proud." A stomach-dropping thought occurred to him. "Omigosh. Imagine if I were wearing headphones. New rule, I'm never listening to music here."

"My Fairies aren't supposed to wear headphones anyway. Which, immaterial, sorry." Adriane tutted. "Seriously, though, are you okay? It's crazy he showed up, like he heard our plotting or something."

"Right? He did say it was very unusual and not to expect it again. But then, that's what you basically said. I'm like a dog placed in his third 'forever' home. It's going to take a long time for me to trust again."

"Odd and oddly specific, but illustrative."

Sen pushed up to lean against the dryer. "To answer—yes. I'm okay. I was startled, of course, but nothing happened, and we're in the clear. I might use cotton swabs to dust the carved front door and fill the time next week instead of drawing, though."

"I'm glad you're okay, but I bet you're also totally wrung out now. Fight-or-flight adrenaline rushes have that effect." Adriane paused and keyboard tapping sounded for a bit. "You have my permission to leave early if you want. I just made a note in the job file, even."

"Thanks, but I have to finish the wash, and I'm on the hook for redoing the master bath vanity. I dumped everything in the cabinet onto the floor when I heard him coming, and it's still on the floor."

"Nice move." Adriane hummed. "You know, Ballard did say something about your attention to orderly detail. Keep that up, and not just as a clever ruse."

"Sure." Sen would, but not because Adri asked.

The action-and-reward blend was too good to ignore. He grooved on reorganizing anything. He was nosy and curious about the little things other people chose to keep in their lives, and he wanted to know more about Morgan. All three together? Bliss.

"Awesome. I'm so sorry that happened, but I'm glad it's all okay. For your sake and mine." Adriane let out a breath. "Just one last thing."

"Lay it on me."

"What does he look like?" Adriane's giggle almost conveyed a whiff of shame. "He's got that sinful, purring, husky-voice thing, which is all I have to go on. Not to say it didn't give me a lot of ideas and a half, but still."

"Handsome. Very early thirties or very late twenties. He's got kind of a young Paul Newman quality." Sen flapped a hand. "But… hunkier."

"Oh." Adriane sounded disappointed.

Sen let her be. She was thinking he wouldn't be interested, based on his past types and stated preferences. As with his painting, he wasn't ready to share what stirred in him from meeting Morgan.

"I should probably peel myself off the floor and get back to work." Sen tucked the phone under his chin and spun on his butt so he could transfer the wash to the dryer.

"Me too. The work thing, if not the floor. Thanks for calling to let me know, and we're still on for group Sunday brunch. Right?"

"Double right." Sen pushed to stand and started the dryer. "Are you and Hubs swinging by after, to get the table?"

"Yuppers. I'm excited. Dan stood up straight for the first time yesterday," she chirped. "Oooh. Since you've met him, that means you can sketch the elusive Ballard for me or describe him in detail. Bye, sweetie."

"Later, gator." Sen disconnected and spread his hands on the dryer as it got warm.

In the recycling bin were small and sturdy cardboard boxes from a men's toilette delivery service. Sen assessed them and then grabbed all four, got the heavy-duty shears from one of the drawers he'd just redone, and returned to the master-bathroom vanity. As he cut the boxes in half to use as storage trays, the visage of the young man he'd imagined returned and superimposed over the painting he'd worked on since the week before.

Sen fell back onto his heels and caught his breath.

Adriane had jokingly asked for him to draw a picture of Morgan—and he already had.

He was careful and thorough in his task, but he went quickly, did the same with folding and putting the laundry away, and then gathered his things and left. He didn't quite flee, but he didn't linger, and once the house alarm activated, he pedaled hard for the nearby wildlife refuge.

Sen did believe in signs and the power of prescience, and tried to be receptive when either nudged him. Call it intuition or second sight, serendipity or synchronicity. Whatever. Sen didn't quibble about the semantics. His nomadic, crystal-using, tree-hugging parents had taught and encouraged him to keep the proverbial third eye open. The practice still served him well and he always listened, in case the world chose to whisper its important secrets into his heart.

He was a wanderer, but he never drifted. He'd lived a lot of places and might appear to others as having no plan or true ambition, but that wasn't true. By nature and nurture, he was meticulous and impulsive, practical, passionate, and open to possibility. That might have been contradictory on paper, but in practice, Sen thrived. He came to New Orleans following guidance shown to him in overt and subtle ways—proof pinned to his corkboard. The friend he traveled there with knew a mutual friend of Adri's, who led him to both the gallery and then Greycote.

That made Morgan the next link in the chain. Perhaps the endpoint—the hook. Or would it be what reeled him in?

Sen rode the main loop in the wetland refuge and focused on the schirring of the tires over the cinder path, the sluggish lapping water, and intermittent bird cries. Summer lay in wait and, sooner than he'd like, would cover spring with its heavier mantle. The wind carried its promise of heat and the aroma of thickening humidity.

When Sen got back to his apartment, he avoided the painting. Standing at the sink, he drank two glasses of water, washed his face and arms, and stop-started attempts to fashion a dining table replacement. Eventually he realized he had no ideas for making a new table because he wasn't going to get one. He wouldn't be there long enough for its absence to matter. With that admission the noise cleared from his mind and the painting beckoned.

Sen approached it as though it were a skittish animal whose trust he was trying to gain. There was so much more to it—it wasn't just a painting—but he didn't yet understand its message and meaning. He dusted his fingers over the oilcloth and then rolled it up and folded it behind the easel, as if asking permission to enter, envisioning the layer upon thin layer of color and narrow lines that he had slowly built into an image and then a face. The process invigorated him, a change from his usual method of starting with the portrait and then laying the background in. As the face began to reveal itself, he'd shivered, and in moments of contemplation of where to place another line or block of color, he called on impressions of dappled sunlight in the trees around the lawn at Greycote.

He sucked in, held his breath, and confronted the painting. Then he let his breath out on a bewildered laugh.

The man in the painting wasn't Morgan. There was no chin cleft or curls of thick hair, and he was thinner and graver than Morgan. Sen had done him in greens and grays—like the house's verdigris porch and trim work and shutters, he realized—but those colors didn't seem like Morgan to him. No. Morgan was power-suit black, like granite, with pinstripes and a burnt orange pocket square and an assertive red tie. Why, then, had he thought he'd somehow painted Morgan before they met?

Sen walked back several steps and studied the canvas. Then he walked an arc, left to right, to see it from several angles.

At about a forty-five degree angle the strongest feature was the eyes under their heavy brow and the surrounding abstract colors. They jumped out at him and demanded attention. Sen had worked the paint with solvent, so it was thin, and let it run everywhere so there were blossoms and drips and overlapping areas of color and shape. Then his brushstrokes implied outlines and darker layers that created contrast and brought out the portrait. He'd been happy with the painting and the new technique, and planned to do more, but really studying it told him it was finished.

He had painted Morgan—the eyes and powerful gaze were undeniable—just not the Morgan of today. The voice he heard calling his name while trapped in the storm vision belonged to that face. His long-awaited signposts might have arrived, and he was painting them.

Sen could embrace it or run.

Running held definite appeal, but the signs didn't lead anywhere but back to Greycote and to Morgan. He had to keep going and see it through to its end—the hook or the switchback return—or he might never be free. Nothing had led him from New Orleans yet because he hadn't figured out what he'd been brought there to find. The thought of leaving without discovering why Morgan persisted in his thoughts ripped a piece of him away. He had to learn, or he would never be whole.

"So, then, let's see what we find," he said to the painting of other-Morgan.

Sen moved other-Morgan to a drying easel, set up a blank canvas, and began to paint. In minutes he had four brushes going, one busy in his left hand and the other three at the ready, held between each finger of his fist like splayed claws.

Hours later the unknown young man had emerged. He hadn't done it on purpose, but he understood it as inevitable. He painted past dawn and well into midday without overthinking or stopping the flow. The young man demanded to be painted in similar colors to other-Morgan—with added hints of apple green and turquoise and pale yellow. He daubed a wide brush against the canvas and pulled up blisters that broke to weep color, the darkest tones leaving watery patterns behind and lightest becoming floating halos. Sen made a series of them in rapid succession and varied the colors to mix directly on the canvas. He paused to watch the last one swirl with color and then break, and he stilled his hand.

He stopped when he couldn't automatically feel where to put the next stroke, dropped the brushes in an old pickle jar filled with turpentine, and walked to the far wall to study the painting.

"Hello there," he said from afar and tilted his head. "And now—who are *you*?"

To his relief the young man wasn't another iteration of Morgan. But nothing else made sense about it, including the sudden, insistent presence of the young man in his mind. The portrait had sharp features and hazel eyes and wasn't a classic beauty. But the young man possessed true allure. There was something familiar about him as well, but not in the eyes, as with other-Morgan, or in any other tangible feature Sen could name.

Sen looked at the young man, ethereal and coming forward through the background colors. He looked at other-Morgan, who was grounded and veiled by the color washes except for his pronounced gaze. The two paintings belonged together—not as a diptych or complementing series, but as an obvious couple. An undeniable match.

He didn't know what to make of any of it, so he poured a cup of yesterday's coffee, made it palatable with an equal measure of milk, and went out on the landing.

"What the fuck."

Sen believed in signs—the power of prescience. He paid attention and listened and had gotten good at recognizing and reading them. Most of his life decisions were informed by following cues the world offered, and he didn't regret that.

Never had any predictive or guiding forces infiltrated his very being. But having just painted that young man from out of nowhere, from something greater than his creative spirit, indicated the current signs came from him—his head, heart, and very hands. Two portraits of unknown people, painted after encounters in a house. Or did the encounters depend on Morgan?

Sen sat lengthwise on the top step and dropped his head back against the wall.

"What kind of useless, meaningless signs are these?" he asked his coffee, the muzzy air close around him, and the setting sun.

Frustrated tears welled up and spilled over, and he let them fall. Sen couldn't be sure whether the two portraits were all he'd get, or where their presence would lead. He had no idea where to begin to decipher them, their message, or their direction. If they were the only two, then what? Give them to the gallery, keep them for a lifetime's interrogation, burn them in effigy and walk away? If more were brought to life by his hand, did it matter who they were and why they came into his life?

Sen didn't know where to start. He fervently wished for the easy answer and for it to be over. But the idea that it might end scared him like nothing else ever had.

Chapter Four

Sen entered Greycote with trepidation the following Wednesday, but he encountered only silence. That disappointed him, and then he got annoyed at being disappointed.

He cleaned, found a sticky note asking if he would reorganize the towels in the guest bathrooms, and he did so. He didn't cotton-swab detail, but he vacuumed the pristine area rugs in the guest rooms and mopped the rest of the house. Then, when he had twenty minutes left, he allowed himself to stand and stare out the windows of the turret room, and then he escaped unscathed.

For no good reason he kept the note—brief and impersonal and signed with a cursive *MB*—stuck on his fridge. The bright square of blue caught his attention throughout the week. He slept okay, landed a gig painting a portrait of a couple who had recently bequeathed a small fortune to a private historic-house museum, and hovered around the decision to invite the gallery owners over to see the strange paintings.

His hours at Greycote and his contact with the note elicited no other visions or portraits, so he got on with his work. At home he couldn't shake the feeling that other-Morgan's gaze followed him and that the young man patiently waited for something. When he managed sleep, they showed up in his dreams, whispering to each other or following his journeys through mazes and caves and castles, watching but always just out of reach.

He zoomed around what had become familiar corners and curves, turned up the driveway, and parked his bike. Another week had wrapped around and he was back again. Sen noticed the side door was open to the screen, and knots tangled low in his belly.

"Sebastian?" Morgan called in answer to the squeaky screen door. He stepped from his study into the hall, wearing the casual-clothes version of a business suit, and looked up from an overstuffed three-ring binder. "Good morning. I didn't want to startle you."

"But I thought you were never here?" came out instead of a polite greeting. Sen stood in place with his back to the screen door and grimaced. "Ugh. Well, that was awful. I'll just go dust the attic or hide in a cabinet."

"The attics are empty, although there might be a cabinet here big enough for you." Morgan quirked a half smile. "Don't worry about it. Here I am again, unexpectedly. Also, through life and all my dealings with people, I've come to the sound conclusion I always prefer an uncalculated response."

Sen nodded. "I'll keep that in mind." He continued down the hall but stopped short of pushing past Morgan.

Neither of them spoke, and Sen shifted his stance and tried not to stare and absorb every detail for comparison to the portrait. Morgan's demeanor didn't exactly encourage chitchat, and Sen wasn't one for forcing small talk into silence. He also didn't want to blurt out another awesomely awful bon mot.

Morgan tipped the binder into one wide palm and tapped the page. "The team I lead just successfully wrapped up a significant milestone in our project, so my boss's boss gave us the rest of the week off. It was compulsory." His deep voice was dry. "Don't worry about cleaning in here. I can telecommute, so I'm going to shut the door and get lost in work."

"Now would the boss's boss approve of that?" Sen gently teased.

"Without question." There was no answering humor in Morgan's tone.

Irrational disappointment flooded Sen. This not-at-all-his-type guy had come to life in his art before they even met, then made his whole body throb at first contact, and was apparently made out of cardboard. Morgan's flat statement required no answer, and Sen didn't know what to say, so he waited to be dismissed.

"I won't keep you." Morgan drummed his fingers and said, "Just pretend I'm not here."

"Impossible," Sen whispered.

His gaze flew to meet Morgan's quizzical expression, and he stammered. Then for a brief, wonderful, and terrible moment, he thought Morgan had reached out and caressed him. His cheek, throat, and arm all burned from the ghostly sensation. He shivered and flattened to the wall.

"What I mean is, you should be the one pretending I'm not here. I'll be quiet as a mouse." Sen managed a grin and moved without going anywhere, because Morgan still blocked the hall.

"Maybe so. We'll endeavor not to bother one another. How's that?" Morgan stepped back when Sen shifted again, and the binder overweighted and tipped onto the floor. It bounced hard enough that the rings opened and several pages slithered free.

They crouched in unison. Sen chased the pages that had spilled to one side as Morgan got the others, and they met in the middle with messy stacks of paper.

"Here," Sen said and took Morgan's pages, shuffled the bundle, and then rapped it on end, using a ruffle-and-curl method he'd perfected for squaring paper. He smiled and held the neat pile out. "I can't do anything about the order, but this way they're easier to handle, and at least you won't have crumpled edges."

Morgan nodded. "Thanks." His fingers curled across Sen's under the paper.

Sen blushed—something he wasn't prone to and hadn't done in years—and Morgan's gaze darted from his throat to his cheeks and followed the rise of color. Morgan's eyes darkened, his pupils dilated within swirls of flinty gray, and his grip tightened. Then he leaned forward on one knee and kissed Sen.

The kiss was brief, dry, and shattering.

Relief and longing surged into Sen. He twisted a hand in Morgan's shirt and repeated, "Finally, finally," and watched the storm in Morgan's eyes. Sen wanted Morgan's kiss.

Morgan cupped Sen's cheek and tipped forward. He stared at Sen's mouth and the rapid pulse in Sen's neck, and then looked heavy-lidded into Sen's gaze. His eyes flew wide open, and he snapped upright. The color drained from his face, and he went rigid and tumbled backward onto his heels.

"I'm so very sorry." Morgan stood abruptly and retreated a pace into his study, his breathing harsh but controlled. "I honestly have no explanation for doing that and hope it didn't offend you. But if you want to leave and clean another day, when I'm not here, or leave and ask to be replaced, I understand completely."

Sen barely heard what Morgan said. His mind reeled on overload, and he began to crawl. Then he clambered from his hands and knees to both feet and lurched down the hall and into the kitchen.

Flashing, quick-cut images and spoken phrases assailed him faster than he could register. He dumped his bag on the center island and flipped the sketchbook to an empty page. Then he rapidly drew gestural lines and raced to capture the essential impressions of the speakers and their words.

He quickly sketched other-Morgan and the young man, using line work without picking up his pencil to connect them, framing the top of the page. Four other faces clawed forward through the fray of swirling pictures and sounds of clanging metal, hoofbeats, and low-spoken words. Sen's hand moved with a will of its own. He had no control over what he drew—hatched lines, dark single strokes, undulating contours. Fog built up around him as he worked, shrouding him in shadow and the odor of distant places, long forgotten. The chaos began to lessen and allowed him to draw each face, one at a time, and to linger over the curves and planes of their features—features he recognized in faces so familiar but without name. The voices quieted to whispers, less frenzied and no longer overlapping, but he couldn't hear what they said.

"Sebastian?"

Morgan saying his name broke Sen's reverie. He gasped and dropped the pencil, and its whap and roll on the counter thundered in the sudden silence.

"Sorry." Morgan held up both hands and moved away. "You didn't hear me from over there." He indicated the far corner by the open entryway to the kitchen.

Sen hummed in neutral acknowledgment but couldn't look at Morgan. He traced and retraced a disembodied pair of eyes, soothed by the continuous movement.

He had no more explanation for his rush to draw than Morgan had for their kiss. What could he even say? *I drew you before we met, but it doesn't look like you. Your touch conjured others, people I don't know, and I was powerless not to draw them too.* Or that he wasn't upset by the kiss and wanted more, despite their barely knowing each other and their seeming lack of interest otherwise?

"Are you all right?"

He looked at the pages jammed with images—faces, miniature landscapes, a jewel-topped walking stick. No. He wasn't all right. Yes. His body hummed with inspiration.

"I'm fine. It's really okay—all of it—so you don't have to worry about anything." Sen fiddled with the pencil and squared his shoulders. Maybe in that moment of contact his weirdness had surged enough to bleed over and affect Morgan. He smiled ruefully and tapped his forehead. "Inspiration never picks a convenient time to strike. But I've learned the hard way not to ignore it. Why bother with normal social interaction when I can be full-on artistic eccentric?"

Morgan studied him, seemingly unconvinced, but he finally nodded. "Thank you. And again, I want to offer my apologies and say that if you want to lea—"

"No," Sen interrupted. He couldn't leave. He just couldn't—not Morgan, not the faces he'd drawn, not the things he seemed to unlock there.

Morgan's brows went up, and he nodded. "Okay, sure."

Sen tried for less intensity and said, "We're moving on. Remember? It's all just fine." He dashed a confident line to give one of the four people he'd drawn flowing hair. She would be painted in ochres, greens, and gold, and those earthy, burnished colors would reflect in her eyes and skin.

"Hmm." Morgan's brows beetled, but he shook his head and then relaxed. His gaze fell to the sketchbook, and he seemed tugged on a string to come back to Sen's side. "May I?"

"Please do." Sen's invitation was genuine. He still wasn't ready to share anything new with Adri, but he wanted to drag Morgan to his studio to show off everything.

Morgan smiled. It looked spontaneous and real. "You're quite skilled. In only minutes and with minimum details, I feel like I know these people, just from these few lines."

Sen tingled when Morgan's long fingers traced one of the portraits—the young man with sensitive features and a sensuous mouth who belonged to other-Morgan—and his breath caught as Morgan's touch lingered on the lower lip. Morgan frowned, and a shadow passed across his face. Then he straightened.

"Quite skilled sounds pompous and condescending, doesn't it?" Morgan didn't wait for an answer. "I spend so much time in them, I forget not everything is a boardroom." He tilted his hip into the island and turned to Sen. "You're really good, and I like these. I'm glad you didn't let the inspiration get away from you."

"Thank you. And thanks for providing inspiration," Sen said and then shrugged. "Err, the house—your house—it makes me think of who could have lived here over the years." That sounded reasonable enough.

As he spoke, Morgan shifted closer until their thighs pressed together, and Morgan's fingertips traveled from the drawing up Sen's hand, arm, and neck, and then rested lightly at the jut of his jaw. Sen lifted his face and swayed toward Morgan, and Morgan's eyes looked drowsy. Sen rolled his hips, and Morgan made a broken noise, but then reared back.

"I don't—I'm…." Morgan fisted his hands and crossed his arms. "I don't know what." His fingers flexed against his sides, and he looked anywhere but at Sen.

That worked out, because Sen needed a moment to compose himself and not vibrate out of his skin. He closed his eyes and worked to rein everything back in—their kiss, the apparition of those faces, his insistent desire to touch Morgan again—because what the hell?

"Do you like strawberries?" Morgan's voice cracked, but he shifted to face Sen and released the tight hold of his arms.

Sen grasped the line Morgan offered him to get back to some sort of equilibrium. "My favorite."

Morgan nodded. "Do you drink coffee?"

"Intravenously."

"Nice." Morgan sputtered a genuine laugh. "Same. Do you avoid carbs?"

"Only when they're mean to me."

"A fair policy." Morgan's lips quirked up, and he drummed the countertop. "It's just, I went shopping and actually got more than frozen dinners this time, and I meant to tell you, from the start, to help yourself to a cinnamon roll or making coffee while you're here working."

"Well, now if there are no cinnamon rolls on Wednesdays future, I'm gonna be disappointed." Sen shut his sketchbook and laid the pencil on the cover. "And thanks. That's very generous."

"No guarantees on baked goods—I get whatever's on day-old markdown. And nothing to it. I'm sorry I didn't think to mention it before." Morgan's gaze fell on Sen's hand, still on the sketchbook. A shadow passed over his brow. "And I should leave you alone and get back to work." He paused, swallowed, and then spun on a heel and strode from the kitchen.

Sen fell forward onto the island and buried his head in his arms. "That all went super great," he muttered as he listened to Morgan gathering the forgotten binder and papers, and then the study door shut with a decisive click.

He supposed he could leave—supposed it might be for the best if he did—but he'd made his decision. Sen stowed his messenger bag on the breakfast nook table and gathered his cleaning supplies.

The master suite didn't take long to clean. Sen stripped the bed and remade it, doing his all to ignore Morgan's scent in the sheets and aftershave in the air, and to keep the work impersonal. He put sheets and towels in the washing machine, headed back upstairs, and decided to scrub the guest bathroom. A little distance from Morgan wouldn't hurt.

Sen didn't watch the time, but he'd been at it long enough that all the unused surfaces were sprayed, wiped, polished, and buffed, and he had begun to organize the vanity drawers when Morgan knocked on the open door.

"Uh, hi?" Morgan held two steaming mugs. "Here." He set one of the mugs on the counter and then stood in the hall. "I read an article that antioxidants are good for you. I read another article about green tea being high in antioxidants. Then there was that all-important third article, about green tea being good for you because it's high in antioxidants."

Sen nodded. "I heard that too. I tasted green tea once and liked it, so I kept drinking it." He grinned and had a sip. "Mmm. With ginger and honey. Nice."

The tension making his head light, his shoulders and neck into knots, and his stomach like lead dissipated as he looked at Morgan. Just seeing Morgan warmed him with inexplicable gladness and relief. He stared into the tea. Green with ginger and honey, exactly what his mother recommended.

Morgan seemed on the point of going, but instead he asked, "Don't you take a lunch break or anything?"

"Nah." Sen thought about the snacks in his bag and the hours he'd already wiled away in the turret room on days when he was alone. "I had breakfast, and it's only four hours. I just tough it out." He drank half of the tea and returned to the middle drawer.

"You have a real knack for that." Morgan leaned on the doorframe and watched Sen work. "I think the last cleaner did the same as me when she had to deal with the linens—grab or stuff, slam the door, and run."

Sen chuckled. "Mom says I never wanted toys as a kid, just a pencil and paper, books, and something to arrange, rearrange, and re-rearrange. Like a cat who disdains fancy toys in favor of the box they came in." He finished the middle drawer and did nothing with the empty bottom one. "I was a menace with the tub of odds-and-ends Legos we had."

"I bet. I've seen you in action." Morgan skidded his gaze from Sen to a shadow box of shells on the far wall. "And don't all kids end up with tubs full of those after they lose bits and pieces from the sets?"

"Actually that tub was all we had." Sen made a line of round paper-wrapped soaps. "Every town we stopped in with a thrift store or Goodwill, we'd get what they had—Legos and books—which was awesome," he said with enthusiasm and real affection. "Since nothing went together, that meant everything could go together, so I could make whatever I imagined."

Morgan mulled that over, and then accepted at face value the curious detail Sen had dropped so casually. "Hunh. Nice way to do it. Not like me. I always wanted sets, and then they sat on a shelf after I finished them, so I could bask in their whole, undisturbed perfection. My favorites were the houses and skyscrapers." The corner of his mouth lifted and teased out a dimple. "It wasn't a shock to anyone that I became an architect."

Sen didn't miss the parallels to the near-pristine house he got paid to clean. He glanced up, and when Morgan hesitated, he smiled. Morgan accepted the invitation to continue talking and slid along the doorframe to sit.

"But I was the same with books, reading whatever I could." Morgan rubbed the back of his neck. "In between tearing around, playing sports, and the dance classes Mom kept me in until I was thirteen, and my room was a knee-deep maze. It's not that way now, because I'm an adult and everything, but it helps that I keep belongings to a minimum." He closed the bottom drawer. "So, do you clean because you're a starving artist? Or are you a personal organizer who draws?"

While Sen considered the most diplomatic way to answer, Morgan studied him.

"Ah. Or are you a working artist who did a cleaning favor for a friend and don't want to put her in a bad light?" Morgan raised a brow. "Loyalty—very admirable."

Sen clucked his tongue. "It has gotten me into trouble more than once." He reopened the middle drawer and held up a decorative soap shaped like a pineapple. "So did you make yourself a workaholic to avoid this shell of a house? Or are you a workaholic who just has to live somewhere?"

Morgan took the soap between his thumb and finger and twitched it in front of his gaze. "I didn't even know these were here." He tossed it back in the drawer, stilled, and then fitted it back into the space where it belonged after Sen's organizing. "Am I allowed to answer 'neither'?"

"Of course." This time Sen wasn't apologetic about speaking his mind. He could tell Morgan wasn't bothered. "Totally a dodge and completely dissatisfying, but of course."

"Most kind." Morgan turned to look across the hall and into the adjacent bedroom. "So you've been here several times and have gotten a feel for the house. Is there anything particular you like about it?"

Sen nodded. "Oh yeah. The third floor gable room—I call it the turret room. Awesome light and views. It's restful." He skipped right over all the other things that room had been. "And the small detail of a rabbit curled on an acorn—it matches the carvings on the main doors—sat over the door. Do you know what I mean?"

"Yes." Morgan glanced out into the hall and up, as if he could see the little guy. "Yes. He's a favorite of mine too."

"Why do you ask?" Sen asked.

"I'm always curious about people's impressions and takeaways about homes—any structure really. What details pop out and what the eye passes over. Yours especially, being an artist." Morgan had a drink. "It helps me build a mental portfolio of things people appreciate, and don't, in houses and libraries and skyscrapers. Or whatever."

"Ahhh." Sen understood. "I always want to know what paintings or pieces someone was most moved by in a museum or an exhibit, even if the movement was toward repugnance."

Morgan's eyes brightened and crinkles deepened as he smiled. He drained his cup, and Sen followed suit. They sat there until Morgan shifted, stood, and then held out both hands. "Here."

Sen uncrossed his legs and planted his feet. His hands fit into Morgan's to nest, and the rises and hollows filled one another. Morgan hefted, Sen levered, and as he stood, their hands turned so their fingers intertwined. Their contact didn't provoke any images or staring faces. Rather, it comforted Sen and settled his heartbeat as his breathing evened out.

He pulled back and blinked. Then he assembled the cleaning supplies and lined them up on the counter in order of descending height. His hand shook, and he tightened his jaw. It ached being away from Morgan, but he had been dangerously close to closing his eyes and leaning on Morgan's chest.

"All okay?" Morgan asked. He ran his knuckles down Sen's arm and then took light hold of Sen's hand.

Sen wanted to pull away and say stop—at least he felt he should. He could offer no reason why Morgan's brief kiss and very presence appeased instead of annoyed him. But oh, was he appeased. His tiredness from sleepless nights turned mellow, almost to contentment, and his racing thoughts subsided. He glanced at Morgan's hand and then at Morgan's eyes.

Morgan didn't seem to know he still had hold of Sen's arm.

"All is great." Sen shrugged. "Disorder makes me twitchy" sounded good so he said it.

Morgan hummed a laugh. "Yeah, I gathered."

His eyes shimmered as he gazed at Sen, and his mouth got soft. He moved closer, and Sen didn't retreat, but a bottle clattered to the floor when he reached for Sen's other arm. Morgan frowned. He swallowed and shook his head, and the shimmering colors faded. He cleared his throat and picked the bottle up.

"When I learned work was transferring me to NOLA, I bought this house. I do like it—a lot—but it took tons of rehab to make it livable, and I oversaw that process from several states away. Which is fine for the major stuff, when you trust your contractor. But I also needed it to be turnkey, as soon as I arrived. Ergo, I left the finishing touches to an interior design firm." Morgan waved at the bathroom and its beachy theme. "When I got here, work demanded priority. I haven't even lived here very long, at that. Then you arrived."

"So I did," Sen said, and beamed in answer to Morgan's smile. He wondered whether Morgan noticed their perfect fit as they stood together, and how familiar it felt.

Morgan's nose almost stroked Sen's cheek as he tilted his head from side to side and lowered his voice. "Your eyelashes are so long. Long and curly."

Sen ignored the comment about his lashes and the urge to duck his head and flutter them. Morgan tightened his grip, and Sen realized they were still holding hands.

"That explains a lot about the house. I had you pegged as a workaholic who bought a showplace you didn't care about."

"I am something of a workaholic, when work requires it. But I'm not married to the job, and I do know how to have fun. I have fun having fun, even." Morgan rubbed his thumb over Sen's, and then he looked down, let go, and retrieved the mugs.

"Now those you should leave to me." Sen pointed at the mugs and opened his hands. With purpose, he went around Morgan and down to the kitchen. Otherwise he would linger forever in the dim hallway, soaking in Morgan's warmth and their inexplicable rapport.

Some people you just clicked with. He knew that from a lifetime of traveling. But he'd never experienced such instant chemistry—the way his nerves zinged whenever he and Morgan touched or how he could read Morgan's expressions and inflections, and how Morgan was getting his.

He'd let Morgan invade his space and wanted to invade right back. Usually he called guys on that kind of shit—kissing him, excusing it, promising to chill, and then showing up moments later to chat. He didn't play games or play the fool. But Morgan he allowed for no good reason, and no good explanation why. They didn't even know each other.

So of course when Morgan followed him to the kitchen and slid onto one of the barstools at the island, he glowed with pleasure and mocked himself for it.

He loaded the dryer and cleaned the kitchen with methodical care. Sen didn't have anything to say, so he didn't talk, and neither did Morgan. But as he worked around Morgan, his glow didn't fade and the silence wasn't awkward. The company was nice, and when he stole a peek, Morgan looked relaxed, almost half-asleep. Sen moved on to the powder room, emptied the trash in the study, and returned to the buzzing dryer.

"Someday you'll have to show me your origami-level secrets," Morgan said while Sen folded everything.

"Why would I do that? Then you wouldn't need me." Sen snapped a towel and folded it in thirds and then in half. He knew he'd look up to Morgan staring at him.

Morgan had stood, walked around the island, and definitely stared. He advanced a step, then seemed indecisive about closing the gap or retreating.

"I'll just get these put away." Sen made an untidy wad of the fitted sheet, stacked everything, and stumbled upstairs. "Ridiculous," he huffed as he crammed sheets and towels onto his neat shelves. "Stop it."

Stop obsessing about what it might mean. Stop getting weak in the knees just from the sight of him. Stop thinking you know him because nothing has ever felt so right as when you touch.

"Stop," he bit out and closed the linen closet with some force.

Sen paced the hall and checked his phone. Twenty minutes remaining. He killed fifteen doing nothing upstairs and returned to an empty kitchen. Sen made a final sweep, grabbed his bag, and walked with purpose down the hall. Morgan lifted a chin at Sen from the study. He was engrossed behind the computer, and Sen escaped in a muddle of relief and annoyance.

He pedaled fast but got home before all his frustrations were vented, so he kept going until he began to tire and looped back to carry his bike up the stairs to his apartment on shaking legs.

Sen did his two-glass water ritual, had a shower, and then fell into bed. His sleep schedule hadn't regulated at all to accommodate his Wednesday morning hours, and he needed a nap.

Not ten stubborn minutes later, he got up with a groan to appease his racing thoughts and restless energy. He went for his sketchbook, but it wasn't in his bag.

"Dammit," he huffed.

He didn't think Morgan would mind or complain, but he wanted to look at what he'd drawn. Several minutes of trying to recapture the faces and images later, he sighed and threw his pen down.

"What were you trying to tell me?" he asked the abortive drawings.

In answer, the colors he'd seen for the long-haired girl washed over him.

Sen nodded and concentrated on her—her contentment, the confidence of her gaze, her spicy scent, and her regal bearing. He set up a new canvas.

"At least you aren't Morgan," he said and loaded paint on a brush. Then he stilled.

Sweat beaded on his neck and behind his knees, and he shivered.

He covered the canvas in color washes, then carved the portrait using thicker lines where the washes intersected. The earthy girl started to shimmer to life.

Only one way to find out.

CHAPTER FIVE

"TELL ME again why you haven't found a replacement and I can't quit?" Sen drained his sangria and poured a refill.

Adriane pushed her empty glass at him for more lemonade.

"It's only been four weeks. I can't just magic up another Fairy. Finding just the right candidate isn't that easy." Adri lounged back in the chair. "And, uh, since Ballard likes the job you're doing, specifically, I'm going to need another favor and have you train your replacement."

"To do what? Organize the beers in the fridge by type with all the labels turned front?" Sen shook his head. "They won't need training, and to go back a step, four weeks is a long time. That's a month, Adri."

"Have you been doing that? With the beer and everything? Eh. On second thought, don't answer." She considered something. "Four weeks vacation in an all-inclusive with my in-laws—yes, long time. An eternity, maybe. To find a new employee? A blip." Adriane pouted. "Another month? Please? I will get someone as soon as I can."

Sen frowned. He didn't have a good reason to give Adri for why he wanted to quit, and he wasn't going to open the can of worms of trying to explain. "Week to week," he countered. "With the understanding I might need for any week to be my last."

"Did you get spooked from him being there the second week? I'm sure it was a fluke. It's not cutting into your art, is it?"

He got spooked, all right. Sen ate a wine-soaked hunk of pear to buy time. "Not yet, but the group show is only getting closer." He squeezed Adri's arm. "I'm reminding you and using my words, mostly. We don't want to get stuck in a resentment rut here."

"Point, and I get that." Adri tapped her rings on the glass and sighed. "Fine. And thank you for still doing it. Really. I'll go back to cleaning myself if it comes to it."

Guilt twinged, but Sen tamped it down. He was the one doing the favor, and Adri's business wasn't his job.

"Did you ask me to impromptu dinner and buy me drinks to soften me up so you could quit?"

"Pretty much. Yup." Sen topped her up with the last of the lemonade.

Adriane tsked. "Evil. Cute, smart, and evil."

Sen grinned. "Birds of a feather."

She clinked their glasses together.

Pinpricks lifted on Sen's skin, and something pulled outward on his ribcage and drew his whole attention. He looked up and over and right into Morgan's eyes.

"And who is that?" Adriane asked in the faraway distance.

Sen half smiled when Morgan did. He held on to his chair so he didn't get up and run across the street to where Morgan stood after exiting a neighboring restaurant.

"Well. Oh my." Adriane leaned into Sen. "Do you know him? You're practically vibrating." She made a considering noise. "Waaaait. Do you *know* *him* know him? Are you finally dating? Or at least getting some? And with someone so... that?"

Sen grabbed her sleeve when her wave turned into motioning Morgan over. "That's Morgan," he hissed and held on. "Morgan Ballard."

"What?" she squawked as he pinned her arm to the table. "That's Mr. Ballard?"

Morgan's gaze slid to Adriane, and he dipped his head in curt acknowledgment and then turned away. Sen's ears roared, and his pulse rioted. He gripped the table and almost hauled it with him to chase after and confront Morgan, but after several breaths, he managed to stay seated and not shout curses at Morgan's retreating back. Anger faded to hurt and, at the core, betrayal.

Of what? Their quasi-friendship, built on brief encounters?

Sen grimaced and forced the normal motions of taking a drink and agreeing with whatever Adri said.

"He's gorgeous. Wow. Just think, we haven't been to this place in ages, and tonight of all things, we kinda run into the guy kinda in question." Adriane got distracted by her phone and tapped a reply message. "It's the hubs. Phoebe enjoyed being chauffeured around enough to fall asleep, so he's swinging by to get me. Want a ride home?"

"Nah, I'm good. How's he feeling?"

"Better. He'll be back to endless hours wrestling claims and wrangling paperwork in no time." She wrinkled her nose. "Throwing his back out hanging Phoebe's mobile didn't convince him to give it all up and learn carpentry. Which I suppose is for the best. And are you sure about a ride? He won't mind."

"No thanks. I need to stop at the store on the way home."

Adriane's eyebrow arched. "And that would preclude us giving you a ride how?"

"It wouldn't. I know." Sen fanned his hands out. "I want to get some air—walk off dinner, and dessert, and our second dessert."

"Wait. Is this why you want to quit?" Adriane sat straighter and gave Sen an assessing look. "You're starting to like Morgan and don't want to like him more? Or you think you can't like him more and work for him at the same time? It's not like I have rules against fraternization. Or is it a power imbalance thing?" She frowned. "He hasn't been a jerkface to you, has he?"

"No," Sen laughed. "He has not been a jerkface. We've barely interacted. And you really got going there. No, listen. I want to quit because working for you isn't my job." He waited until that landed, gave her a speaking look, and stuck a tip under the empty sangria jug. "Let's go wait for Hubs at the corner. It'll be easier on him."

"This feels like a subject change, but I'm not going to ruin my mellow by arguing." Adriane tucked herself under Sen's arm as they walked and dozed while they loitered near a lamppost.

Hubs wasn't long in arriving.

"Heya, Dan," Sen greeted him and helped Adriane into the car. "Still fighting the good fight?"

Dan made slashing motions and light saber sounds. "Always, brother. Just yesterday I toured a storefront we're thinking could be The Place. Awesome location, doable price, doesn't need a crapton of work."

The Place referred to Dan's dream of opening a craft beer bar. Dan and Adri had been scrimping and saving toward the goal longer than Sen had known them.

"Nice. That's awesome. Big change from insurance." Sen almost recommended talking to Morgan if Dan needed remodeling advice, but he didn't want to bring him into the conversation.

"Yeah, I'm totally psyched. I can feel my toes again too, so there's progress all around. Adri's parents are coming to coo over Phoebe, which will give me time to pore over my business plan while sitting at a desk and everything."

"Glad to hear you're feeling better." Sen shut the door and put his head in the open window. "Thanks for letting me date your wife."

"Thanks for treating her so nice," Dan said with extra twang and eased the car into gear. He was big and burly and had played football to pay for college—the visual opposite of Adri in so many ways—and he doted on her utterly.

"Dinner was so tasty, and I love the little bug more than my life. But wow, was it nice to have a few hours not ruled by Phoebe. I'm exhausted." Adriane kissed her fingers and landed them near Sen's nose. "And you'll work tomorrow?"

"Yes, and as long as you need—within reason," Sen stipulated. He patted the doorframe. "Have a good night, Dan. Everybody home safe and sound, now."

"That means you too, buddy," Dan said. He checked on Adri, then Phoebe, and poked the car out to merge with the slow-moving traffic.

Sen stepped back, and as he watched them drive away, it began to rain. Not a hard or cleansing rain, but the kind where humidity reaches its saturation point, takes form as drizzle, and then fades back into a blanketing haze.

He wandered in the direction of his apartment without haste, needing space and for his head to be less of a mess. He'd asked Adri to dinner as a distraction, but when his circling thoughts of Morgan wouldn't be quieted, he brought up needing to quit. On an ordinary day, guilt would swamp him for dodging her, but he didn't have energy for guilt.

Sen had paintings good enough for the show, but none he wanted to share yet. He dreamed about storms, desert landscapes, and twirling in someone's embrace across opulent ballrooms, and he woke every morning with Morgan's name on his tongue. He cleaned Morgan's pristine house on tenterhooks, waiting for Morgan or another vision to spring. The ennui had gone, but an exhausting flow of images that demanded to be captured had taken its place. He was past ready to leave New Orleans and start fresh on another adventure, and after the gallery show, he could. Sacrificing the chance to get to know Morgan tore at his heart.

Hadn't he just finished saying they barely knew each other? And wasn't that the honest truth? Even their brief kiss and his pang of loneliness when he found the house empty last week weren't indicators of anything monumental. But Sen couldn't shake the notion he'd found Morgan at that restaurant that he and Adri never went to anymore so their eyes could meet and then… what?

Sen wound around, following the snaked and curving streets, taking the turns and alleys that seemed to tug him in a certain direction. An antique-store window display of miniature globes, opera glasses, hatpins, and pocket watches. Drooping paper arrows stapled to telephone poles, advertising a garage sale. A gurgling noise he couldn't place that led to an overflowing storm drain.

His jean cuffs flopped heavily against his legs, but he remained unbothered by the rain and how it soaked his shoes and squished between his toes or dripped a constant line down his forehead from a hank of hair. The streets were clear of people and the sickly-sweet stench that built over the hot and humid days. It refreshed him and cured his unease, falling steadily and not driven by a storm, cool on his skin but not cold.

The crumbling wall of a cemetery beckoned, and Sen crossed the street and hopped over it. He threaded between mausoleums and beneath the sentry of angels and obelisks to a path. Sen flattened his palm and ran his fingers along details of statuary, scrolls, and the patterns time had etched on stone. It didn't creep him out—the cemetery's energy was clean. He liked the history, artistry, and restful quiet. When the path ended, he hopped another boundary fence, trudged up a shallow incline, and stopped short.

His hackles rose, and he turned in place. The view—the cemetery obscured by trees and the shape of the lawn—had become familiar. Sen squinted at the looming silhouette on the top of the rise and realized he'd walked to Morgan's backyard.

"Wow. That's just perfect and not at all weird."

He laughed a humorless "Ha ha," but even that caught in his throat.

A light came on upstairs at the neighbor's house, and his hand got mired in mud when he dropped to one knee. Sen scanned the yards and then looked back, thinking he could retreat through the cemetery, but a dark curtain of sheeting rain churned toward his position, cutting off his view and his chance to escape.

Sen licked water from his lips and toyed with the direct approach of going to the house, knocking on the door, and asking Morgan for shelter. Morgan might question his sanity, because doing so would be weird, but he wouldn't be hunched over in the backyard, puddles up to his ankles, terrified he'd get caught and look even weirder.

He hunkered into a dorky duck-walk toward the house, as though that would make him invisible and stealthy. He'd call it farcical, but his heart was in his throat, his hands shook, and his breath heaved.

The curtain of rain caught him and whipped around, obscuring the house and surrounding him in shadow. Sen jumped when lightning split the dark. Thunder followed, rolling around in the sky and rattling the ground.

Sen closed his eyes to the stinging downpour and pictured the yard and where the house sat in proximity to his position. He went into a tiptoe run but pulled up short of slamming into a tree. He staggered and almost smacked into another tree, so he stopped, spread his arms, and tried to feel for any others around him.

A branch snapped, and Sen turned, expecting to see low, glowing eyes and get meowed at, because the only thing the inanity needed was a genuine cat scare.

Instead someone approached without hesitation and reached for him—and Sen reached back.

"There you are," Morgan said, as though he'd spent hours searching. Morgan hauled Sen into his arms and a searing kiss. Lightning ripped the sky, and thunder shook their bones.

Sen didn't—couldn't—resist. He poured his confusion and frustration and desire into returning the kiss, spiraling the intensity higher, and dug his fingers into Morgan's damp shirt. Morgan's hold shifted so one arm kept Sen pinned and the other moved so Morgan could angle his jaw and then blister a line of kisses down to his throat. Sen groaned when Morgan tugged at his thigh and lifted it to bend them into a tighter embrace.

Morgan's kiss was restless and seeking. He tasted Sen's cheeks, nipped at Sen's neck, and with each return to Sen's mouth, his kiss became harder and hungrier. He grabbed at Sen, let go, and then held on tighter, as though afraid Sen would slip from his embrace, and hurried to fill the ache of being too long denied.

Sen shushed Morgan's protests when he broke contact so he could rebalance—body and mind. He wrapped both arms around Morgan and laid his head on Morgan's chest, as he'd wanted to do since they met, content, bemused, and heedless of the rain. He marveled at how they filled and complemented one another, with hollows and curves matched and met, just like their hands. They swayed, and Morgan nuzzled Sen's temple, kissed his brow, and then pulled back.

"When will I see you again?" Morgan asked.

"I could just stay?"

Sen wanted to stay, either to stand there holding Morgan or to go inside, it didn't matter. Being together. Touching and completing the circuit of their connection and calming the ache in his heart mattered. The portrait of the young man flashed in his mind, animated with life, nodding and urging. He whispered for Sen to surprise Morgan by stealing another kiss.

Lightning flickered and revealed Morgan's expression, which was filled with sorrow. His features warped and melded into those of the first portrait Sen had painted after the false storm from his vision.

Morgan leaned his forehead to Sen's and whispered, "And I would have you stay, if the decision could be ours alone to make." His voice had a different cadence and quality, huskier and more formal. He pulled Sen to him again and their kiss spoke of bitter restraint and good-bye. Then Morgan made a tortured noise and tore himself away. "Promise me soon?" he demanded as he retreated. "Promise to take care and do nothing foolish until then."

"Soon, yes. Of course," Sen agreed, because he had no clue what was going on.

Thunder rumbled, the wind kicked up, and Morgan disappeared into the shadows.

Overwhelmed, Sen sat on the ground right where he stood. Morgan should have returned to yell at him, because sitting in a puddle under a circle of trees in a thunderstorm was the height of foolishness. Jagged lightning forked close to the ground, and Sen squinted at the dark, where low branches took on the animated movements of bodies, arms and legs. Something flashed among the trees, reminiscent of that knife and its heat, but he dismissed it as an illusion created by a very real storm. Sen gritted his teeth and got to his feet. Then, hands on knees, he leaned on a tree trunk.

Exhausted bewilderment kept him from pursuing Morgan into the house. Sen teetered on his feet, checked for cats or Morgan or whatever else lay in wait, and then darted around the side door, down the driveway, and ran home. His whole body shook nonstop—from exposure and fatigue, he tried to rationalize—but even safely back in his apartment, the shaking didn't subside.

Sen poured two shots of bourbon instead of water and downed them in quick succession. The alcohol burned his throat and soured in his stomach, and he let out an involuntary breath, yucked, and wiped his mouth. But he reveled in the concrete physical sensations.

He fumbled through a hot shower, exhausted and tipsy, and then he face-planted into bed to lie in a miserable, brooding lump. The gazes from the portraits he'd painted were heavy on him, and he turned his back. Sen wanted to be drunk and to be left alone in a swimmy nowhere.

"Oh, no," he moaned when it occurred to him that he had to get up and go clean in a few hours.

Sen snapped on a dim lamp, cast about for his laptop, and did some Internet searching on Morgan. He had to learn more about Morgan, the house, anything, and that gave his restless mind something to do.

He found an architect in greater New Orleans named Morgan Ballard quickly enough—the only one in the area—a lot of bland professional mentions, neglected social media accounts, and a brief career portfolio on his firm's website.

"No help," Sen grumped at the computer. He'd hoped to find a dating profile or something, but there was no clickbait "Can You Guess These Ten Secrets About Morgan Ballard" quiz to take. Which, too bad.

He shut the laptop and slid it back on the floor. Then he curled onto his side so he could study the finished portraits while they observed him. Even with his annoyance, their presence comforted him, and after a while he was pulled from bed to stand in front of the man with Morgan's eyes, which were filled with the same sadness he'd seen earlier that night in the real Morgan's gaze.

"Why are you here?" he implored, but the portrait remained silent.

Sen had painted three couples from their strange visitations and their intrusion on his mind. Two of the portraits—an earthy girl and her young man companion—emanated satisfied pleasure. The first two, so suffused with loss, contrasted all the more painfully. Anything else he tried to paint had stayed elusive, despite his referencing the quick sketches he'd drawn in Morgan's kitchen.

He stood in front of other-Morgan. "Do I know you?"

Sen tried sketching, but nothing wanted to be doodled, much less called forth. He tried to sleep, but that didn't work. Sunrise interrupted his nonconversation with the paintings, and he tore away, made double-strength coffee, and headed back to Greycote.

Storm debris littered the streets but hadn't inflicted damage on the house. Sen parked his bike and stared into the far circle of trees in the backyard but found no telltale mark or even a trace of what had happened there with Morgan.

"Hello?" he called as he let himself into the house and walked down the hall.

"I'm just leaving," Morgan answered from the kitchen.

Sen heard clattering, and Morgan cursed. He followed a trail made up of a briefcase, a laptop bag, an accordion file folder, and a suit jacket hanging from a hook on the study door. When Sen walked into the kitchen, Morgan was sticking a cup under the coffeemaker with a piece of toast in his mouth and stepping into expensive shoes.

"Overslept," Morgan said around the toast. "Damndest thing. I don't think I've overslept since freshman year of undergrad. Maybe the storm got me. I had terrible dreams." He forgot his toast, frowned, and seemed to pick at his memory while he studied Sen's face. Coffee dripped and sizzled on the element, and Morgan blinked and then straightened. He pulled the mug from the coffeemaker, had a long slurp, and then put the mug back. "Good morning."

"Seems not." Sen went around Morgan's hubbub to put his bag on the breakfast table. Then he stayed there, waited for some reaction, and tried to pick up any cues of awkwardness.

Morgan mumbled an eloquent *hmmpgh* while he gobbled the rest of the toast and then threaded a yellow tie, patterned with gilded olive-colored florets, through his collar. "Was that your sweetie?" he asked, flipping his collar back down.

"What?"

"The woman you were with at the restaurant—the French bistro place with a twist." Morgan frowned. "Is sweetie too much of a throwback word? Or...?"

"Oh." Sen clicked with what Morgan was talking about. "That was actually Adriane. You know her, or at least you've spoken before. She owns the Fairymaids. And she's married, but not to me."

Morgan's "Ah" sounded entirely too satisfied.

"Let me," he said and batted Morgan's hands away from mangling the tie. He adjusted the ends, looped once, then twice, and made an expert knot. "I leave the tightening to you," he teased, but couldn't move away when Morgan smiled.

Their positions echoed those of the night before, and Sen arched his spine so he didn't lean in when Morgan's hands briefly landed on his shoulders. The colors of the tie were the colors Sen had used to paint the earthy woman and her young man. Sen blinked at it and stared while Morgan examined his work.

"Perfect, thank you." Morgan strode down the hall for the suit jacket and then returned to finish his coffee. "Extend my apologies that I didn't come introduce myself. I was entertaining people we really need on our side to complete our big project here."

Sen nodded. "Sure. And that explains why you were in a place so exclusive. Were they suitably impressed?"

"I hope so. God loves fools and expense accounts, let me tell you." Morgan scanned the kitchen and then motioned for Sen to follow as he went back toward the study. "Ugh. I've left such a mess this morning, but I have to go. I'm so late."

"Good thing I'm here to clean." Sen laughed aloud. He shooed Morgan to the side door, held it open while Morgan gathered and juggled everything, and then held his breath when Morgan paused. He waited for Morgan to explain the night before or acknowledge him creeping in the yard, how Morgan found him, and their searing kisses.

Morgan cracked a grin. "Touché," he said, and nothing more. His dimple faded and his mouth softened as he stared at Sen a moment too long. Then he shook his head. "There's something I want to ask you, but I can't remember what."

"Well, if it comes to you, write it down and leave me a note for next week." Disappointment filled the hollow crash of anticipation, but Sen managed a smile.

"Right. Good thinking." Morgan stepped out the side door and then turned and regarded Sen. "Do storms scare you?"

"Do storms scare you?" Sen countered.

Morgan stiffened, and his gaze hardened.

"Did you have a bad experience in a storm?"

"You damn well know the answer," Morgan hissed and showed his teeth. He stared at a spot just over Sen's shoulder, and Sen watched dark clouds billow in Morgan's eyes and spread to surround his head and then body in a grotesque halo.

Sen retreated and made calming sounds. "Storms don't scare me," he whispered, seized by a sudden chill, but he steadied his breath and kept shushing.

Morgan grimaced, and a hint of blood appeared in his nostril. Then his brow furrowed, and the dark cloud started to break apart.

"Storms have never scared me." Sen opened his hands and watched, fascinated, as Morgan's posture relaxed, and the shutters lifted from his eyes.

"We had quite a storm last night. I think it gave me nightmares." Morgan frowned and rubbed the bridge of his nose. He looked back at Sen and smiled. "Do storms scare you?"

Sen swallowed and briefly closed his eyes. Then he answered Morgan's repeated question as though their previous exchange hadn't happened. "No. Never have. I was the kid who had to be pulled inside and given a scolding when storms really started to bear down. They're beautiful and fascinating and can pass without incident or destroy everything."

Profound silence followed his answer, and then Morgan stepped back into the house.

"Yes. That's it exactly." Morgan's eyes danced with shared pleasure. "I've always loved them, but lately they've really gotten under my skin. One of my favorite things is falling asleep to a storm. You know?"

Sen warmed again and nodded.

Morgan licked his lips. "Right. Of course you do. But lately I can't stand them, and who knows why. Not really the most convenient development in New Orleans during springtime." His smile turned rueful.

"Right, right," Sen echoed.

Morgan continued to stand there, and Sen teetered on edge of grabbing his expertly tied necktie and strangling Morgan until he explained what the fuck was going on or until he forced Morgan into a kiss. The nosebleed, the cloud, and Morgan's obvious confusion stopped him.

"I hope you figure it out," Sen grated.

"Thanks. Me too." Morgan hesitated. "And now I'm for sure late and for sure have to get going. Have a good day."

"Yup," Sen answered without trying to be heard.

He watched Morgan hustle across the driveway to the detached garage and lifted his hand in answer to Morgan's wave.

Sen left the shadow of the portico and went to stand in the circle of trees. He spread his arms out wide and closed his eyes in readiness for another vision or some answer to reveal itself.

Wind rustled the leaves, and he yelped when something tickled his face and arm. He tensed, opened his eyes, and then growled and flicked the trailing

Spanish moss away. Sen turned and glared at the house. The back wasn't as ornate as the front, but that didn't diminish its presence. The curving line of the gable and windows in the turret room met the long main center wing that spilled out into a terraced patio. He searched for signs of hidden rooms, ghostly figures in the upper windows, perhaps a cellar that had been buried over, but didn't find any.

Sen looked to the cemetery, as though an apparition would helpfully rise up, wave him over, and impart long-held secrets. Instead the scattered clouds parted, and the sun blanketed the crypts and graves with warm, tranquil light.

He huffed and went back inside.

Sen started in the kitchen. He attacked, using his frustrated energy, slung Morgan's coffee mug into the sink, emptied the coffeemaker, and scrubbed the spot on the counter where the machine lived. He wiped everything down and even scraped gunk from the toaster's crumb drawer into the trash. He hand-dried the mug and a butter knife, idly wondered when Morgan had gotten butter while putting it away, and scowled at the takeout containers and the bag of baby carrots in the fridge.

He swept and mopped everywhere, working his way upstairs, and then he checked all the rooms down the hall and back. The master bedroom loomed, and he hesitated.

"Just go in, loser," he said. Then he propelled himself in and braced to see evidence of what had made Morgan linger in bed.

The room was the same as every other week, including the two dented pillows on one side of the mattress and all the other pillows still under the blankets on the other side. Morgan said he had terrible dreams and gave no indication of being restless due to company, but Sen had dreaded that as the cause, and didn't realize it until then.

Sen sank onto the corner of the bed and let out a long sigh. His scattered thoughts wanted to land and roost on the memory of their encounter the night before or pick at Morgan's behavior that morning.

Morgan had seemed genuinely no-big-deal casual, to the point where Sen wondered whether their kiss and strange conversation had even happened. But then Morgan had asked about storms, tracking Sen's blush when he mentioned falling asleep to them, and had trouble leaving. If it were anyone else, Sen would get direct and ask what was going on.

He forgot how with Morgan. No matter his resolve, their affinity and his contentment in Morgan's company overruled his confusion and doubts. He forgot they hadn't known each other forever and a day and demanding answers fell from importance. Then they parted, and in Morgan's absence, every question and worry rushed back.

He centered his breathing until his calm returned, and then he got up to snoop in Morgan's stuff. Something he had resisted like a champ so far, but no more.

For Sen, snooping was like poring over specimen cases in museum archives, learning about someone from the artifacts of their life. He was also nosy and curious about everyone and the things they chose to keep, because he had grown up without many belongings. From the towns they rolled through to the hand-me-down clothes, books, and toys he quickly outgrew, owning stuff had no importance in his worldview.

Oh, he had plenty of treasures, but everything fit in an old-fashioned, hard suitcase the size of a laptop case he didn't open often. Other peoples' stuff—piles of books, accumulated mail, dust collectors, and antiques—all of it fascinated him. He wanted to know what was inside kitchen cupboards, the decals on the china and the porcelain figures in a dish hutch, and whether the contents of bookshelves were well read, for show, or slowly being phased out for bigger televisions. Finding out what Morgan collected and kept was an itch he'd been tempted to scratch since he walked into this house.

"Boundaries," he chided as he approached the dresser. "Respect the boundaries."

Each drawer had clothes in it—shocker. And in each drawer the clothes were crammed and messy—double shocker. Sen didn't redo them, though he wanted to. Snooping was one thing. Reorganizing dresser drawers for Morgan to find later and probably feel creeped out about was another.

Which should give him pause. Sen was pragmatic in his approach and followed a code. He was snooping, not prying. Messy drawers told him a lot. He didn't need to read old letters or a diary to learn the story. Even if he wanted to.

Pocket squares and boxer-briefs filled the top drawer. Sen didn't linger. The other drawers were a mishmash of athletic socks and brightly colored striped socks, ratty T-shirts and long-sleeved thermals, sweatpants and comic-book-character pj's. So Morgan had more than power suits and power casual clothes.

Sen already knew where not to look—the closet, bathroom cabinets, and under the bed held no secrets or intriguing caches. Sen dusted as he went from the dresser to the chest of drawers, and peeked inside to find them crammed with sweaters and workout clothes. Then he moved on to the bedside tables. He didn't open those drawers. Bedside tables could reveal a lot, and most of it really none of his business unless he'd been invited to share the bed.

Perhaps most telling was how little Sen found. Plenty of things bought and belonging to a set—the armoire, dresser, chest of drawers, two chairs, lamps, and side tables—filled the room but offered up no personality or preference. Morgan couldn't fold to save his life, and tossed receipts in a plastic bin on the floor under a chair. Truly personal items were sparse. He had expensive watches and cufflinks, a surprising number of scarves, and an expired coupon for kickboxing classes.

Sen had no right to feel disappointed, but he did. He fingered a mother-of-pearl cufflink and then snapped the armoire shut. When he turned in place, he noticed the padded chest at the foot of the bed had hinges.

Inside he found a small, square box almost lost in the depths of the chest. Sen flattened his hand on the lid and wondered what Morgan kept in there, protected from the otherwise spare and utilitarian house. It reminded him of his old suitcase, and that made his belly flutter and his heart clench. Sen curled his fingers and cradled his hand against his chest. He bit his lip to stave off a fleeting, hot rush of tears, and removed the lid.

Sen dropped the box and scrambled away. Then he backed against the far wall. He'd wanted to learn a secret or insight about Morgan, not get totally creeped out. His gaze stayed riveted to the chest as his insides lurched and saliva filled his mouth. Dizziness felled him, and he sat, his head tipped against the wall, swallowing rapidly and denying what he'd found. When he could breathe without his guts pinching, he gathered his resolve and crawled to the chest.

Dramatic music tracking his movements and discovery would be ridiculous, but he'd have preferred that to the calm quiet of the house. He balled his hands into fists and tightened them until they stopped shaking. Then he reached in and pulled the box onto his lap.

There wasn't any rabbit's blood, or a whole rabbit, or cut-and-pasted mixed-letter manifestos, or whatever other over-the-top scariness he imagined would be in a creepy horror box. Thinking he could have discovered much worse offered cold comfort, but it steadied him, and his shock faded into baffled wonder.

"What is this? What are you doing?" he asked while not quite touching his drawings framed in the box. Sen hadn't noticed that page missing from his sketchbook, but he had definitely drawn them, frantic to capture the portraits he'd visualized after Morgan's brief and shattering kiss in the hall.

If that weren't strange enough, only two of the portraits from that page had been saved, and one of them was torn to bits. Sen recognized the bits as other-Morgan, piled in the far corner of the box, banished, but unable to be separated from the young man. Guilt, anger, and desolate sorrow vibrated from the pieces in palpable waves. The despair cut through Sen's unease at finding them.

Sanity and self-preservation should have kicked in and insisted he run and never return. But Sen didn't want to run. He wanted to wrap himself around Morgan and confess to snooping and finding them, but he wasn't afraid.

Sen skimmed a fingertip over the young man's familiar features, and sparks traveled up his arms. Then wet ground replaced the carpet as white light pushed from behind his eyes.

He looked up into the rain and heard shouting, but he wasn't strong enough to rise or answer. Warm lassitude spread from his middle to his limbs, and he forgot the ache in his side. As the world grayed at the edges, he imagined his lover's hand taking his, and he smiled and murmured hello wrapped in good-bye and allowed himself to let go.

Gentle but insistent noise nudged Sen's awareness, and he muttered and curled further onto his side. Drool cemented his hand to his cheek, and his head pounded and his neck ached. Rain pattered against the windows, and he levered upright and lurched to look outside. Sun dappled the yard across the street, and the rain sprayed and then slowed. He craned up to see the sky and a passing cluster of low-lying dark clouds. That was real rain, and the carpeting was just carpet, not wet ground. He wasn't bleeding or dying or even creeped out anymore.

He located the box and, without touching the drawings, he replaced the lid, returned it to the dark corner of the chest, and shut it inside. Sen stared at the chest and then dragged his gaze away to check his phone. Four twenty-seven.

"Damn." He grimaced in accusation at the dent he'd left in the carpet. He had just enough time to make the bed and scoot to avoid the risk of being there when Morgan got home.

He finished, left, and biked home in a fog. Other-Morgan's sorrow stayed with him, heavy against his ribs and leaden in his heart, and he stood in front of the portrait and whispered "Sorry," again and again.

Morgan's eyes gazed at him from the painting and forgave his rash action. Sen didn't understand it. Morgan had the creepy box—wasn't it for Sen to forgive? But he felt guilt and sadness clinging to the portraits on the wall, cluttered in his sketchbook, and in the box. Morgan probably didn't understand it any better than he did.

Other-Morgan and the young man stared back at him, and he waited for them to explain. But they remained implacable. His mind raced and demanded answers, but there were none. Exhausted, Sen touched each canvas a last time and then went in search of painkillers, an unadvised drink, and some stolen moments of oblivion.

CHAPTER SIX

"THESE ARE exciting paintings." Lars moved forward, tilted his head, and then stepped back several paces. "Movement, color symbolism, compositional aspects—all dynamic. And the portraits within the work here are compelling enough that they'd stand on their own. Together it's something very special."

Sen rocked on his feet and hid his nerves. Lars had once mentioned Sunday afternoons were slow because everyone was at church or dining out, so he'd chanced to swing by with two of the new paintings to take advantage of an empty gallery and its bored owners.

"She has a real Mona Lisa quality going on, with her enigmatic smile." Bharti crossed one arm to prop on the other and tapped her chin. She was the other half of the gallery and really the one with final say-so. "I'm in agreement. Very exciting."

Lars lifted his glasses from their perch on his nose. "Not right for the group show, however."

"Not in the least." Bharti nodded. "You have more, you said?"

"Yes. Four others—two pairs—but each is a different portrait." He talked through the crushing weight of their words. He'd brought the green-gold girl and her young man, the happy ones, the accessible ones. "I have pictures on my phone, if you'd like to look." Sen didn't want to show them. They included the first portraits that he still wasn't ready to share, and he didn't want them to request one painting in particular.

Bharti waved away the offer and turned her back on the paintings. She walked a diagonal to the far wall, studied them, and then slowly returned. Eventually she gave Lars a nod.

"You said these are part of a larger series?" Lars turned to face Sen. "So you're currently working on more?"

"Oh yeah. Busy with several others," Sen answered, skipping to the end so they didn't think he was worried about the means.

Lars moved to stand close to Bharti, and as they talked, competing factors crowded for Sen's attention. What did they mean these weren't right for the group show? Would the source of inspiration continue? Did it require contact with Morgan, and could he paint facsimiles of them, if not? He could continue to paint and make something similar, but their soul would be missing.

The portraits represented the quenching of his long creative dry spell. What if pushing for more ended up risking the gift?

"Could you paint twelve—six pairs in all?" Bharti interrupted Sen's spinning thoughts as she moved next to him.

"I'm sure I can. Do I need to?" Sen looked from Bharti to Lars.

Lars flicked his glasses away once more. "Absolutely. If you agree to a solo show with us, of course." He joined them and stood to Sen's left. "We agree these are phenomenal, and we want to represent them. In fact we believe this collection of yours is strong enough and perfect for our Emerging Artist spotlight, a two-week solo exhibit that does exactly as billed. It comes on the heels of the group show and highlights a star from among the constellation. Which gives us, what? Just long enough for you to work and us to prepare then launch mid-June, I believe. Since you have these and others, we can select the right ones for the group show as lead-in."

"Teasers, if you will. And these are lovely, but we should have two with more weight, more oomph. All you need to do is keep working, and we'll do the rest." Bharti put an arm around Sen. "Are we railroading you? Overwhelming? I'm so glad you brought these in to show us." She squeezed Sen and then returned to the paintings. "There's so much going on with them. I feel like I'm listening to private conversations and peeking into others' lives. And we think our clientele and the critics will agree."

"Dependent on you agreeing, naturally. And checking in with us as to your progress and our expectations that the subsequent pieces will follow in this vein." Lars retrieved his phone from a pocket as it rang. "Please, think about it," he said to Sen. Then he stepped away to take the call. "Hello? Yes. Now is a good time."

Sen wanted to do cheerleader kicks or run full speed through the streets shouting victory cries or fall over and lie on the gallery floor as they repeated and reassured him their offer was genuine.

"Wow. *I'm* so glad I brought these over," he said to Bharti. "In case it wasn't clear, yes, I'm interested. Is there more you need from me besides a huge *Y-E-S*? Thank you?"

"Certainly, but I'll send it all in an e-mail. Read over the fine print, call with any questions, devil's in the details, and so forth. You know." Bharti's grin broke her cool, assessing eye and professional façade. She grabbed hold of his arm and said, "Sen, these paintings are wonderful. It feels like a real breakthrough, and we can't wait to see the others and get started planning and staging the show. So exciting."

Sunshine bounced and streaked across the gallery floor when the front door opened. Sen's pulse jumped and his nape tingled.

"Come in, come in. Good timing. We're just finishing up." Lars fanned a manila folder in greeting.

"Afternoon, Lars. Hello, Bharti," a familiar voice greeted. The rhythm of his quick footsteps mirrored the pace of Sen's heart.

Sen turned slowly to find Morgan with Lars. Bharti offered a cheek, which Morgan kissed. Then she eyed them when Morgan smiled at Sen.

"Do you know each other?" she asked.

Sen's gut dropped. "Yeah. Sen cleans my house," Sen imagined him saying. But Morgan inclined his head and his smile changed to encompass the room.

"Yes, I have had the pleasure. We've met professionally, in other circumstances." He moved to get a better view of the paintings, but Bharti stepped in front of him.

"No. No peeking." She arched her brow in answer to Morgan raising his. "Why ruin the effect of seeing them at this opening, hung and lit beautifully?" Bharti leaned in and handed Morgan an announcement postcard. "Bring your friends and wealthy clients."

"I can do that," Morgan said affably. He pointed toward the paintings. "And these are in that show?"

"Something of mine will be." Sen tilted his head at Bharti. "We're still negotiating what."

"Then I'll definitely come." Morgan's gaze lost focus. He blinked and asked, "Those sketches you did—are your paintings related?"

The careful tone Morgan used to reference the sketches, done in his post-kiss state, told Sen that Morgan remembered their short kiss in the hallway weeks before. Morgan acknowledging it, however indirectly, rattled and excited Sen.

"Yes. Good memory," Sen said and searched Morgan's expression for any response.

Morgan nodded. "I look forward to it."

"Maybe you don't need these after all," Lars said and handed the manila envelope to Morgan. "Here's a happy coincidence. Sen is a talented commercial artist as well. You've sought our recommendation for local artists, and here I can recommend him, and you're already acquainted."

"And why didn't I think of this in the first place?" Morgan asked.

Bharti shook her fist in mock threat. "Just remember we're his priority."

"And standing right here," Sen said dryly.

"Sorry," Morgan said, only to Sen. "I hate when people do that to me. The pleasant surprise of finding you here made me get ahead of myself."

"Hmm." Sen tried not to smile, but totally smiled. He broke from the spell of Morgan's eye crinkles and jawline and said, "I think we're pretty well ironed out here, so I can be on my way. Is it all right for me to leave the paintings here?" He didn't want to, but he had to get out of there. Dan had given him a ride over, and he couldn't take them home on his bike.

"Certainly." Lars clasped his hands together. "They'll be quite safe until you can collect them, or leave them in our keeping entirely until your show."

"Unless you want them for reference. Whatever's best for you." Bharti pointed toward the back brick wall. "We'll leave them in the racks for when you decide, and we can make arrangements to have them returned."

"I could be the arrangement?" Everyone looked at Morgan, and he opened his hands. The manila folder jutted out like a fan. "This is what I came for, and you said you're finished. It seems logical."

"Providential, even," Bharti said. She walked to a dispenser of brown paper bolted to the floor in a secondary space and tore two pieces from the huge roll.

Sen took one piece and they wrapped his paintings. Then they all shook hands and exchanged the polite business promises that people make after such meetings. Then Lars held the door for them, and they carried the paintings to Morgan's car.

"Wait—my bike."

"Will also fit in my car." Morgan cupped a hand under Sen's elbow and kept them moving. "But for the time being can stay where it is. Lars gave me an idea, something I'd like to discuss with you."

Morgan led them down a side street to a sensible Volvo, and they stowed the paintings and then stood on the sidewalk.

"Do you have time for coffee? And to discuss things?" Morgan swept a hand around behind him. "There's a nice café a short and pleasant walk from here. Explaining this shouldn't take long, and then you can decide where you want yourself, your bike, and the paintings delivered." When he dimpled and added "My treat," it was easy to agree.

They nabbed a two top outside the casual and cozy café. Sen ordered an iced coffee and nothing else, so Morgan made up for that by ordering an assortment of bread and pastries with his black coffee.

"So, in brief, I need to commission illustrations of the historic property my firm will soon finish restoring. Interior and exterior vantages, and some detail sketches of the wallpaper, tin ceiling pattern, banister carvings, and so on. We prefer using local talent—artists from outside the firm—and I had approached Gallery Paon for recommendations. But if you're available and interested, I think my search is over."

"And before it even began." Sen paused when the waiter brought their order and didn't pretend he would pass on the pain au chocolat. "If you want to consider the artists Lars assembled, I don't mind. You might find someone more suitable."

Morgan shook his head. "Impossible," he said, and then he blinked as though shuttering away a memory.

"I mean someone whose work is more suited to the task. I'm not a draughtsman."

"That's precisely our motivation for getting an artist." Morgan considered the basket of goodies and selected brioche and loaded it with whipped butter. "We use the illustrations for visual reference and marketing, but they're primarily for on-site enrichment. So they need to have an interpretive flair. Blueprints and specs and invoices have the raw data, but not the soul of a place, which is what I want you to capture."

"Would you have asked me before getting Lars's recommendation? When I was only a starving artist who cleans?"

"I'm not sure." Morgan weighted one hand. "I thought about it, and thought it was a good idea, but I didn't want to put you in a tight spot or make you feel beholden to say yes."

"Okay, good answer. I respect that." Sen had a drink and sucked an ice cube so he didn't say yes outright, but he wanted to. "How many illustrations? And what's the time frame?"

Morgan's eyes gleamed. "Twenty-four, none large-scale, and we're committed to a May 31 completion date. No later than May 15 for the finalized illustrations."

"Compensation?"

"We start at five hundred per piece, but that's further negotiable, depending on your current commission rate. With reimbursement for expenses and supplies." Morgan sipped his coffee. "The building, rooms, and samples for the detail pieces will be at your disposal."

Five hundred times twenty-four sounded enormous, but given the work involved and what his time and talent were worth, Sen wouldn't mind pushing for a bit more. He did some quick math and determined the job could pay for the solo show and then some. Agreeing would put him under pressure, but his creativity and output were perverse and thrived by being pushed. The painting inspiration came to him in bursts, anyway, so he could stagger work on the illustrations amid those fugue states. He could also turn down random commissions and not sweat where money for more stretchers, canvas, and framing would come from. A lot could happen in two and a half months, and when the push was over, he could answer the wanderlust and move on.

"Can I please consider the offer and let you know my decision on Wednesday?"

"Most definitely. You can leave me a note." Morgan smiled and cut a piece of lemon pound cake in half. "I appreciate you even considering it."

Sen ate the other half, and they finished, paid the bill, and returned to the dorky Volvo.

Morgan checked on the paintings. "So, shall we retrieve your bike? Or would you like me to meet you somewhere?"

With Morgan in the street and Sen on the curb they were the same height. Sen's mouth burned, and nerves fluttered under his warming skin. He should run, remember the creepy ripped-up pictures in the box, and shout no, nope, no way would he work with Morgan on anything.

"I don't need to leave a note," Sen said, instead of shouting, and at Morgan's look, he added, "About the illustrations. Yes, but it's conditional."

Morgan raised his brows and waited.

"Gallery Paon offered me a solo show, and I accepted. The group show I'm already part of will be settled with something I've already finished, so it won't interfere, but I suddenly have a lot more obligation on my hands. The illustrations will get done by the deadline, and I'll do my best to give them immediate priority. But the pace won't be nonstop, and there will be days I'm not available."

"You have? That's awesome. Congratulations." Morgan leaned forward, his eyelids lowered, and the surrounding noise of the street faded away as he laid a light hand on Sen's arm. Then he drew back and shoved his hands in his pockets. "Seriously, that's great. It's a real accomplishment, and they're well connected. These, I'm guessing?" He motioned to the paintings in the car.

Sen nodded. "Yes. And several more. Which is why I'm telling you, in case you want to change your mind and offer the job to someone who can give it their undivided attention."

"I trust you. I want you," Morgan said, and his gaze again fell to Sen's mouth. He cleared his throat. "If you can manage your time half as well as you do linen closets and kitchen-utensil drawers, I have not one qualm about engaging you for the project."

"Okay." Sen patted his thighs and let out a breath. "Okay, good."

"So that means you're doing it?"

"That means I'm doing it." Huge mistake to agree, but what was life without some glorious regret?

Morgan punched a victory fist. "Nice. Which, speaking of linen closets and such, leads me to something else."

"Oh?" Sen wondered whether he was about to be fired from cleaning for being hired to make art.

"Since I oversee the illustrations project, I of course have access to everything that needs illustrating. Would it be easier if we set up a workspace for you at the house? I can bring the samples home and save you the time of carting them around. And you also won't have to juggle painting and drawing at your place, if your studio isn't amenable." Morgan tapped his fist on the car's back window. "The third floor is empty, and several rooms get great light. You're comfortable in the house already, and you know, again, that whole 'I trust you' thing."

"That actually sounds really good. What about Wednesdays?" Spending more time in the house and with Morgan would be dangerous, or the best thing ever—both?—and Sen couldn't resist.

"If you want to keep that up, by all means, keep doing it." Morgan moved closer and squeezed Sen's arms. "But the illustrations are my priority, and the paintings yours, so if you get overwhelmed, just give notice. It's Adriane's responsibility to find someone else."

"Eminently practical," Sen said. "I should really start tomorrow, if there's something for me to start on."

Morgan held Sen's arms and stared. He rubbed circles with his thumbs and traced Sen's face and shoulders and neck with his gaze. Goose bumps rose on Sen's skin, and he swayed under an onrush of belonging and rightness as the noise around them faded away.

"There is something." Morgan's eyes were heavy, and he leaned closer. "Isn't there?"

Other faces, similar and somehow familiar, shifted in and out to displace Morgan's intense gaze. Sen watched in fascination until it made him dizzy, and he shut his eyes and shook his head.

Morgan let go of his arms. Sen opened his eyes and returned to the present in an abrupt drop.

"I'll make certain there is something for you to start on." Morgan cleared his throat. "And don't worry about getting there any earlier. Come at the usual time. We can discuss the basics, and then I can head in to work." He got his keys out. "So, where to?"

"Let me get my bike, and I'll show you."

As he pedaled back to the car, he realized that maintaining contact with Morgan provided the sole and sure reason he hadn't quit working for Adri.

He might be confused and wary, but more than anything, he wasn't ready to lose Morgan. His body, his bones, and his intrinsic self knew there was something between them and more to discover, and he wouldn't abandon the chance to find it.

Morgan smiled and waved as he approached, as though they hadn't parted minutes earlier. He took the bike, secured it to the bumper rack, and then popped the passenger door open and settled into the driver's side.

Sen gave directions and commented on things they passed, as though they were old marrieds running to the grocery who didn't need to fill every second with chatter. He guided Morgan to his place, and they got his bike and paintings unloaded and stood together on the sidewalk.

"Well." Sen balanced his bike against a hip and stuck out his hand. "See you tomorrow."

Morgan stooped in a mock bow and accepted the handshake. "Tomorrow, then. Have a good rest of your Sunday."

Sen didn't move, and Morgan didn't either. Then Sen huffed, leaned the paintings on a big planter, and walked his bike along the side path.

"Need help with the paintings?" Morgan called after him.

"Nope. All good, thanks. See ya soon." Sen propped his bike against the side of the house and then hunched in so he wasn't visible and waited for Morgan to leave. He heard a car door shut and the engine start, and Sen crept back out and had to wave, because Morgan had waited to drive away.

He relayed his bike and the paintings up the back stairs and then had to stand in silence for a while to take in everything the day had brought and changed. He had to get his current paintings seen and approved for the group show and extricate Morgan from his life, his awareness, and his every thought. Instead the sun was setting on one less day to produce for a solo show, a series of illustrations, and a return to Morgan.

The long wall overlooking the garden space of the main house had windows at each end and nothing in the middle. He hung the first two portraits—other-Morgan and his young man—at the far left. Next to them he hung the earthy woman and her companion. All the portraits sprang from the visions he had when Morgan kissed him, but the other two portraits weren't quite finished. They needed layers of color, and he needed to soften the edges with solvents, but they wouldn't take much longer. They would join the others on the wall and leave blank spaces to be filled. He would build the series while they were on view for study and comparison.

Two portraits for sure done. Sen didn't include the other-Morgan couple in his count, just in case he decided they should never be shared. Leaving possibly ten more that relied on chance and unknowns and were inextricably tied to Morgan.

"Easy," he said and tried to believe it. The first few had flowed so well. Good thing he believed in fate and taking chances on the unknown.

Sen nodded at the couples and then got the coffeemaker started. He changed into painting clothes, threw himself into taking stock of supplies, made lists of what else was needed, and got organized.

CHAPTER SEVEN

SEN WENT to bed wired, lay awake for hours, overslept, and woke to a rainstorm.

"Shit." He stumbled from bed wrapped in blankets and tried to get dressed, eat something, and put together what he'd need for his meeting with Morgan.

He stubbed his toe on the futon and hopped around, grabbing a mishmash of things as water hammered the roof. Then he stopped, straightened, and looked outside.

"Maybe I shouldn't go," he said, his gaze drawn to the portraits. "I mean, c'mon. Listen to that."

Morgan could hardly blame him.

Lightning filled the room and thunder cracked and rattled the paintings. Other-Morgan slipped from his wire and hung crookedly. Then a reverberation of thunder knocked the painting to the floor.

Sen hurried over. "You okay?" he asked and then rolled his eyes.

He righted the canvas, and it burned his hands. Dread and dire premonitions rode his veins and began to fill his heart. Sen shoved the painting against the wall and tried to massage the numbness from his hands and arms. Bursts of scattered lightning warped the faces staring at him. Warning clanged in his chest, and he swore Morgan called to him through their accusing gazes.

"Fine. I'll go."

Sen shoved a change of clothes into a backpack, put on canvas shoes, shorts, and a long-sleeved tee, sheltered under a poncho and ball cap, tore downstairs with his bike, and got moving.

The alley quagmire gripped the tires with mud-slinging suction and created a cascading wake as he sped through streets transformed into rivers. Sen skidded and hydroplaned, crossed onto the sidewalk as needed, and reached a dark and quiet Greycote. Once under the portico, he parked his bike and shed the poncho. The rain had soaked everything but his backpack, and his shoes were filthy. He tucked them next to the side door and went in.

"I'm so late. I'm so sorry," he said as he entered, and his skin tingled.

Sen ditched the backpack and his sodden clothes and slipped into the tank top and sweats he'd packed. Thunder rumbled, and the vase in the wall niche vibrated as he passed.

Maybe Morgan had gone to work thinking he wouldn't come in this weather. He checked his phone—no message—and left it and his cap on the kitchen island.

All the appliance clocks were out, and he flicked a light switch to make sure. No power. The storm strengthened, and shadows lengthened as he went upstairs. Sen snagged a towel from the closet and scrubbed his hair while he checked the master bedroom.

The slept-in bed reassured him, but no T-shirt sat rumpled in the corner. He continued down the hall and peeked in each room until he was at the window overlooking the side yard. Rivulets of water coated the glass and made it impossible to tell whether Morgan's car was in the garage. He should have looked before he came inside, but he hadn't thought of it.

Sen paused at the balcony and listened for movement or a hint of someone else, but rain and thunder blotted out the rest of the world. He closed his eyes and *listened*. He didn't feel alone. An undercurrent of unrest, deeper than the violent storm, inhabited the house and filled it with tension.

He tossed the towel down the service stairs into the kitchen and climbed the narrow flight to the third floor, dragged as if by force to the turret room.

Sen's bare feet made no sound, and he opened his mouth to call hello but couldn't speak. He pushed into the room without hesitation, and lightning blazed—white and blindingly blue. Thunder growled as the lightning continued to flicker, and Sen blinked unseeingly.

"You came? Even in this? Why would you take such risk?" Morgan's voice was harsh, and he spoke with a strange and formal inflection—the same as when they'd kissed in the backyard.

Morgan laughed, a short, strangled bark. "And now that you are here, I want to demand you tell me where you have been, what took so long to come to me, and whether you understand I am nearly out of my mind waiting for you. In this. At all."

"I appreciate your concern—"

"Appreciate?" Morgan loomed into Sen's space and took hold of his arms. "I have been watching out that window for hours, imagining you discovered and taken from me, or hurt trying to get here, and you appreciate I have concern?"

"Yes! And I'm sorry I'm late." Sen's vision swam with ghostly afterburn. He couldn't make out Morgan's eyes, and the dark clouds appeared to creep in past the windows in a low slinking haze. "But I'm fine. It's just rain."

"Just rain," Morgan mocked, and the storm punctuated his point with a shard of lightning and percussive thunderclap.

Sen jumped, and Morgan massaged his arms.

"No. It is I who must apologize." Morgan sighed. "As I said, I have been here waiting, allowing fear to prey upon me, even believing the absolute worst had finally happened. But here you are, and we are safe. Forgive my anger. There is simply so much danger, and I am overcome each time I think of you brought to harm."

Sen didn't have to answer the impassioned, old-fashioned words, because Morgan kissed him. Sen straightened his arms and flattened his hands on Morgan's chest. They staggered and lurched sideways. Then Morgan clamped an arm around Sen's waist, walked them backward, and pushed Sen against the wall. He leaned in and brushed their mouths together. Then he stayed there, breath warm and supplicating on Sen's lips, and waited.

Sen remembered that embrace—the risk, devotion, and thrill—and a force beyond his own reason twisted his fingers into Morgan's shirt and pulled.

Morgan crowded between Sen's legs, lapped at Sen's rain-wet neck, and bit and sucked behind his ear until he shuddered without cease. Sen got his hands inside Morgan's shirt and raked his nails up Morgan's sides. He chuckled knowingly when he got a familiar growling purr in response, and he tilted his wrists and flicked Morgan's nipples with his thumbs.

"Damnation," Morgan stuttered past clenched teeth. He tugged Sen's legs to wrap around his hips and got a hand down the back of Sen's sweats. He traced the length of Sen's cleft with a finger, lingered at the notch, and then circled the dimple at the small of Sen's back with a maddening, feather-light touch.

"That's good," Sen breathed, losing focus and shorting out as Morgan worked that secret hot spot without mercy. His legs jerked when Morgan combined sensations and returned to the raw bruise blossoming behind his ear while he continued to stroke his ass. Sen braced his shoulders on the wall and unbuttoned Morgan's shirt.

"God," he said. He shoved Morgan's shirt away best he could, mapped the heat, texture, and strength of Morgan's neck, shoulders, and chest, and kept babbling. "I've wanted to touch you for so long, wanted to bring you to me, into me, and kiss—for you to kiss me again—since we met."

"Shhh," Morgan said as he trailed kisses across Sen's face. He hovered over Sen's gasping mouth, his breath tickling as his lips caressed Sen's with the barest touch. His hands continued their lazy torture as he kneaded the grooves of Sen's hips and quickened Sen's desire.

Sen writhed, lifted his hips, and moved so his pants slid to the swell of his thighs, and he made short, breathy pleas when Morgan stroked the exposed tip of his cock.

Morgan licked the corner of his mouth, and Sen dug his fingers into Morgan's flesh until he was driven to beg, "Morgan, please…."

"Please what, dearest?" Morgan's tone was indulgent and exultant and on the edge of control.

Sen growled. He curled a hand in Morgan's hair and pushed away from the wall, tightening his legs and falling back so Morgan stumbled and had to grab hold of him, and he devoured Morgan's mouth.

He rolled his hips as they kissed, and Morgan responded and ground into him. Sen angled enough to get leverage to yank Morgan's pants undone and parted Morgan's fly so they made contact as Morgan followed his lead to align their groins. Sen groaned and rounded up for another kiss, knotted his other hand in the hair at Morgan's nape, and held on. Sen wanted them naked—to feel the hard weight of Morgan's cock dragging on his belly—but it would have to do. He couldn't wait any longer.

Morgan grasped both their cocks together and pushed Sen up against the wall. Sen lost his breath as Morgan's powerful thrusts shortened and sped up, and his whole being coiled tighter and tighter at his center.

Sen looked up while Morgan watched him, and began to shake. With want. With delirium. With recognition. With the desperate need to come.

Morgan's gaze reflected his needs and matched them, gave him solace and permission. Sen nodded and twisted. His back arched as he pulled at Morgan, toes bunched and knees locked as he came. He sagged to the wall but didn't let go of Morgan. Instead he skimmed his hands everywhere and murmured encouragement as Morgan worked to finish.

Sen kissed the sweat from Morgan's temple, caressed his sides, and then pinched and teased Morgan's nipples. Morgan heaved into Sen and shuddered. His whole body trembled with the strength of his release. He whispered nothings into Sen's mouth and kissed Sen's nose and earlobe and the spot behind Sen's ear. After several sluggish breaths, Morgan gathered Sen in his arms and tipped backward to sit on the very end of the chair.

They flopped over and scooched and rolled until they were lying together, Sen still cradled against Morgan's chest as the storm still raged outside. The dim room was restful, and Morgan's heartbeat steady and sure under his palm.

"I've missed you."

Morgan kissed his brow and draped his shirt over them as a makeshift blanket. Sen had never felt safer or more content.

SEN WOKE up alone and knew the house was empty. Rain pattered the windows, but the strength of the storm had passed. His heart sank, but he tried not to jump to conclusions. He folded the shirt that had been tucked around him and sat up.

"Oof." Dried sweat, mud, and stink clung to him, and his head pounded like a hangover. He needed a shower and gallons of coffee and to find Morgan.

Sen snagged the waistband of his sweats bunched around his knees and pulled them up as he stood. He righted his tank top from its weird, balled tangle at his neck, slid his arms in, and then searched the house in a reverse of that morning. But he found no sign of Morgan.

"Did I imagine that too?" he said, overlooking the foyer as his words echoed back to him.

At the side door, he slipped into his shoes and dashed to the garage. No Volvo, which, not a surprise. But he agonized through several undecided minutes and then gathered his stuff and biked home. The streets were quiet and clear, and he didn't bother to wear the poncho.

Morgan hadn't left a note, hadn't texted, hadn't anything. Should he consider that a good sign or a blaring klaxon of imminent doom? Maybe Morgan didn't do the morning after, or didn't think about it as a morning after, since they would see each other again. Or maybe he wasn't a note leaver, or who the fuck knew.

He showered until the water ran cold, ordered apple fritters and bread pudding from his favorite soul food place, and channeled everything into painting.

Meeting and clicking, being a natural fit, but only friendly, the kisses and lingering glances that seemed to lead nowhere. Storms and shadows. Morgan's strange turns of mood. Then going at each other like they'd never see each other again and his enthusiastic acceptance of Morgan's possession.

Unwanted elements, shapes, and colors were conjured onto the canvas, mixing with what should be there, so he scraped it, started over, and painted the same thing again. Sen grunted and set everything down, shifted the easel to accommodate two canvases, and worked on two portraits at once.

"Maybe you'll tell me something. Who you are." Sen stabbed and scoured the paintbrush against the canvas. "Who I am."

Paint and solvent dripped from one to the other as he worked, lines dragged and interconnected as the faces were created from layers and washes. The palette was rusts and blues and grays, gray-green and white, and the paint thin, drizzling, and running across the canvas like water.

The other vision portraits were traditional three-quarter poses, each looking out from the same center, some into the world and others toward each other. These two men emanated from the inner sides of their respective canvases, meeting at the middle and connected at a mutual origin point on the inner corners. But they were at odds and inextricably linked and lost in a storm.

Sen couldn't tell where the paintings were coming from—whether they were tapping another vein of ghostly inspiration or his fraught confusion over Morgan bleeding out. It didn't really matter. The portraits were in him and belonged with the rest. He painted rapidly and without indecision as one day melted into another.

The rain at last spent itself and broke apart in time for a murky, colorless sunset. Sen dropped his paintbrush.

He hung the paintings on the long wall of portraits at the opposite end from the others. Then he ignored them and literally turned his back to clean the studio area and meditate over the simple act of rinsing his brushes with care. He cleaned himself too, soaping to the elbows and cleaning the effort, fatigue, and spattered paint from his skin. The apple fritters were cold, and he ate all six in a row and swallowed them down with fresh coffee.

Sen stretched, checked his phone, got changed, and then napped for a few hours. The nap was necessary but not refreshing, and he groaned and stretched and then curled up and stared at nothing for a while.

The new portraits watched him, and the apartment smelled like a meadow wet from rain, not the sweet and pungent blend of oil and turpentine.

"What?" he said from bed, not looking at them. Every face he painted played on a flipbook animation when he closed his eyes.

Sen threw the blankets back, pushed up, and walked to the wall.

"Assholes," he rebuked their silence. "This could be a reality show, you know. Self-Portrait of a Young Artist Losing His Mind."

Even other-Morgan appeared hidden and more inscrutable, and he cursed their existence.

He stepped into a pair of shoes, snatched up his wallet and Moleskine and pen, and fled. Heavy air and the waking chatter of birds greeted him, and he ran in the opposite direction from Greycote.

A curved bench appeared as he lost steam, and he collapsed onto it and sat until the sun broke the horizon and passed the trees. As he watched the dawn, the charged anger left him, and he saw it as if on a line, returning to the storm couple he'd just painted. Sen rubbed his eyes as weariness took its place.

Burst of energy spent but still teeming with crowded thoughts, Sen let his busy mind roam on the page and sketched in freeform. Sen drew whatever came to him—words and questions and pictures. He drew a temple that resembled a pyramid, a disembodied arm holding a hawk, art deco filigree, and two figures on horseback. A pair of eyes began to form, and he crossed them out. He drew sand dunes like an ocean, the ocean shore, a circle of trees, and a knife.

The eyes returned, and he let them through and wound up outlining their shape over and over again. As he did, the eyes lost definition, and sharp corners became rounded. He picked up the pen and remade just the shape. It resembled an infinity symbol.

He turned to a blank page and wrote *Infinite*.

Sen read it several times. "Yeah, infinite wisdom," he scoffed and snapped the book closed.

The walk home seemed long. He got a croissant and a fruit cup from the corner shop and ate it sitting on his apartment landing to delay the inevitable.

Inside smelled like oil paint and turpentine again. The portraits were quiet.

"Maybe that's it. Maybe I have solvent and heavy metal poisoning, and I'm hallucinating."

Sen grabbed his phone and shot a text to his mom. *Was I like the Sixth Sense kid growing up?*

As he got dressed, his phone dinged several times.

No, see you were alive.

And never mentioned dead people.

But you always had a way about you—you know things, honey.

It's okay to listen.

Good enough advice if anyone were actually talking. Sen replied with a thanks and then gathered himself and his stuff and headed to Greycote.

CHAPTER EIGHT

"SEBASTIAN? HEY, just in time." Morgan stepped from the open garage and waved as Sen rode up the driveway.

He waved back and parked his bike, and then went to Morgan, like normal. Like his guts weren't in knots and he wasn't angry and wouldn't throw himself into Morgan's arms at the slightest encouragement.

"Yes. Today I'm actually on time." He offered a wan smile.

Morgan didn't take the cue. "I snagged a drafting table from work for you. Mind helping me carry it inside? We can get it set up in whatever room you want."

Sen had a good look at Morgan, so clearly exhausted, and some of his belligerent pique subsided. "Still not sleeping well?"

"Is it that obvious?" Morgan stifled a yawn and nodded. "I have no idea what's up, because usually I'm a champ sleeper. I even asked my dad if he was holding back any childhood night-terror and sleepwalking habits."

"And?"

"And negative on that count." Morgan shrugged.

"Hmm. Yeah. Sorry it didn't lead anywhere."

"I'm not sure if I'm more annoyed or relieved. Worth checking, I thought, although now he's a bit worried about me." Morgan tugged the desk past the back bumper, and they wrestled it upright on the driveway.

Sen knew the feeling.

Morgan put his hands on his hips. "I'm thinking we go in the front door, right on up the main stairs, and then to the third floor with it. It's not heavy, but it's awkward. That way we'd have less turns to make and we don't have to negotiate the tiny back stairs."

"Sounds like a plan." Sen didn't wait for Morgan to say anything else. He hefted the back side and let Morgan lead, and they got the table onto the second-floor balcony with minimal fuss.

"Do you know what room? The corner one, maybe?" Morgan asked in an even voice and without any particular expression.

"No," Sen shot back. He shook his head when Morgan knitted his brows together. "Uh, all those trees and it's on the west end, so. How about I go up, have a look, and decide. Before we carry this up there."

Morgan made to follow, and Sen pressed his hand in the air.

"Won't take a minute," he said as he charged up the flight of stairs that adjoined the balcony. He didn't need to be up there to know he would choose the empty bedroom just off the stairs to the left, on the other side of the house from the turret room, but not right on top of the master suite. A complicated but necessary matrix.

Sen loitered a few minutes and then ran back downstairs. A burst of gladness rippled out from his solar plexus when he saw Morgan standing there waiting for him, tired but smiling.

"Get it figured out?"

"Not even close." Sen waved a hand at Morgan's confused expression. "That is, yes. I chose a room, but they're all really great, so I'm already waffling on the decision."

Morgan nodded and let him lead. They got the drafting table squeaked past the one tight turn, and on into the bedroom. Sen directed and they centered it under the double windows diagonal from the door. He'd get the best light and limited shifting shadows from the hallway.

Morgan pivoted and locked the tabletop flat again and lifted his chin toward the backyard. "Nice view. Kinda surprised you went with this room, but it is bigger, and you're right about no trees too close."

Sen drummed the table, and Morgan looked out the window. They stood for too long without speaking. The silence wasn't uncomfortable or bad, but that was the problem.

"Thanks for that. I was racking my brains trying to devise some kind of pulley system to haul this up here on my own." Morgan smiled. "Okay, I'll go get the other stuff."

Sen nodded, went to the windows as Morgan left, and thunked his forehead on the glass. How bad would it be to quit everything on the spot—and was it worse he didn't want to?

When Sen heard a crash in the hall, he rescued a desk lamp and its trailing cord as it fell from on top of the large box Morgan carried.

"Whew—thanks. That's obviously for you to use, and these are some of the samples." Morgan set the box down and then left again. He returned with a stool for the drafting table and a rectangular folding table, which he set up. Then he unloaded the box on it.

Sen untied the cord, set up the desk lamp, and stared too intently at the ripple of muscle in Morgan's shoulder, the length of Morgan's fingers, and the cut of Morgan's profile. He huffed, plugged in the lamp, and went to stare out the windows again.

"And then this," Morgan said and handed Sen an oversized book. "One catalog from a past project, and I brought several others. There." He pointed at a stack on the floor under the folding table. "Thought you'd appreciate seeing some of the other illustrations done for us. There's a spec sheet for the minimum dimensions and approved archival materials, all that, here."

Morgan gestured to the table where he had set out lengths of carved wood trim, wood appliqués, plaster medallions, wallpaper samples, scallop-fretted shutter locks, and an assembly of other bits and bobs that elevated an interior from basic to a showplace.

"French and Spanish, and Victorian and Rococo—this building is your basic beautiful kitchen sink." Morgan held up a small brass cherub. "He and his twin just hold the staircase carpet runner in place and keep dust out of the tread corner."

"Wow." Sen took the cherub, turned it over a few times, and noted the notch where the connecting brass rod would fit to cross the stair to its mirror-image cherub.

They reminded him of the portraits he'd just finished. He put the cherub down behind a pinewood corbel.

"These are all models for the restorers, so don't be precious with them. There's calipers if you need that kind of precision, and this thumb drive has digital shots of the details, in situ." Morgan fished both from the box and held the drive out for Sen.

"Guaranteed not corrupt?"

Morgan's eyes brightened. "Guaranteed."

Their fingers bumped when Sen took it. He stuffed it in a pocket and left his hand there. Morgan twitched and then set the box under the table with the catalogues. The twitch was damn satisfying to see.

"So, get acquainted with everything. This represents the central motifs and is the bulk of what we want illustrated, though there might be a few additions. Sometime soon we'll plan a site visit, and you can go there whenever needed, on your own." Morgan absently rubbed his finger against his thumb. He trailed a glance to look at Sen's hand and then stopped. "Questions?"

Oh. So many.

"None at the moment, but there'll be a list soon enough." Sen followed Morgan from the room, down the stairs, and into the foyer. "I'll do some initial thumbnail sketches and leave those for you, and we can go from there."

Sen would clean, sketch, and leave before Morgan got home from work.

"We definitely can." Morgan's smile froze, and his gaze dragged from Sen's neck to his mouth and back.

Morgan stood in the darker hall, Sen framed in sunlight that spilled through the second-story windows, providing Morgan a good look at him. Sen flushed hotly when he remembered the huge purple red hickey behind his ear.

"The other morning… I'm sorry we missed each other." Morgan licked his lips and a nerve ticked in his jaw. He frowned, stop-started in a jerk toward Sen, and then shook his head. "I expect it was the storm—I worried about you biking in that mess but figured you'd know better than to think I'd expect you to slog through it. And I knew I'd see you today." He rounded his shoulders and sighed.

Sen wanted to forgive and soothe and tell Morgan to just shut up and go to work. He wanted to know what the hell was going on. He wanted to drag Morgan to bed—clear the air, muddy, or poison it—but one way or another end their awful, polite friendliness.

Instead he edged in the direction of the kitchen. "I should really get cleaning, given how much drawing I also need to get finished today."

Morgan reached for Sen, drew back, and then turned the other direction. "Right. I'm keeping you from work, and I'm late for my own."

Sen heard the mantle clock ticking in the sitting room. Morgan just stared. Sen's hickey burned, his headache had returned, and he still wanted to lean in and rest in Morgan's arms.

"What?" Sen's tone was sharp but weary.

"I'm forgetting something." Morgan's strain showed, and his whole frame slumped. "I don't know what. I just know I am."

"About the job? Cleaning? The storm?" Sen watched a nerve jump in Morgan's temple, but nothing dramatic happened, so he pushed. "Something that happened during the storm?"

"Yes." Morgan closed his eyes and clenched his jaw. "It's about a storm—at least my nightmares have been."

"Maybe talking about them would help."

Morgan didn't seem to hear. His eyelids fluttered, and he held himself tightly coiled, arms drawn up and hands fisted against his chest. Confused sensations and strange sounds, low and garbled, emanated from Morgan and collided with and soaked into Sen's skin.

He closed his eyes and could almost see what Morgan chased. He could almost hear what Morgan tried to track down. Bright light flashed, followed by a deep rumble. Sen opened his eyes.

Morgan stared at him unseeing, pupils blown and irises stormy and cold, shaking all over as a trickle of blood ran from his nose. Tendrils of black clouds fell from the staircase and pushed up through the floorboards. Sen thought he heard shouting.

He lunged forward and caught the blood with his thumb, licked it without thinking, and gripped Morgan's arms.

"Morgan?" he called and tightened his grip. "Morgan, answer me."

"Sebastian?" Morgan blinked several times and looked at Sen. His eyes cleared, and he searched Sen's face. "What was I saying? I can't remember."

The transformations and Morgan's distress disturbed Sen enough that he wasn't sure he could push further or would try again.

"Then let yourself off the hook and forget it entirely." Sen tried for jokey but fell flat.

Morgan wiped his nose with the back of his hand. "I thought nosebleeds came on from dry weather. Maybe it's drainage." His mouth worked, and he shook his head. "Wish I could just let it go. But I'm not myself when I'm around you. I feel like there's nothing you don't know. Which makes no sense, I realize that."

Sen nodded and retreated. "So get to work, write it down when you think of it, and tell me later. It's okay."

"Okay." Morgan frowned, hesitated, tapped his fist on his thigh, and nodded. "Text me if you have questions about anything."

Sen didn't watch Morgan go.

He scrubbed, tidied, made the bed with hospital corners, washed the dishes, and finished by loading the washer. Cleaning calmed him, with its straightforward and reassuring steps toward a definite goal and end. Once it was finished, he brought his messenger bag of art supplies to the third floor.

He drifted toward the turret room without intending to but didn't get past the doorway. The room and its diffused light and the chair in its place appeared unchanged. Sen wished for evidence of his and Morgan's passionate encounter there but couldn't find a trace—not even scuff marks on the floor.

He scrubbed his face with both hands and went to set up his workspace.

"Enough," he said, lengthening the vowels and gaining volume until he shouted off the *gh* into the foyer.

That felt better.

He sat on the stool and lined up his pencils, eraser, and sharpener. No shadows invaded the room, and he listened but only heard the expected noises outside the open windows.

Sen flipped open the sketchbook, chose a finial reminiscent of a pinecone emerging from curlicues and leaves, and went to work with a soft-leaded pencil to sketch it in quick, broad strokes. As he filled the page with the palm-sized object, showing various angles and highlighting aspects, he pictured it completing wrought iron curtain tiebacks or a chandelier.

There were way more than twenty-four items on the table, so he decided to ask about that. Sen started a list on a piece of scratch paper and kept drawing. Next was an ornate light-switch cover—not nearly as interesting as the finial— and then a wood rosette.

Sen looked at the spec sheet and the scratch-paper list and then put the clothes in the dryer. He made a cup of coffee and sat at the breakfast nook to read over his scribbled notes, and he had another cup of expensive coffee.

If he weren't so messed up inside, he would be grooving on his job. Paid to touch, explore, and archive the treasures of a grand place far outside his experience, a gig to make art and snoop, really. Sen needed the money and would enjoy the work. He vowed he'd figure out how to deal with the rest, in whatever way.

But he couldn't ignore Morgan's connection to Lars and Bharti, the coincidence of meeting Morgan at the gallery and getting two opportunities that would culminate at the same time. They were signs, or at the very least, strong indications.

He also couldn't ignore Morgan's state—exhausted, disassociating, physically affected by whatever was happening. Sen had to follow more than signs at that point.

Sen washed his mug, dumped the coffee pods, and finished up. When he put away the sheets and linens, he noticed some of the towels were not quite right. Morgan had attempted to refold them his way. Sen made a little noise— half sigh and half meep—and stood patting the stack.

"That jerk," he muttered without heat. And leave it to his foolish heart to flutter.

He paused by the master bedroom, and after a minute, went in. Sen opened the chest and found nothing. The small box and its contents were gone.

Sen closed the lid and didn't know whether he should be relieved or disappointed. Sitting there provided no answers, so he got up and returned to his workroom.

His pencils and such could stay, but he packed the spec sheet, two catalogs, and the list in his bag. Sen tore the three pages of rough sketches from the book and put them on the kitchen island for Morgan's perusal, grabbed the trash and recycling, and went home.

A nap tempted, but then he wouldn't sleep that night, and he needed some semblance of a daytime schedule from there on. The paintings he could do whenever, but he wasn't about to show up at Greycote at three in the morning saying he'd woken to a rush of energy ready to tackle drawing doorstops. Add in the unresolved issue of him being in the house with Morgan longer than he had to, and it seemed for the best that he not get fuzzy and mellow sketching in the house while Morgan slept.

He ate the last of the bread pudding and an apple, added items to the materials list as he thought of them, and then tried to work on the two portraits in progress. Sen mushed and overmixed paint into every shade of brown, scraped his palette clean, and started over. He squeezed the tube of titanium white and hit an air bubble, and it spat double what he needed onto the palette. The burnt umber had separated and crusted at the opening and wouldn't budge.

"Awesome." Sen let the palette drop onto the floor. "Awesome and exactly what I wanted and just so awesome." He stood and side-arm tossed his handful of brushes onto the work table, where they knocked over a jar of dirty water.

Sen's expression flattened, and he glared at the portraits. Then he sighed, cleaned up the mess, and texted his mom.

Yes! Call came the reply.

Sen made a nest of pillows and blankets so he could sit on the bed in swaddled comfort, leaned against the wall, opened Facetime, and watched the screen.

"Hello, sweet pea," she answered and smiled into the phone.

"Hey, Mom," Sen said and sighed.

She resituated and propped the phone on the table she sat at, and Sen had a sweeping view, in the background, of the converted school bus he thought of as home and his hometown in one. They'd gone everywhere in it, including through Canada and up into the wilds of Alaska. Sen was pretty sure his dad had researched making duck boats to see whether they could make it to Hawaii. Or at least the Keys.

His mom was fifty-two and wore her hair in a long silver braid and every last wrinkle with sparkling charm. Her eyes were lively and mild. She and his father had never married, but they'd been devoted and together since they met at nineteen, homesteading on patches of land big enough for the bus and a garden. Sen hadn't known his traveling childhood was unusual until he left it behind.

She said that year would be their special year—their golden palindrome—because he was twenty-five. She made jewelry. Some pieces sold for hundreds of dollars, and other pieces she gave away. She acted as the bus's head mechanic and had taught Sen the value of reading anything that crossed your path, and to approach to the unknown with kindness instead of fear.

"How is everything? You look good," Sen said as she tilted the phone. A wave of longing hit him. He'd struck out on his own at eighteen, without regrets, but there were moments when he wished he'd never left. In recent weeks there had been about one thousand of those moments. "Hi," he said, and a wibble escaped.

"Everyone and everything is fine. We're heading west after a stayover with Celie—did she tell you we visited?"

"She texted me some pictures." Sen grinned. "Birch looked ready to move in."

Sen had a sister, Thea, who was two years older, and his brother, Birch, was younger than him by ten years—the oopsie kid his parents were thrilled to get. Celie was his eldest sister. She made crazy-interesting fiber art, high-end all-organic stuffed animals, and ran a small farm.

"Oh, yeah. Birch met all the alpacas and worked the loom, and he's feeling very at one with textiles and the land. We told him he could stay back for a while, but we're on our way to SoCal and you know, sun and beaches won." She grinned. "Can't say as I blame him. And how are you? How's that persistent ennui coming along?"

"Better—much improved. I've had some breakthroughs, and the cleaning gig has proven interesting. Go figure." Sen drummed his fingers. "I have a solo show in June, with a big-deal gallery doing the group show of New Orleans artists I told you I was sticking around here for. I brought in recent work—you haven't seen these yet—and they offered it on the spot."

"Honey, that's wonderful! We'll come for the opening. Breakthrough for sure." She leaned away and returned to the frame with both hands wrapped around a huge mug. "Thea just threw this. I'm loving the glaze colors she has going. One day all of you should do a show together."

Sen raised an eyebrow. "Let me get through this one first. I've also taken on a pretty intense illustration gig, basically due the day before I hang the solo show, so matching Thea's enormo-abstract bowls and Cee's wall rugs will have to wait. Maybe… well, I should have turned down the illustration thing, but it'll upfront pay my expenses and then some, so if nothing sells at the show, I'm not in the hole."

"You should have turned it down?"

"It's a lot of work, and you know me—one day into it and I'm already charting the calendar and planning everything out to the nth but feeling like I'm a day behind. But I like work, and it's good work, so I'm good."

She had a drink and then leveled a Mom Look. "What's the matter, really?"

"I don't know." Sen frowned. "There are a lot of pieces, and I can identify the pieces, but I have no clue what the picture is, if the picture is the problem, or if I'm trying to put the picture together wrong."

"Part the first, then." She held up a finger. "Wait—Busy Bee, hand me my notebook, please. Thank you." The blur of Birch's arm came and went, and she tugged a pen from the spiral binding and poised to write.

Sen rolled his eyes but didn't tell her not to diagram it. "Producing twelve good paintings in two months for the show." He paused and then said, "Can I just go on? Or are we discussing these as I unload?"

His mom made a go-on motion.

"Producing approximately twenty-four architectural illustrations. More like illustrations of architectural stuff, but still. Then having to do them while I prepare my show. And I'm ready to leave New Orleans, but the solo show will keep me here longer. But I'm not sure where to go next, which I tell myself to stop thinking about, since it doesn't matter yet and only distracts me."

Sen waited for his mom to finish writing and look up.

"Right. So there's all that. Then there's the guy who hired me to do the illustrations. I really like him, and I thought he really liked me, but suddenly that's all changed. And it changed after I was hired, so, awkward. Plus I'm working in his house—he set up a studio space for me to draw and not spill over into my paintings—and it's a huge house, and I like the house, but now the guy I want to be with, and am confused about, lives *here*."

She reviewed her notes. "Is that all?"

"That's the highlights. I was going to be orderly and break it all down in a list to tell you, but it's a mess in my brain, and I can't unmess it."

"So you called me."

Sen conceded that. "So I called."

She tipped back and closed her eyes. "Do you want to say hello to your father? I need to take a quick walk with this."

"Yes, please. And not just as a filler to your wisdom sandwich."

"Luke? It's Sen—come say hello." His mom slid from the bench seat and the view of the bus-house opened to more light.

He gazed at the key visual hallmarks—the tiny kitchenette, the seashell mobile, the carved wooden masks over the windshield. They were constants from his first memories. But the bunk beds he'd shared with his sisters were now shelves, and with only three people, the general assembly of belongings had thinned.

"Nice of you to give your mother something to do," his father said as he sat. His speech had a careful intonation, his person a runner's build, and his olive-plus-tan features were those of a handsome nerd. "I'm eavesdropping of course, so congrats on the show. It's definitely not the art or work burden giving you doubts, and let me know if I need to have a talk with this guy."

Sen laughed. "Thanks, Dad."

His dad so wasn't that sort of dad. It was possible he'd show up, make friends with Morgan, and then explain to Sen everything he'd misinterpreted. His dad was also the supportive, respectful, and chill sort he wouldn't trade for anything.

"So after your shows the world'll open up to you again. Where to next?" He fished their ancient road atlas from under the bench and flopped it on the table. "Hmm. Before NOLA you were in San Fran and then Charlotte. You could go international. Or New Mexico, and finally give Taos a try?"

"Maybe." Sen had left home with the intention of getting to Taos but hadn't made it there yet, with no regrets. "Anywhere good in Montana? I can hit up all the compass points and then go interior. And I'm tired of living in a sauna."

"Someplace near Yellowstone. Besides, Missoula is too obvious." His dad ran his finger along what Sen knew were interstates and secondary roads. "Livingston? That has a certain regal bearing, doesn't it."

Sen hummed but didn't ask any of the usual questions they bandied when discussing his plans. His dad closed the atlas and held Sen's gaze. He could feel the weight of it through the phone, and the camera, and the miles.

"You really don't know, do you?" His dad made room when his mom returned. "Not even one matchbook to scent the trail?"

Sen had moved to New Orleans after offering to road trip there with a friend. The friend returned to Portland, but Sen stayed. For months leading up to their trip—well before the invitation—he couldn't escape mentions of the city. Hurricane glasses from a popular bar left unclaimed at his apartment after a party. An erroneously delivered travel guide, sent to him at Jasper Street instead of someone on Jasper Lane. Stacks of vintage NOLA postcards and napkins given to him when he posted a call for collage materials at a local art supply store. Then the trip, and on the way, he met a trucker's dogs, who were named Mardi and Gras, in West Virginia, and the Alabama B&B they found by chance was run by a transplant from New Orleans.

"Nope. Nada. It's almost as if, when I decided I'd stay through the group show, my compass turned off." Sen lifted his hands from his burrow of blankets in surrender. Since he'd been in New Orleans, all the connections he made brought him to Morgan.

"It could have. Or you're too distracted to notice." His dad waggled a finger. "Could be you have to wait and be led this time."

Sen made agreeing noises and decided he'd bang his head on the wall after they hung up.

"Your mom's thoughts are crowding the bus and me out of the conversation, so I'll say good-bye." His father glanced at his mom then half stood. "Have a little more patience, and it'll come. We're here if you need us." He waved and Sen waved back.

"You're not worried about the art, deadlines, or skidding into another creative block. So let's dispense with those parts." His mom held up the notebook. Several words were crossed out and two things were circled. "That leaves This Guy and Still Here, and I think Dad just nailed the Still Here part."

"Leaving the guy." Sen groaned. "I'm so disappointed in myself for the cliché."

"It doesn't have to happen to everyone, but there's no shame that it's happening to you." She tossed the notebook aside. "So?"

Sen made big hands. "Remember that day in Death Valley when we were scorched on the salt flat and then it snowed up in the mountains by the charcoal kilns?"

"That day was awesome."

"Yeah, well, that's also the level of 'blows hot and cold' we reach. Which, not awesome. Something isn't right, but to tie this all the way back around, I have no idea what." He hesitated to say more, but he had to say it to someone, and his mom would understand. "It's bigger and scarier than anything I've felt before. So, that's not helping either."

"Are you threatened or anxious about this?" She was progressive, encouraged her kids to seize life, and the family was beyond nontraditional, but she sounded like any other mom, worried about her child.

Sen smiled. "That's the thing. All I feel with him is good stuff. He's an old friend I don't know anything about yet."

"Then get to know him. That's what it seems like you need, and that's fine. But go past the good stuff, because only having feel-good time can get in the way just as much as misunderstandings."

"Ugh, Mom." Sen pursed his lips.

His mom snickered. "And be careful with the bigger stuff. Go get your cards read or something. You never know." She raised both eyebrows. "Did we do anything but go in a big circle? Have I helped at all?"

"Logically, I'm not sure yet. Emotionally, heaps." Sen let out a long breath. "Thanks, Mom."

"My pleasure. I'll pay attention to the tea leaves and light a guiding candle for you."

"And say hi to the squirt for me," Sen added.

Birch ran to the phone and yelled, "Hiiii!" then ran away again.

"All right. Good-bye. Love ya."

"Love you too, and update me." His mom kissed her fingertips and pressed them toward the camera. "Bye."

Sen threw his phone to the end of the bed and sat in a drained heap for a while. Then he eased from the pillow fort, made dinner, and ate out on the landing beyond the gaze of the portraits.

Just picking up the palette and sitting with it in front of the paintings frustrated him, and talking with his mom still filled his head with noise, so he put it aside. Sen went and leaned onto the kitchen counter to doodle and process their conversation. He didn't need to consult cards. He would pull answers from his drawing.

He bore down with the flat of a pencil, and soon dark clouds framed the page. Then he added wisps and tendrils to invade the blank center space. Sen paused, went back over the curlicues and insidious lines with his eyes, and acknowledged that, yeah, it did scare him.

A lot.

Sen darkened the clouds with a pen, adding highlight and shadow, nearly black at the edges but lighter toward the middle. He didn't know how to draw thunder, but he heard its distant rumble, and here and there he left the punctuation mark of lightning forking across the paper.

He let the pen wander in looping shapes, then stopped after he'd written Morgan's name in exaggerated, stylized cursive, somewhat obscured by the clouds.

Sen tapped the pen.

Morgan was caught up in it too. Maybe he was the key. Sen weighed the likeliest options—leave, or stay and somehow get them both through it. He went over Morgan's name and repeated it several times. Despite everything, he wanted a chance with Morgan. They were too well matched to give up yet.

He liked Morgan's eye crinkles and easy humor, Morgan's smarts and sincerity, his wide shoulders and strong hands. Heat spread across Sen's body, and he wondered what it would be like to be with Morgan untainted by confusion and doubts.

Sen ran a fingertip over Morgan's name, feeling it and blurring it. Then he made tiny circles to fill the center area. The circles developed and morphed, until he wound up drawing two cherubs intertwined by long, swirling bunting. Their gazes were serene, but they were framed in a mandorla of overlapping ovals where those piercing eyes lurked—the infinity symbol.

Sen flipped the pen down.

"Ha, ha," he said and looked over at the portraits.

He picked up the pen, and in the bottom left corner of the page, he wrote "two more." No ideas roared forth in his mind, and no inspiration came from the cherubs floating unconcerned through a storm. Eight portraits represented a great start, but he needed twelve.

Sen had to tally that with his reasons for staying in contact with Morgan.

He ripped the drawing from the book and pinned it to his corkboard over the postcards and truck-stop placemat. That felt right. Then, needing air and pleasant distraction, he went to shop for art supplies.

CHAPTER NINE

MORGAN NEVER did think of what he wanted to tell Sen. At least that's what Sen assumed when he showed up to clean a quiet and dark Greycote and found a complete lack of any note from Morgan after days of silence.

Sen resolutely did not watch the door of the gallery, but from that determined avoidance, he gained hyperawareness of every movement. Voices drifted over the tribal house music as people circulated and made the rounds of seeing and being seen at the opening. The long rainy day of preparation had turned into a rainy night, and wet sounds from the street and sidewalk flowed in through the propped-open door. A good-sized crowd braved the weather, coming and going in a steady stream, but the rain and Morgan's absence preoccupied Sen.

"Okay. What's up?" Adri came around Sen's shoulder and pushed a champagne flute into his hand. "You've haven't done anything but stare at the door since I got here twenty minutes ago. I'm not sure you even noticed we arrived."

"I did so," he lied. He scanned the gallery and found Dan wandering around with Phoebe, who seemed more into the paintings than her father. "Phoebe's dress matches yours. That's so delightful and soccer-momtastic of you."

"Sen." Adri maneuvered into his line of sight. "You're distracted and kinda miserable at the opening of your own show. Did you overhear someone savaging your paintings? Should you subtly indicate who I should shake Phoebe at after her feeding?"

"Group show," Sen corrected and didn't acknowledge the rest. He shoved a slick postcard at her and smiled. "My show is next month. I'm still getting used to the idea of it and freaking out over it a little, and isn't the card pretty?"

Adri gave his show announcement a cursory glance. "Yes. Very pretty." She pursed her lips. "Is that what's bothering you? It'd be just like you to allow obsessing over an upcoming show to ruin your enjoyment of the current one instead of taking a minute to celebrate both."

"Something like that."

A tall figure darted into the gallery, and Sen's breath seized. Then he let out a ragged sigh. Not Morgan.

"At least drink your champagne." Adri got closer. "I'm not the only one who can tell you're miserable, and that's not a good look. Just saying."

Sen drank too fast and snorted as bubbles pushed up his nose.

Adri patted his back and snickered. "There you go. Already better."

He rolled his eyes and sipped champagne, but tried to appear more composed. It shouldn't matter to him whether Morgan came or not. But it did matter—a lot. That in turn annoyed him. The show itself couldn't even provide some appeasement, since it had changed to represent a stepping stone for more opportunities and work. Which meant more time spent in New Orleans and a good portion of that time already consigned to being with Morgan. Then he returned to thinking about Morgan and back to square one.

"Thanks for coming, by the way." Sen pointed across the room at the table of nibbles. "Have at least five mini cheesecakes before you go. They're delicious."

More people ducked into the gallery. None were Morgan, and Sen's tension ratcheted up.

"Are you waiting on someone? Is your family supposed to be here?" Adri looked to the table and back and took Sen's empty glass. "Hold that thought." She darted away and returned with more champagne and a plate loaded with cheesecakes. "Okay. Answer."

"Since they're so close together, I told the fam to delay until my solo show. It's that or have them likely staying here for the next month. Which, no. I'll be glad to see them, but." He let the word hang meaningfully.

Adri nodded. "Oh, I get that. So, then, who are you really definitely not at all watching the door like your eyes are magnets for?"

"Magnet eyes? That's just really odd and kinda creepy." Sen choked out a dry laugh and ignored Adri's frown. He searched for something to say to distract her. The hair on his arms stood on end, and his spine tingled.

Wind swirled into the gallery, ruffling the tablecloth and spilling piles of programs onto the floor. Mist carried in on the wind and wet Sen's face, and thunder rumbled like a sleeping beast coming to life. Morgan appeared, wild-eyed, in a short-sleeved shirt and slacks and soaked to the skin. His gaze landed on Sen, and the air crackled.

Sen knew that look. He also knew he had to intervene before Morgan started rambling or ravaging him right there in the gallery.

"Here you are, here at last," Morgan said, voice deep and lilting. He strode in, crowded close, and took Sen's arm. He seemed unaware of anyone else in the room. "I have searched and searched."

Adri's eyebrows arched, and she glanced from Sen to Morgan and back again. "Uh, what's all this? Everything okay?"

"I honestly don't know." Sen burned where Morgan had hold of him. Heat radiated in all directions from the point of contact. He resisted the powerful urge to press against Morgan and wrap them together. "I'll uh, text you later, but everything's fine. Take this, please." He thrust his champagne at her and led Morgan from the gallery.

He left without a second thought, abandoning the final minutes of the opening, his bike, and probably his sanity. His spike of frustration and anger passed quickly, replaced by anxious bewilderment and doused by the rain as they walked. Sen stopped under a store awning and searched for Morgan's car but didn't see the Volvo. He checked Morgan's pockets but didn't find any keys.

Morgan gripped Sen's arms and shook him. "I have been beside myself. We were to meet, and then you were not there." Anguish flitted across his expression, and he cupped Sen's face in his hands.

Sen gave in to the urge to embrace Morgan. He held on, his confusion and Morgan's relief all mixed up in his heart, and Morgan pulled him closer. The storm had cleared the streets and curtained them from view.

"Have you lost faith? Did my silence stay your desires and keep you away?" Morgan combed his hand in Sen's hair and then held Sen's cheek to his shoulder.

"It's weird you didn't talk to me. It's confusing, and it pissed me off. But it's also weird when you do, so I'm giving up trying to decipher the messages," Sen answered. Morgan wouldn't remember anyway.

"I am doing all I can. I wish for more." Morgan kissed along Sen's temple and jaw, and Sen convulsively tightened his arms. "For a different time where we need not fear or hide."

"Yeah, how about today?" Sen snapped, pulled back, and then massaged Morgan's tense shoulders in contrition.

Morgan searched his face. He stared and then seemed to drift away.

They couldn't walk the distance to Greycote, not with Morgan in that state, the threat of lightning overhead, and the storm flooding the streets. Sen called a car service, kept hold of Morgan while they waited, and then bundled them into the backseat and apologized for the wet.

The driver grunted and didn't pay much attention. He'd undoubtedly seen weirder and had worse.

Morgan went into a trance state during the ride, muttering things Sen only caught snatches of, and had Sen's hand tucked between his on his lap. The contact appeased Sen as well. Despite the weirdness and his trepidation, all he wanted was Morgan, and he had no wish to part.

He thanked and overtipped the driver, hauled Morgan out, and propped him against the wall next to the side door.

"Good thing I know this house so well. Right?" He kept one arm around Morgan's middle while he entered the key code.

Morgan didn't answer.

"You're freaking me out, you know that? Which is saying something, all things considered." Sen eased the door open and didn't turn on any lights. He guided them to the master bedroom.

"Here," he said inanely and stood Morgan in place. Then he ran into the hall and grabbed several towels. Several more tumbled out onto the floor, and he didn't bother to tidy them. He scrubbed his hair and then scrubbed at Morgan, and managed to get Morgan dry and changed into sweatpants.

Morgan went through the motions, slack and unresponsive as Sen prattled encouragement and comforting nonsense sounds. He knocked the stupid bolster pillow and decorative pillows to the floor, turned down the covers, and avoided thoughts of mostly naked Morgan and himself. He got Morgan to the bed.

"Okay," he whispered. "You're home and safe and you just need to sleep. And then, well, and then things probably won't be fine. But hey, you'll have slept." Sen patted Morgan's chest and impulsively lifted onto his toes and kissed him.

"Stay." Morgan came to sudden life and caught Sen's wrists. "Promise you will stay." He walked forward, and his intense gaze looked through and past Sen, to something Sen couldn't follow. "Promise me."

Sen nodded. "Shh. Of course." He wouldn't stay, but those were the only words that formed.

Morgan backed him against the bed, and Sen shifted to coax Morgan around. But Morgan tugged, and Sen toppled over, got pinned under Morgan's weight, and lost his breath. Fever emanated from Morgan's clammy skin. Sen grunted as he kicked off his shoes and tried to grab the blankets with his toes.

"This is crazy. I'm crazy." He said it aloud, full voice. "There will never be enough green tea with ginger and honey for this. You beg me to stay and don't even know I'm here."

Morgan answered with a long exhalation and burrowed closer.

For the first time it occurred to him that he might be the one taking advantage of Morgan, somehow. The thought made him sick.

"Maybe I should have run and not returned, so we never met," he said into Morgan's hair and squeezed his eyes closed. That thought made him even sicker.

Morgan moved restlessly. made distressed noises, and tightened his hold on Sen.

Sen soothed and rubbed Morgan's back, but that didn't appease Morgan, who grew more agitated.

"I'm right here." Sen combed his fingers through Morgan's hair. "Right here and I won't go anywhere. Everything's fine."

Morgan muttered but then sighed and settled to the side, his arm heavy over Sen's middle, his face tucked into Sen's neck.

Sen put his hand on Morgan's and let out a long breath. He forced himself to go over their encounters and, most importantly, how it all felt on a gut level. The unerring answer was it all felt right and allowed—even if beyond his understanding and control—and he knew in his heart nothing had been forced or taken or trespassed. Still. He wasn't suddenly less anxious for answers or more able to clear the shadows between them.

Relief filled him but didn't make the strangeness less strange or Morgan's distress easier to take.

Sen stared at the ceiling and listened to the rain. Then stress, ragged nerves, and Morgan's slow breath and warmth overcame him, and he drifted to sleep.

He woke curled into Morgan's side, and the storm had faded to gentle rain.

"Déjà vu all over again," he sighed. He indulged himself by lying there a moment more. It soothed him to watch Morgan sleep. He was sheltered from all bad things in the warm fit of their bodies.

Ever since they met—even before their first meeting—Morgan had been his moon and sun, drawing him like the tide, emptying and filling him by turns.

Morgan's fever heat had passed, and he didn't stir as Sen slipped from the covers. He sat on the bed, leg pulled up and folded along Morgan's back, and thought through what he wanted and what he wanted to do.

It *was* crazy and crazy-making. Sen fantasized about quitting cleaning and hastily finishing the illustration gig. He imagined packing up and leaving New Orleans and all of it behind. He imagined telling Morgan good-bye. Sen visualized everything in rich, painful detail and went over it several times to perfect the words to say and the steps to take. He got it so perfect and exact that he knew he couldn't do it.

"I should wake you up with breakfast," he whispered. "That is, if you had any food in this house."

Sen reached to shake Morgan's shoulder but shied away. Early morning in bed without the memory of the night before wasn't exactly the conversation he wanted to have. That, and Morgan's confusion at his being there would gut him.

He swept his hand down to press over Morgan's heart, and he kissed Morgan's cheek. He heard distant yelling, the clash of metal. The rain picked up tempo.

His pulse surged, and Morgan grew restless.

"Shhh," he breathed, and he stood and leaned over to smooth the worry lines from Morgan's forehead. "See you Monday."

Morgan rolled toward him, briefly caught his hand, and then settled into deeper sleep.

Sen broke away to find his stuff. He tossed Morgan's damp clothes into the bathroom corner and stood in the hall. The room's shadows seemed to darken and envelop the bed, shuttering Morgan from his view. He pressed a hand out, palm open to say "Good-bye" and "Rest" and "This isn't over."

He crept downstairs through the house, dropped his shoes on the driveway, stepped into them, and started walking home. The dry pavement and fresh scent suggested the rain had stopped a while before.

Last night presented new circumstances. This thing had triggered in Morgan, even outside the boundaries of Greycote, but Sen had no visions during it.

Sen scuffled and went cold.

In Morgan's arms he dreamed vivid, intercut images of other lives and familiar people he didn't quite recognize. They spoke in languages he couldn't identify, and he answered fluently while they walked through parlors, sculpted gardens, untamed forests, and sand. He'd been seared by the heat of the sun and buffeted by stinging winter winds, on horseback and then on a cliff overlooking the sea. Someone he knew more deeply than words and his own heartbeat remained at his side, changing faces and clothes and landscapes, but always the same.

A blaring car horn shook Sen from his reverie. He stood in the middle of the street, and an annoyed woman in a beat-up minivan honked again.

"Sorry," he called and waved.

Sen didn't have a sketchbook. He'd left his bag at the gallery. So he picked up his step and began to run.

He sped up the stairs, fumbled in a pocket for his keys, and pushed into his apartment. Sen grabbed the nearest thing, charcoal and a large, thick pad of newsprint, and sketched his dream—urgently because it was already less distinct.

French? he wrote inside the hasty blocking of the parlor interior. Ocean waves split around the parlor and then the cliff rose above it, and he made two dark hashes at its promontory. Sen drew a rabbit and filled it in with stippling. He grunted and dragged the heel of his hand over it, but then pulled back and closed his eyes. He drew topiaries, bathed in sunshine, in the shape of fanciful animals from the formal garden. He drew a second rabbit, a fountain, and a sandy pathway that turned into a desert.

Sen continued to doodle, but the remnants of the dream proved elusive and slipped from his hand. He finished the silhouette of a carriage, tore the page from the pad, and taped it onto the wall with the others. It had become quite a collection.

Echoes, repeats, and mirror images threaded through every drawing. Sen could identify storm clouds and eyes, even if he didn't understand them. But trying to study the drawings and divine meaning was like reading a code without the cipher.

He used his knuckle to start the coffeemaker and washed his hand. Charcoal dust mixed with the water and formed dark clouds in the sink. He watched them drain away. He'd figure it out. He had to. His inexplicable, yet undeniably perfect fit with Morgan had to be the key to his sanity, and he wouldn't abandon it.

CHAPTER TEN

"GEM OF a place, isn't it?" The man waiting for Sen gestured across the planned gardens and brick drive and stuck out a hand. "Hi, I'm Jerry, and this is Nicole. We're the other leads on this overhaul with Morgan. He showed us your preliminary drawings, and we're all really excited about them."

Sen had had an uneventful weekend with no painting, no dreams, no vision. And no Morgan.

He shook hands with Nicole and Jerry, and they motioned for him to precede them into the old hotel. Reading the binder full of project notes and history he'd found tucked into the samples box, he learned the current project was rescuing the building from previous incarnations and restoring it to its original glory. After the hotel went bust, the building was converted to a sanitarium and then a TB hospice, and then it stood empty for years, until a developer came and chopped it into apartments.

"You'd never know it was anything but this," Sen said as he took in the splendor. The lobby ceiling was domed and covered in gilded plasterwork, and an enormous double staircase rose from the center. Cherubs connected by rods on each stair to either side of the plush crimson carpeting drew his eye.

Nicole grinned. "There is no greater compliment." She crouched along the wall and pointed out an imperfection in the floor Sen would otherwise have missed. "This is all that's left of an interior join for a built-in put here by the hospital, and the apartment owner added another layer and used it as an office. We matched the stone as closely as possible, but the first was quarried centuries ago, so there are some unavoidable tells. But we're here to resurrect, not obliterate the past."

"If you're interested there are pictures—tons of pictures—of every single thing excavated during the demo, cleaned out after, and whatever we put back in here. Some will be featured on our website after the job is complete, but if you want to root around in the digital archives, let one of us know." Jerry leaned in. "There's usernames and passwords and everything. I'm sure Morgan would share his."

"Share his what?" Morgan waved from the second floor. He wore jeans and a dress shirt with the sleeves rolled to the elbows.

Rationally Sen knew he should stay guarded, but seeing Morgan made him light up inside. He waved back and then curled his fingers to his palm and schooled the huge grin that threatened to eat his face.

"Access to the megadump," Nicole said and beckoned Sen upstairs.

Morgan met him at the top landing, where the staircase split to continue its climb to the left and right. He smiled. "Oh yeah. Sure. So, what do you think?"

"He spoke the golden words," Nicole said. "And considering his critical artist's eye, that makes it even more satisfying."

"I do wish I'd seen the before and during stages, though." Sen surveyed the entire entryway, filled with chandeliers and crystals reflecting light in all directions. Windows surrounded enormous carved doors, and colorful marble and white plaster went in all directions in gilded sensory overload. "Ruin is fascinating and beautiful in its own right. Then to see it brought back, that's a poetic dichotomy people like me can't resist."

Jerry spread his arms. "This is what I enjoy most, the view when the work is nearly finished and before anyone has tramped in to dirty up the place."

"There were trees and plants and whole microclimates in here. The moss-covered solarium was stunning." Morgan inclined his head and smiled, and after a pause he went on. "We spent weeks poring over city archives—old photographs, older drawings, the original plats and plans for the hotel—rebuilding her from memories. Coax her out, learn her secrets, then make her whole again." His gaze held Sen's, and he said softly, "I'm so glad you're here."

"Me too." Sen stared and then remembered that he brought his camera and started taking pictures. "I know there are plenty already, but these are for me."

"Makes sense. Your eye needs to learn and understand the place too." Morgan gestured to encompass the greater space. "Take your time. We'll let you wander and go in anywhere you want. We're done with the hard-hat stage, so you won't fall through the floor or anything."

"Oh." Sen had imagined wandering around with Morgan.

"I thought you wouldn't want us hovering." He pointed across the stairs and balcony to a deep-set doorway. "It's early, and we work until six at least, so have at. We'll be in there if you need anything."

"Yes. Six at least. We're in the tedious stage you don't want any part of— paperwork and final sign-offs," Jerry said while walking away. Nicole followed him down the hall.

Morgan caught Sen's arm. "This is okay?"

"This is totally fine." Sen snapped a picture. "Go to your tedium. I'll just be waltzing about not doing tedious things and enjoying every minute."

"Not to rub it in or anything." Morgan curled his lip, but Sen could see he was fighting a smile. "Come and find me for lunch. Around one," he said, and it seemed like an impulse.

"You're on." Sen hesitated, and Morgan didn't move. Then they both took a step, and Sen laughed. "Was there something else?"

Morgan nodded but made a helpless gesture. "Yes. And I have no idea what."

Sen's chest tightened. "Was this the thing you were forgetting to tell me that I told you to just forget entirely?" He tried for a light tone, but sounded wary.

"Yes. Whatever that might be." Morgan shoved his hands into his pockets and looked away. "I've tried to, you know. Right now with us together and talking, it's not there, or at least it's no longer important. But whenever we meet or are about to part that niggling little *something* returns. I can't shake it, and it's starting to make me feel a little crazy."

"Turn a teacup over on your countertop." At Morgan's expression Sen spread his hands. "It's something my mom always recommends—when you're trying to remember something, get a teacup, turn it over on the countertop or table, and leave it there. It'll collect your thoughts and then let you know. So, on your first impulse to turn it upright again, do it. Whatever you're trying to remember will be there, inside, and return."

Morgan frowned. "I've never heard that before, but I'm willing to try."

"Hey. You never know. It's worked for me a few times, even if it's just a mnemonic device that helps unlock your brain." Sen raised an eyebrow. "A coffee mug might work in a pinch—I don't think you own any teacups."

"Let's hope so, because I think you're right. I'll update you." Morgan turned away. "One o'clock."

Sen nodded. "See you then."

On a whim he took a picture of Morgan and caught the moment as Morgan turned back to look at him. He peeked from behind his camera and waved. Morgan sideswiped with a hand as though to send him along, and Sen managed to unmoor and get moving. He glanced around, assessing and planning, and then decided to go all the way to the top floor and work down.

The hotel was a massive square with two blunt wings, composed of six main stories and two more for staff and storage tucked in the eaves. He started there and marveled at the flourishes even the utilitarian areas had been given. Wide wood-plank flooring, stained with a dark border, expanded the rooms visually, and windows and hardware were plentiful. Modern touches were discreetly added—fixtures, outlets, and cable jacks—with every other room divided into closets and bathrooms.

Sen discovered four different staircases leading this way and that, and passages inside walls that would conceal staff movement from the guests. He walked up and down the halls, looked into the rooms at the rear and the front, and then went down. The job contract stipulated he draw ten interiors, but allowed some creative latitude, as he could choose rooms from a suggested list. He would also illustrate four exterior aspects, and the angles to draw the front, sides, and back from were up to him. Those were straightforward, and he planned to draw the front as if sitting in a carriage on approach, head-on but looming grandly. The side views would be boring but with enough angle to hint at the wings and break up the blocks, and the fourth illustration would focus on the formal gardens at the back.

He didn't have the ten interiors set, but he jotted "grand entry" and "solarium" in his notebook. Because it was a hotel, he would draw one of the suites and one of the communal spaces. Then maybe the salon, and if he had his way, one of the plain bedrooms. The rest would reveal itself to him as he worked.

The third floor had a smaller balcony, and Sen leaned over it to see into the room Morgan had pointed out.

"Hi. Don't let me scare you into falling onto the stairs and cracking your head open," Morgan said from behind. "I'm going to put my hand on your back, because I'm nervous, even if you're not."

Sen craned around and laughed. "Sorry. I wanted a picture and didn't realize how far out I'd gotten." He eased down and turned, and he tingled to his scalp when Morgan's hands settled on his hips. "I can't get over this place. The box of samples you brought isn't even a tenth of all that's here."

"We each pick favorite things, and we call the illustrations 'highlights' for a reason." Morgan glanced from Sen's mouth to the thump of his pulse in his throat and then to his eyes.

"Nothing cursed or haunted, though, I'm guessing?" Sen asked without sounding serious. "I mean, you never know with old buildings and New Orleans—killer combo."

Morgan's eye crinkles showed up in force, and he shook his head. "Nope. At least none I'm aware of. You're safe." He arched an eyebrow. "That is, so long as you say you didn't slide down the banisters or hang from the window niches to get a better angle. And please don't hang from anything else."

"I actually didn't. No lie." Sen instinctively tilted his hips, but after their thighs pressed together, he cleared his throat and jerked back. "Is it one already?"

"Let me see." Morgan checked his watch. "Quarter of, so no tardy demerit."

"I'm almost disappointed—that would be my first." Sen grinned. He liked that Morgan had come looking for him.

"You were never late to class? I hate to cast aspersions, but I find that hard to believe." Morgan started to massage Sen's hips but didn't seem aware he was doing it. "Not even once, because something was jammed in your locker or you got distracted in the library?"

"Sounds like *you* were." Sen repressed a shudder and shook his head. "Mom didn't believe in negative reinforcement." At Morgan's blank look he said, "Homeschooled."

"Hunh." Morgan tightened his hand and then slid away and started toward the stairs. "Lunch is here."

"I'll be down in a few. I'm almost done on this floor. Then I don't have to backtrack after we eat." Sen trotted along the balcony to the far end. "Start without me."

Backtracking wouldn't bother him, but he couldn't take another minute of Morgan's subconscious, potent intimacy. Sen flattened his hands on the thick balustrade and tried to center his breath and quickened pulse. He frowned as he watched Morgan descend away from him.

"Your body remembers, even if you don't," he said. But he didn't know who he should address.

The middle floors didn't take as long to explore. Sen soon rounded the staircase onto the second floor and headed into the side room pointed out before. In the center sat an enormous table ringed with freestanding whiteboards and full of drawings, laptops, and a clutter of takeout coffee cups. A graffiti of lists, random thoughts, and a hierarchy of prioritized tasks covered the boards in various writing styles and scribble, interspersed with reference pictures. A side table held more samples and paperwork.

Morgan stood at the windows by a makeshift table that held flavored water and pizza boxes. He handed Sen a paper plate, and they loaded up. Then Morgan led them through a connecting door into a cozier room over what would be the main entrance. A length of plywood stacked on plastic crates created a table, and conference chairs from the other room clustered around it. Sen sat, devoured two pieces, and finished a water in a few gulps. Since Morgan was doing the same, he didn't excuse himself for wolfing down everything he could reach.

"Did you grow up on a farm or somewhere remote? Or was homeschooling a religious or a social choice?" Morgan asked, a bit more carefully.

"None of the above." Sen attacked a third slice of pizza and opened another water. "My folks are total hippies and wanted to live off the grid long before 'living off the grid' was a thing people said. We traveled almost nonstop my whole childhood, so nontraditional school just made sense." He shrugged. "I'm sure experts would say I'm supposed to be stunted, or whatever, but no way. My childhood was amazing. Plus I didn't know different, my parents are smart and cool, and since it was up to us, I graduated early."

"I was homeschooled." Morgan gave Sen a look. "Dad didn't travel nonstop, but we still moved a ton. During middle school he was reassigned three times, so in the end, it was easier for me to cram at home and then test in at the base schools—more or less bypassing actually going, but getting credit—so the next year I could go into high school without a problem. It was a year early, but my dad was finally stationed somewhere long enough for me to get continuity through my sophomore year. Then junior year the home thing again, until the last half of senior year, when he found a school to stick me in so I could graduate and get a diploma from somewhere real."

"Base schools?"

Morgan's dimple appeared. "Army brat. Probably the diametric opposite of total hippies, but not so different for us, when you get down to it."

Sen considered that. "Agreed."

"Growing up like that is a lot of why I love this job so much." Morgan's gaze was drawn outside. "I make stable homes, and I make my mark in a place that will last long after I'm gone."

That caught Sen's attention. "Either that's really maudlin and Lord Byron of you, or it's practical, and I'm not connecting why."

Morgan laughed. "Gone as in to another location—city, state, country— to work on whatever project my firm has taken on. With long vacations between them."

Sen snickered. "Ahhh, right. Growing up a vagabond made me into an adult vagabond."

"Same," Morgan said with a nod.

They grinned at each other.

"And you know, that's a lot of why I make art?" Sen tilted his hand so Morgan could see the corner of the pizza box Sen sketched on as they talked. "I've always been a doodler, and my family keeps up our end of the total hippie bargain by all being artist types, but I also sketch and paint to have some remembrance of all the places I've been. Like, my sketchbook is the diary and the work I sell is the public record."

He didn't ask if that made sense, because he knew it had.

"We both make art for and about where we've been," Morgan said, tapping the doodles. He bumped into Sen's hand and ran a fingertip up and down Sen's finger. Then his eyes got heavy.

Sen let out a low, anticipatory breath and rubbed Morgan's finger with his thumb. When he licked his lips, Morgan's pupils widened, so he did it again.

The air charged around them, and Morgan covered Sen's hand with his and leaned in, enticing Sen to lean in too.

"Hey, boss." Jerry poked through the door and smiled at them. "Are you guys done? Nicole is already back to it, and I think if we grind away, we can leave by five."

Morgan jerked away, and Sen bit back a frustrated noise.

"Thanks, Jerry. Leaving by five sounds great." Morgan wadded up a napkin, frowned, and straightened. "I still can't remember what I meant—need—to tell you."

"It had to do with storms and stuff, I think," Sen tested.

Morgan nodded, and his brow furrowed. "That sounds right. It's just on the tip of my tongue, but then I try and just say it, and it always eludes me." He closed his eyes, concentrated, and began to shake.

"It's really fine," Sen interrupted. He could feel Morgan's tension, annoyance, and desperation to push, though.

Morgan's eyes snapped open, and he stared past Sen as the storm started to gather behind his gaze.

"I did say you could forget it entirely. Really, it's fine." Sen touched Morgan's arm.

Morgan blinked and shook his head, and his eyes began to clear. "Which is generous, but doesn't absolve my brain from hamstering for all its worth to run it down." He scoffed. "And believe me, the brain hamster is tired."

Sen followed the lines bracketing Morgan's eyes, dimples, and mouth.

"Believe me, I do." Sen tore his gaze from Morgan's lips and gathered their lunch detritus. "I'm about done with my self-guided tour. Is it fine if I head out after, or do I need to check in with anyone?"

Morgan followed him into the adjoining room and out to the balcony, but he stayed a step back. "Yeah. Please text me or yell upstairs that you're going. That way we can lock up and not lock you in." He arched his eyebrows. "And I won't have to worry you've done that cracking-your-head-open thing."

"I said I wouldn't. I even promised."

Morgan gave him A Look, so Sen caught his grin between his teeth and looked down, until the desire to giggle passed.

"Okay. I'll text." He got halfway down the main stairs and turned. "Wait, so if you travel for this job, and this project is nearly finished, are you moving when it's over?" Sen didn't fear Morgan's answer.

"Yep, as soon as my house sells." Morgan came around the balcony and down two stairs. "Then I'll bounce around a bit, maybe go visit my dad, then see where I'm assigned next."

Sen's heart sped as excitement shivered through him. "And that explains why the house is fully restored, kept pristine, and unlived in." He paused. "Again, not a dis, it just made me curious."

Morgan nodded. "I've rented or done long-stay hotels before, but there are so many houses in need of rescue here, I couldn't pass up the opportunity." He descended another two steps. "Jerry and I went in on a few in some of the lower wards, and I was going to live in one of those, because they're smaller and more practical, but we had needy buyers knocking on the door the day construction began. So I took the big house. No immediate demand, and it'll definitely move once I put it on the market."

"That's awesome and clever. Awesome for the people who get to buy improved houses and clever for you to think of living in places that way."

"I guess so. Mostly we have fun doing it, and it keeps our wits sharp." Morgan gestured at the hall. "Not everything is on this scale and with this budget."

"I hear you. There's some street art out there with my tag on it," Sen said and winked. "I've done volunteer construction while living here." He climbed up a step. "Too bad none of the houses you guys did."

"We make it a point to hire local, so we wouldn't have overlapped with volunteer groups." Morgan made it to the step Sen stood on and smiled. "But you ended up in my own house, and it occurs to me, if things hadn't gone that way, the big house would be sold, and I wouldn't feel justified in hiring a cleaner for a small place."

"You don't really need one either way."

Morgan made a negating sound. "The amount of dusting alone would beg to differ. This way it's maintained and ready to go when I am. A small house I could clean in a Saturday and call it even."

"And we're back to you not hiring Adri to hire me." Sen dared to fiddle with the lowest button on Morgan's shirt collar. "Which would be tragic," he said to tease, but turned serious.

"Sophocles level." Morgan caught Sen's hand and slipped his thumb into Sen's palm. "I wouldn't learn ninja towel folding or be able to wear matching socks, and I'd be lost without my amazing illustrator."

Morgan circled his thumb until Sen's blood hummed. Two faces shimmered and coalesced in his mind's eye, and he pictured them standing there, as he and Morgan were, face-to-face and holding hands. They were serene and certain and surrounded in rosy light.

Sen had to swallow and clear his throat to say, "Thank goodness for coincidence."

"Is there such a thing? I'm not sure anymore, and I always preferred the ideas of fate and destiny."

Sen tightened his hand. "Yes. Yes, me too." A question rose in his mind, and he moved away. "Where did you live before New Orleans?"

"Portland."

"Really." Sen's ears roared. He'd moved to New Orleans from Portland. He blinked. "Portland...?"

"Oregon." Morgan's gaze fell to their hands, and he let go and stepped back. "We overhauled a gorgeous mansion built during a timber boom. Much different than this, in appearance, but underneath, the same process, full of history and memories to tease out."

"I want to see it." Sen added, "And I assume it's on the website and in the megadump?"

Morgan nodded. "I've never revisited any of the projects, and suddenly I want to," he said, quiet but firm.

Sen clenched his jaw to hold back a tangled rush of emotion. He felt a lift and then a crash of disappointment. Morgan had been in Portland, but Oregon, not Maine. He seemed to be forever navigating uneven ground in Morgan's presence, between their comfort with each other, his pleasure in Morgan, Morgan's inability to freely be the same, and his desire to kiss Morgan and say, "You don't have to understand, because I sure don't, just kiss me back, please."

He drew his shoulders up and let out a breath. "You won't get out of here by five unless I get out of here now. I'll text when I've left and talk to you soon."

"True enough, and good. Sounds good." Morgan's gaze followed Sen down the stairs and seemed to reach even around the corner.

Sen rushed through the remainder of the hotel with the heat from Morgan's hand imprinted on his palm.

As he left he looked back from the street to get a final impression of the hotel. Morgan watched him from a window. Sen waved and then biked to a café he frequented near home. There he e-mailed his mom to tell her it still scared him, was definitely only just about the guy, that Morgan was a nomad too, and he was still processing their talk. He attached the preannouncement for his show at Gallery Paon and then ordered a second Americano.

He sketched under a mellow, setting sun to capture the atmosphere of the hotel and allowed his pencil to roam to see what rooms stayed with him. More cherubs appeared, and the fountain in the solarium covered in a fanciful moss landscape. The landscape took on aspects of a castle and a cliff overlooking the sea. Then he worked on some outside thumbnails.

Morgan answering "Portland" repeated in his thoughts, and it had him chasing unanswerable questions. Had he misread the signs that directed him to

Maine? Should he have ended up in Oregon instead? If he'd gone to Oregon, would there have been signs to New Orleans?

Sen dashed out several dark hashmarks to relieve a burst of frustration and fell back in the chair. His dad had told him to wait to be led. Maybe the congruency of their twin Portlands leading them to New Orleans was everything he needed to know. It had led them to their present—after they danced around each other, after he wanted to quit, and after that day in the turret room—for a reason.

He wanted more from Morgan, even if he was still learning what. Sen sketched the view of his palm cradling Morgan's thumb, from Morgan's perspective. He considered it, then packed his bag and delivered his mug to the bar. His phone chirped as he stepped outside, and he swung onto his bike and then checked it.

Promising! T-leaves: even full cups won't sate for a while. keep drinking <3

Thirst got quenched but curiosity got sated. Sen didn't miss his mom's point. He texted back a thanks, assured her that his eyes were open, and headed home.

Sen painted with deliberation into the night. He hinged two canvases at the center seam for the couple on the stairs and captured them in their rosy light and surety. They sat together, flat on the easel, as he built layers of color around them, reminiscent of a spring afternoon. This couple was the calmest he had seen. They were elegantly dressed—the man in a frilled collar and the lady in a thin headdress with a pearl dangling over her forehead. He worked the background to look like parchment and ivory, and shadowed the swirls of solvents and paint to mimic plasterwork and carved ceilings.

After several hours he stood back and regarded them. They would need several more hours of work and more layers, but as they dried, he tilted the canvases inward on the hinge, so they could gaze upon each other as they had in his mind. He sagged in relief that he'd been shown another couple to paint.

Sweet, positive energy emanated from the new portraits.

"I'm glad someone's happy," Sen told them, and he started to clean up.

CHAPTER ELEVEN

"HOW'S IT going?"

Sen filled a shadow with crosshatches and nodded. "Pretty good. All the detail illustrations are finished, and I'm closing in on the interiors." He stayed hunched over the drafting table but tingled in anticipation of Morgan's touch.

"Glad to hear it." Morgan came to stand next to Sen and laid a hand on his back. He studied the drawing and gave Sen an approving look. "And I'm glad you pushed to draw one of the upper bedrooms. They're as intrinsic to the hotel and its history as the opulent stuff and just as important to remember. Maybe more, given those who lived in the plain spaces were kept hidden, but were essential."

"Yeah, totally. Aesthetically I appreciate the simplicity and feel of these rooms, but I also like bringing attention to what they represent. Thanks." Sen craned around to smile at Morgan. "Look behind you."

Morgan lifted his hand, turned, and then rested his other hand on Sen's shoulder. As if breaking contact for too long were impossible, and as if he weren't aware of doing it.

Sen had hung each completed illustration on one wall using binder clips and pushpins. That way they were protected, and he could study them while he worked through the next drawings, so the whole series maintained continuity.

"Whoa. They're really impressive, displayed like that. Gives me an idea of how to group them in the lobby. I originally thought to hang them in a line on either side of the entryway, but seeing this, I think they should be grouped salon style. Maybe over the reception desk?" Morgan squeezed Sen's shoulder. "You do excellent work, and you're gonna make me look excellent with the boss for finding you."

Sen threw an exaggerated point-and-wink gesture. "You're welcome."

Morgan got the cherub from the table and took it to the picture for comparison. "This is unexpected."

"Hmm? What's unexpected?" Sen capped his pens and stood. He stretched both arms overhead and yawned, and caught Morgan staring at his exposed tummy and hip dents. So he deepened the stretch, arched his back, and rolled his neck. Then he pivoted on his feet and grabbed the next illustration to hang with the others.

When Morgan didn't answer, Sen asked, "Good unexpected or bad unexpected?"

"Good. Very good." Morgan sounded distracted and watched Sen twitch his shirt back down. After a moment he referred to the drawing. "This part here."

Sen had recreated his doodle of two cherubs swathed in bunting in the bottom right corner of the page. All the other required aspects were there. He composed the drawing in two main columns, with front, three-quarter, and side views of the cherub to the left, and on the right a lighter background picture of the staircase with the cherubs highlighted.

"Good is good. It just felt like it belonged, and once I had the pencil sketch down, I knew that call was right. Really pulled the whole thing together—made it more alive than a technical drawing."

Morgan turned the cherub onto his palm. "These little guys were the first element among the ruins that reached out and grabbed me during the initial walkthrough, so I claimed them as part of my research. I learned Botticelli was one of the lead designer's favorite artists and influenced a lot of his motif choices. Including these. Your interpretive drawing here is remarkably similar to the painting he based them on."

"Which explains all the seashells, fruit, and flowering vines. And why they all work so cohesively." Sen grinned. "Neat."

"I see there's a few others, which is super," Morgan said about the scrollwork, the branch heavy with oranges, and a flowering vine included in different drawings. "You have such a sensitive touch in your work and a wonderful sense of place connecting to the hotel." He stepped back and took in the drawings, then returned the cherub to the table. "How many days until you're finished, do you think?"

"Three, maybe four."

"Wow. Not long, then."

Sen laughed. "And good thing too. I still have paintings to paint and frame and schlepp and an artist's statement to write and maybe to sleep once or twice in there." He grimaced. "What ever happened to thinking I had several weeks and plenty of time? I have no idea. It's all a blur. I should probably finish the illustrations in two days."

"Are you stuck with the paintings?" Morgan frowned. "Or is it one of those 'get this out of the way, clear your brainspace, then move on to the next thing' deals?"

Sen was absolutely stuck. He circled the drain in tinkering mode with the finished portraits, bringing them to the easel to add another layer or tweak a detail or mute a color. But he had no insights for the others he still needed to paint. The storm-swept couple continued to unnerve him, but he'd stopped ignoring them. They were familiar in an abstract way, the same as all the others and reminiscent of the rest, but no longer as fraught as on the angry night he summoned them. He remained on the fence about including other-Morgan and his companion, but in the end, that choice might be made for him if he couldn't paint more.

"They're going fine," Sen said, and at Morgan's disbelieving eyebrow arch, he fluttered his lashes. "But I'll be glad to have the illustrations out of the way."

Morgan waved a hand over the table. "Should I leave all this here until you're done?" He nodded and packed the samples when Sen shook his head. "And speaking of needing frames, that reminds me to ask if you have strong thoughts on how to frame the illustrations."

Sen had a critical look at them. "Chunky, gold-leafed cake frosting. With a wide, white outer mat, over a very thin black mat." He paused. "I'm sure you know what I'm talking about with the frosting, because that's very technical frame-speak, there."

"Quite technical. There's a whole cake frosting section in our wood trim and frame wholesaler's catalog." Morgan got his phone out. "I'm putting that in a note, because it sounds exactly right, making a bridge from the black and white illustrations to the lavish hotel interior, but the white mat will give the eye a rest between the two."

"Exactly." Sen smiled, and Morgan smiled, and they started toward each other.

A loud, shrill noise carried to the upstairs, and Sen looked around.

"Right. I put the kettle on." Morgan hefted the box of samples.

"Should I get the catalogs?" Sen pointed at the stack on the floor.

"Sure, if you're done with them," Morgan said and headed into the hall. "Now that we're both in crunch time, I won't see you tomorrow, but I wanted to talk to you about the frames and everything."

Sen made an agreeing noise as they trooped all the way to the kitchen. He got out a shopping bag, slid the catalogs inside, and walked it down the hall to set it next to the side door.

"Well, we talked about it," he said when he returned to the kitchen. He stopped alongside the island and surveyed the breakfast nook. "It's not even Wednesday. You'll spoil me."

Morgan rolled his eyes. "I did say I won't be able to stay and see you tomorrow morning." He set a bowl of fruit salad on the table with everything else, sat in the end chair, and patted the bench seat.

There was no reason for Morgan to come home on a Tuesday to discuss something that could be a phone call or a text. And there was no real reason for Morgan to wait on Sen every Wednesday morning and talk over a mug of coffee, ostensibly to check in about the project.

Sen slid onto the bench and arranged himself so their knees almost touched. Then he sipped the tea Morgan poured.

"Mint just sounded good today." Morgan nudged a plate of sugar cubes over.

"And tastes good." Sen eyed the sugar and dropped two cubes in his cup. "When did you get a teapot?" He poked the turquoise Fiestaware pot. "I like it."

"Found it at a junk shop. Nicole and I went on a whirlwind round of antique, scrap, architectural reclamation, and sundry shopping last week. Decorations and embellishments for the gardens and interior. You know." Morgan poked the teapot opposite where Sen had. "Thanks. I like it too."

Sen nodded and propped his elbows on the table, rested his chin on one hand, and gazed into the sunny backyard. Birds fluttered, and moss swayed in the breeze. He passed over rolls and fruit to nibble a praline, and Morgan snickered at him. Sen had another sip of tea and ignored him, but he felt Morgan's smile and fought his own.

"And you're right. We've talked about the illustrations. So, what's your favorite sport? Sports team?" Morgan started picking blueberries from the fruit salad.

"Uh… curling, I guess?" Sen opened a hand. "I dig their pants."

"A valid choice for a very valid reason." A blueberry got away from Morgan and bounced around, but he nabbed it as it rolled off the table. "Ha. Usually I'm alone when that kind of thing happens."

"Nice. You're practically a ninja yourself. I'm still not trusting you with the towels, but that was pretty good." Sen wanted another praline, but he paced himself with a few pieces of mango. "I suppose you have a favorite sporting team that sports sportingly?"

Morgan grinned. "I live for the annual Army-Navy football game. But I confess I'm not a big fan otherwise. I played Ultimate Frisbee in college, and basketball, but mostly because my school was small and our whole team sucked." He moved a strawberry aside to get to the last blueberries. "And I can watch curling. Come for the pants, stay for the frenzied sweeping."

"I'm saying." Sen punctuated by jabbing the air with a piece of mango.

Every Wednesday they quickly dispatched the formality of business and peppered each other with questions on myriad and random subjects. The week before they'd discussed politics. To Sen's great relief, he and Morgan were fairly well aligned, Morgan liberal where it most mattered to Sen and centrist on issues Sen could accept more flexibility about.

"Favorite book?"

Morgan scratched behind his ear. "Man, I don't know." He waved back Sen's side-eye and said, "I mean, I don't know how to choose, not that I don't read. Comics, graphic novels, sci-fi, anything with dragons, and then nonfiction about World War II and the Dark Ages and the Renaissance."

"Just to name a few."

"A mere few." Morgan smiled. "How about you?"

"*Watership Down*." Sen popped a crumble of praline in his mouth. "And anything else I could get my hands on, really."

"Good fave." Morgan unlocked his phone and tapped something into it. "I should reread that. I only remember that it's about bunnies."

"Smart bunnies, facing turmoil and overcoming hardship while learning the meaning of life, home, and family. I think Fiver—that's the main bun hero—was my first crush." Sen blinked.

"What?"

Sen shook his head. "Nothing." His favorite book recounted the story of a seer rabbit guided by visions to a new and lasting home. Morgan still looked at him, so he asked, "Chocolate or vanilla?" then clarified, "Ice cream."

Morgan answered immediately. "Swirled. Both? Any and all kinds? Can I go with any?"

"I'm a fan of going with any."

"Yeah, me too." Morgan hesitated, and while he refilled their tea, he asked, "First kiss?

"Cindy. It was at a camp bonfire—like a KOA-type place for tents and RVs, not summer camp. I was fourteen, and she was a gloriously self-assured sixteen, and on a summer road-trip vacation with her family." Sen smiled at the memory. "It was brief and awkward, but I liked her freckles and that she smelled like hot cocoa mix. And that she was leaving the next morning."

Morgan cracked a laugh. "That never hurts."

"That same summer I kissed Trevor, a not-quite gloriously self-assured sixteen, but close. We spent a day at the same lake, and I couldn't stop noticing how good he looked in swim trunks." Sen hummed. "And that about sums it up for me—two first kisses in the same summer, but nothing lasting, because we were always on the move."

"Same." Morgan frowned that there were no more blueberries and had a strawberry. "The moving and nothing-lasting thing, I mean. My longest term girlfriend was freshman year of college, after my gawky, dork teen years, but before architecture ate my life." He turned to Sen. "My first kiss was a girl on base—one of the few other kids. We were both thirteen. Tried it, didn't hate it, but didn't try again."

Sen smiled.

"Never a Trevor," Morgan said, and his gaze dropped to Sen's lips.

Sen almost said "Not yet," but Morgan's phone rang, and they both jumped.

"Sorry," Morgan said and wrinkled his nose. He answered, had a brief conversation, and then explained, "Nicole, tracking me down. Seems my lunch hour has been a skosh longer than that."

"Ooh. That's a tardy demerit," Sen said with sparkle, and Morgan laughed.

They finished their tea and cleared up, and Sen stood at the center island and watched Morgan putter. A beautiful day, sitting in a breakfast nook, sharing tea with Morgan. How wonderfully normal. So much so that he could almost pretend it could always be like that.

He clenched his jaw and sighed. Then he started down the hall.

Sen snagged the bag of catalogs, held open the side door, waited until Morgan caught it, and tucked the catalogs in the backseat of Morgan's car.

"Okay, then, dear, have a good rest of your day," he teased.

When he straightened, Morgan dropped a kiss on his forehead.

They stood too close until Sen pushed out a low chuckle and they moved an inch apart. His forehead tingled and his blood sizzled and he opted not to acknowledge the kiss.

"I'm not sure when I'll see you next. Presumably when you let me know the illustrations are complete. I have another dinner schmoozing session with some local politicians and society folk tomorrow night too, so feel free to stay late working." Morgan gave Sen's hair a playful tug, and then didn't let go. "You would be welcome to stay late anyway, but, you know."

"I do. Thanks." Sen leaned into Morgan's hand. He didn't usually appreciate having his hair played with, but it felt good. Out of nowhere he asked, "Where is your dad stationed?"

Morgan didn't miss a beat. "Fort Shafter. That's in Hawaii." He waggled his eyebrows. "Not too shabby, eh?"

"Outright fantastic, even. And the only state I've never been in."

"Really? Well, you'll have to come… to the Islands sometime." Morgan combed his fingers through Sen's hair and went around the car. "It's worth the trip. This is Dad's second stint there."

Sen closed the back passenger door and drummed his fingers on the roof. "Since you know your way around, you'll have to give me recommendations. Places to eat, snorkeling, the works."

"Deal." Morgan stared at Sen and swallowed.

"How old are you?"

Morgan didn't hesitate to answer. "Twenty-eight."

"That's it? I mean, I wasn't quite sure, and my ballpark was around that. But yeah." Sen paused. "I'm twenty-five."

"Yeah," Morgan said like he knew. "We'll reconnect soon. And my pocket is vibrating, so I should really get going before Nicole takes more drastic measures."

"My plan is to leave the drawings here, since I don't want to bike them around anywhere, even in a protective tube. I'll put a sticky note on the fridge when they're all done." Sen patted the car and turned toward the house. "Talk to you in a few."

He went inside but watched from the window as Morgan drove away. Sen took a cup of mint tea into the sitting room no one sat in, and drank with deliberation to calm his happily buzzing nerves and focus his thoughts away from sun-drenched beach daydreams.

Sen no longer wanted to draw, but he didn't have the luxury to go home and moon about Morgan or pick apart their interactions and Morgan's every expression. He washed the mug, went back upstairs, and wrote a final to-do list. If he got grinding and stayed grinding, he could have everything wrapped up by the next day. Practicality had made him attack the job by getting the most complicated and difficult illustrations done first, but at the moment, practicality seemed like a genius stroke. So Sen gave himself a little genius credit for handling the job that way.

His alarm sounded at 5:45, and he unfolded from the drafting table, rolled his shoulders, and clenched his fingers in and out. It wasn't that he didn't want to see Morgan. Quite the opposite. But if he stayed and they got to talking, who knew when he'd leave, and he needed sleep and space for the long day ahead.

Sen didn't want to just leave, so he tore out a sketchbook page, wrote a quick note in the top corner, boxed it in, and drew a rabbit in a top hat underneath, as though it were holding the note as a sign.

The humidity had spiked during the day, and moisture hung in the air. Sen would be a gritty, sticky mess by the end of his ride home. He sighed, hopped on his bike, and got moving before the weather decided to outright rain.

He didn't have to pay attention to the route, so he concentrated on the morning spent with Morgan and compared it to other mornings with Morgan. He thought about how kind and charming and worthy of his time Morgan was.

Sen heard his name. It jerked him from his thoughts just in time to swerve into the gutter and near-miss getting slammed by a careless driver. He wobbled and then jumped from the bike onto the curb, and the car squealed away.

"Asshole," he yelled, and for a moment he swore he saw the flash of an angry, protective gaze in the haze above the street.

He steadied himself, caught his breath, and wheeled the bike into position. The front tire kicked up something reflective, and he leaned over, grabbed it, and stuck it in a pocket.

The lump of whatever throbbed against his leg and seemed to burn through his jeans. He kept touching it, worried it'd jar loose and he'd lose it. Sen raced upstairs, stowed his bike, and dug into his pocket.

He'd picked up a dirtied plastic keychain—a small palm tree and hula girl bookending the word *Aloha.*

"Holy shit." Sen dropped the keychain and stared at it as it stared back at him from the floor. He flexed his hand and rubbed at the still-burning spot on his leg.

Sen left it on the floor and avoided it as he busied himself with a shower, catch-can dinner, and packing snacks and supplies for the next day. He turned off the lights, and the streetlamp gleamed off the dull gold trim on the keychain.

Sen got the broom and nudged it out of his line of sight.

"Whatever. Don't judge," he said to the portraits. Then stood there feeling foolish.

He stowed the broom and went to bed, but stared into the shadowy kitchen and couldn't sleep, so he fired up his laptop and researched the cemetery that bordered Greycote. Everything he found listed it as historically significant. It mentioned several beautiful markers and no recorded paranormal activity.

"Like they know," he muttered and thrust the laptop away.

Sen sat for a minute in the dark, and then he jumped up, got dressed, and biked to the cemetery. The humidity hadn't budged, but the still, murky air seemed disinclined to do more than marinate on the idea of gathering into rain.

He locked his bike a block away and went past a man noodling a jazz riff on a clarinet. The man paused, watched him a moment, whistled lowly, and played a melancholy tune. Its haunting melody paced Sen's walk to the cemetery.

Sen jumped the wall and walked the flagstone and gravel path. He peered past wrought iron rails into mausoleums, pressed his ear to tombs, knocked on vaults, and ran his fingertips across carved inscriptions. Nothing stirred. Even the wind and murky air remained still.

The path, his feet, and the insistent thrum in his head took him to the wall at the bottom of Greycote's lawn. He didn't resist. Sen stared across the moonlit yard and fought the impulse to keep walking.

"Oh, Morgan," he sighed. "What are we going to do?"

A light came on in the house. The glowing squares were high up and floating from his vantage point. Sen squinted and recognized the room he used as a studio.

Morgan approached the windows, but paused over the drafting table. Then he moved to look out over the yard.

Sen's breath caught. He dropped to his hands and knees and tensed against the wall as though to hide. But after a moment, he huffed and peeked over the wall. Morgan was still there, although Sen couldn't see his face.

Dark shadows boiled from the trees and spread to wraith around the house. Morgan flattened his hand on a window, and the shadows crept higher. Then he turned, the light went out, and the shadows retreated.

Sen flopped to sit and leaned his forehead on his knees. He stayed a good while, until it seemed likely Morgan had gone to bed. When he pushed to his feet and looked back, the house remained dark and the moonlight brightened. Sen hurried to get his bike and then sped home.

CHAPTER TWELVE

SEN WOKE ahead of the alarm, devoured half a loaf of butter-soaked toast as he got ready, and having slept on it, put the Aloha keychain in his suitcase of treasures. He'd slept heavily and didn't remember any dreams aside from the clear image of his hand, old and wrinkled, holding the faded keychain. He closed the suitcase lid and sat for a minute to consider what it meant about his future. Was it about Morgan leaving? *Aloha means good-bye.* But he couldn't decipher any clear message.

Aside from a few straggling revelers going to their hotels or for a greasy breakfast, the streets were quiet. Sen biked in thick air that only got thicker as the sun rose over the city. It would rain later, for sure. Nearing Greycote he felt Morgan's absence. Seemed he wasn't the only one making an extra-early start.

An assortment of fruit and a bakery bag full of pains au chocolat sat on the counter with a note. *Missing our morning chat. Love Mr Bun. Happy drawing.—M*

Sen flushed with pleasure and ate several pastries. Then he dispatched his cleaning duties with no remorse for speeding through. He sucked down one mug of coffee and then parked it at the drafting table with a second mug steaming at his elbow.

Some two hours in, he'd managed to do everything but draw. He sharpened perfect points on each pencil, cut and mounted paper for the remaining drawings, and scattered practice sketches on the floor. Nothing he drew flowed or felt natural, and the line quality reflected that. Sen roamed the house—stretching, clearing his mind, hunting for traces of Morgan—and the moment he sat back down to draw, his restlessness returned. He listened for Morgan's car or tread on the stairs, and any movement in the neighborhood caught his attention.

Sen fidgeted, tried another thumbnail sketch, and then dropped his pen, gathered the sketches to dump in the recycling, and went outside.

He circled the backyard, walked around the house, and then sat by the fountain and tried to pinpoint what was getting in the way. There were no practical hang-ups anymore. He had full approval on his proposed list of illustrations, and Morgan liked his style and the alternate directions he took with some of the pieces. That left his solo show, but he could work under pressure, and he would figure out how to meet his obligation to the gallery—whether the strange inspiration continued to hit or he had to fake the rest.

Sen groaned when it occurred to him.

Finishing the illustrations represented closing points of contact with Morgan. He wouldn't be needed anymore, aside from cleaning, and cleaning was also fast approaching its end, whether when he quit or when Morgan moved on.

Sen remembered being about eleven when he realized that moving on also meant leaving people behind. So many friends meant well, and so few stayed friends once he'd gone from their immediate lives. It was part of why Sen had loved, but kept it brief and infrequent, and had never fallen in love.

No sovereign doctrine existed to bar him from staying in contact with Morgan, but Sen knew they weren't friends. Their relationship defied definition, and he sensed they had to become everything to each other or be nothing at all.

"Well," he breathed out. "Shit."

As he sat and listened to the fountain, fat raindrops began to patter down. Sen opened his palms to catch them, and thoughts of his kiss with Morgan in the backyard and then their encounter during the storm washed over him—the heat of Morgan's touch and breath, the perfect fit and friction when their bodies and instincts took the lead, and his safe contentment in Morgan's arms.

When he left New Orleans, he would lose Morgan and whatever the hell they had going. He'd miss it like a limb, like his heartbeat had gone silent.

The rain got heavier and chased him inside. Sen allowed a final circuit of the downstairs and another cup of coffee. Then he returned to the drafting table. His thoughts were quiet, and his hand confident again, but energy and enjoyment were gone as he drew to get the job done.

By late afternoon two more drawings hung on the wall, he'd had a snack and one of Morgan's craft beers, and penciled in a rough sketch for the final illustration. The rain continued to fall, steady and dense, without developing into a storm. Sen appreciated its company and the music it made against the windows and roof. He stood, studied the sketch, and decided it was developed enough to start inking.

Putting everything away except his pens and erasers gave him a break and removed the option for continued fiddling with the composition.

When he lifted his pen for the last time and checked his phone—later than he expected, since most of the day had been dark due to the rain. He hung the illustration of the solarium with the others and stepped back to take in the whole effect. They were good—all of them, even the most recent. Sen exhaled with a mix of pride and relief, and then he packed his supplies and turned off the lights. He left his bag by the stairs, went to the turret room, and inched in until he had his hands propped on the window frame and rested his forehead on the glass.

The only clouds he saw were the real ones outside.

He would miss the room, its light, and its view. Sen didn't think he'd ever build a house, but if he did, he wanted a room like that. Given his ideas of living meant living simply, that might mean the house was a saltbox with a tower. Which, why not?

Sen huffed to fog the window, drew a heart in the condensation, and watched a prism of raindrops collect inside it. He made a deal that when the heart faded, he'd be ready to leave. When it melted away, he scanned the room, nodded, and went downstairs to write a note for Morgan.

Using the blank side of Morgan's note, he wrote: *All done. Upstairs & ready to go. If you need anything else, find me.—S*

His hand hovered as he began to draw a heart to match the one on the window, and he jerked back. He scribbled as the words came to him, but rereading the note, he saw what he meant and the avenues left open to interpretation. Sen was half-afraid Morgan would take them.

When the rain didn't let up, he wrapped his supplies in a plastic bag, stuffed that into another plastic bag, and repacked his gear. Then he got as far as Morgan's study and stood in the hall. He didn't want to bike in the rain. More than anything he didn't want to leave.

Sen drifted into the study. Light spilled in from the portico entrance and allowed him to see, and the shadows matched his mood. There was no furniture other than the desk and chair, not even a second chair in front of the fireplace. He scanned the wall of bookshelves and smiled to see that, even being a light traveler, Morgan owned enough books to fill several. The titles were varied, and even the big coffee table books that highlighted architectural wonders around the world had cracked spines.

He sat at the desk, spread his arms, and ran his fingers over the drawer pulls down one side. The contents held no surprises—binders, hanging file folders, a reference book—and were as sparse as the rest of the house. Sen rolled the chair back and opened the wide and shallow middle drawer. His pizza box doodle was the only thing inside. He lifted it out and felt along the carefully cut edges, put it down again, and then covered it with his palm.

Sen remained like that until the side door burst open. He shut the drawer and stood, then walked around the desk in moments. He thought about the first day he met Morgan and having to reorganize the vanity cabinet. Then he wondered whether Morgan would believe he was in there cleaning, in the dark.

Morgan charged into the study and shed his coat as he walked. He backed Sen against the desk.

"Did you tell anyone you were here?" he asked, and he cupped Sen's nape and hip with his hands. When Sen didn't answer, he dug into Sen's waist. "Does anyone know about us? This?" His words were choked, and once out, his demanding kiss didn't allow Sen to answer.

Sen shook his head and tried to speak—to ask what Morgan meant or how it mattered—and got out nothing more than a needy moan. He gripped Morgan's shoulders and opened his legs to get Morgan closer. Water shed from Morgan's hair, and Sen shivered from the heat of Morgan's touch and the cool rain.

"Missed you, missed you," Morgan said into Sen's neck as he undid Sen's pants and rucked his shirt aside. "Please."

Sen offered no resistance. He wanted Morgan, despite the dizzying switchbacks they lurched past. Whenever they were together, he had no questions and his doubts fled, consumed by the rightness that hummed in his blood and its matching rhythm in Morgan's pulse. Nothing should make this so vital and welcome, and Sen surrendered to it without fear.

While Morgan tugged at his clothes, Sen angled his head to pull Morgan's thumb into his mouth. He traced his tongue on the knuckle lines and nail crescent, softened his lips around the base, and then sucked. Morgan shuddered and made harsh, urgent noises. Sen rubbed Morgan's thumb with the flat of his tongue and sucked harder.

"Damn. You must cease or I am spent." Morgan shuddered and pressed his forehead to Sen's. "Will always keep you. Want you. Find you." He breathed curses over Sen's mouth like a kiss, heightening the intensity and centering their intimacy.

Morgan got a hand up the back of Sen's shirt and went unerringly to the tender span of skin inside the wing of his left shoulder blade. He pinched and then caressed with slow fingers until Sen trembled, and when the sensation was too much, Sen tried to twist away. But Morgan didn't relent.

That was a secret hotspot for Sen, tickly and crazy-making, generating pleasure past his ability to withstand. He'd never shared it, but he had long imagined lovers biting, licking, or laying kisses there, and Morgan's persistence turned him inside out.

"How...?" Sen got out. He panted and shook, his cheek damp when he let Morgan's thumb go. He almost shot off the desk when Morgan bit behind his ear, and curled his hands into Morgan's shirt.

Morgan shushed, flattened his hand on Sen's back, and rocked them as Sen's wild tremors subsided.

Sen kissed Morgan's throat and then rested against Morgan's chest and fought to breathe. "How do you know just where to touch me?"

"How could I not?" Morgan leaned away and withdrew his hand. He tipped Sen's chin and covered Sen's mouth with his in a deep kiss, then tilted his hips, opened his trousers, and gathered their cocks in a fist.

Sen locked his heels, dragged them in, and pressed close as his desire curled tighter and tighter. Sen stayed there until Morgan's breath and movements were labored, and then started lifting his hips to match Morgan's strokes. The wet on their cocks and Morgan's hand shimmered in the dull light, and Sen shuddered as Morgan tightened his hand, twisted, and worked down again. He held on to the edge of the desk and watched Morgan's face—straining, blissful, and rapt on where they met and slid in his hand.

They came, almost together, and Sen caught Morgan when he swayed.

Morgan rested his head on Sen's shoulder and pulled him into a crushing embrace. "Always be safe. Always," he said, his voice ragged.

"Of course. Always," Sen answered as he nodded and ran his hands up and down Morgan's arms and back.

Morgan swallowed and then lifted Sen and staggered across the hall and into the sitting room. He lowered Sen onto the love seat and knelt on the floor between Sen's legs, his arms loose around Sen's hips. Sen combed Morgan's hair and murmured soothing noises, and Morgan sighed and relaxed into him.

The rain and Morgan's breathing hypnotized and comforted him. Sen lolled his head to look down at Morgan and met Morgan's waiting gaze. He smiled and ran a finger along Morgan's nose and then held it against Morgan's dimple. Lassitude pulled him down, and he didn't fight it.

Minutes later—maybe hours—Morgan stirred. Sen peered out one reluctant eye and watched Morgan stand, turn, and disappear down the hall. His movements were abrupt and purposeful, and Sen grappled with the love seat arms and stood to follow. He entered the hall to see Morgan round into the kitchen. Then he entered the kitchen to see Morgan's back filling the narrow stairwell.

"Morgan?" he said and got no response. So he followed, perplexed to see Morgan in bed, on that far side, slipped under a corner of blankets. When he went over and checked, Morgan was asleep.

Sen knelt and noticed the sheen on Morgan's forehead. It was clammy—not quite with fever—and they'd rested long enough to have lost the heat of exertion. Morgan's eyes moved beneath the lids as if searching, and his jaw and hand clenched and released.

This too had become familiar. Storms, rain, fever, and Morgan different yet so familiar to Sen's soul.

He filled the bathroom water glass, set it on the bedside table, and tucked the blankets higher. He almost didn't overcome the powerful temptation to slide into bed and wrap all around Morgan, but he wasn't sure what the morning would bring. That provided him with the impetus to stand, and finally, the strength to leave.

As Sen stood, Morgan reached out and grabbed his wrist. "Safe," he muttered. "Stay careful." He tightened his hand. "Please."

More like a bad dream than a chill.

"Shhh," Sen whispered and pet Morgan's hair. He kissed Morgan's temple, and Morgan's grip tightened. Then white light and heat burst all around.

Sen winced and fell to a knee as scattered images and emotions battered him. Someone's gaze locked in and found him, and he looked back into stormy eyes belonging to that other-Morgan he'd first painted. His expression changed, and his face morphed and shifted, but the hooded eyes stayed the same. The bright, penetrating light mellowed to predawn colors—pale blue and rose— and Sen saw two people kiss and then part.

The vision diffused into floating, afterimage blobs of color that shifted every time Sen blinked. Morgan's hold went lax, and his restlessness ceased. Sen kissed Morgan again and slipped away.

Getting dressed with fumbling hands and a thick head seemed to take forever. He fought each button, elusive sleeves and pant legs, and had to retie his shoes. Sen went back to the kitchen, and without allowing himself to think better of it, added a tiny heart to his note. Then he went outside, gasped in fresh air, and biked home in the dying rain and the hint of the rising sun.

He dropped everything inside the door, dumped the recycling from a brown grocery bag, and sketched, quick and sloppy, the faces he'd seen on it. He was too drained to paint or to continue drawing, but he wouldn't sleep if he didn't capture what he could.

Sen fell into bed still holding the wax pencil and paper bag. He stared at the messy faces and then balled up the bag and threw it across the room, pushed back to his feet, and glared at the portraits.

"I draw all this"—he gestured to the wall of sketchbook pages—"every day. I've painted all of you. And I can't see anything." Sen paced and other-Morgan's gaze followed his movements. "What am I missing? You're staring me in the face, and I still don't know. Why can't anyone—you or actually-Morgan or Mom's stupid fucking tea leaves—just tell me? How can I feel it so clearly but not know why I want and need and am falling in lov—" He choked back the rest.

Sen covered his face with his hands and scrubbed the helpless tears from his eyes. He had to start looking for answers elsewhere. He also had to admit that when the illustrations and his solo show were done and he hadn't figured it out, he needed to give up trying.

Grand plans to unlock it, to save them, and even to save Morgan be damned. He pushed to find his destiny, not his destruction.

When the tears returned, he didn't fight them.

CHAPTER THIRTEEN

"WOW, THOSE are enormous," Sen said as the librarian set two books in front of him.

"Most plot maps aren't small, and these were made before reduction or digital technology." The librarian quirked a smile. "Obviously. Anyway." He flipped the top book into his other hand to open the back cover to find the index. "Given the address you provided, it should be in one of these books. They're searchable here by zip code, street, and plat number, if you know that."

On another day, at another time, Sen would be glad to flirt with the cutie with the black-rimmed glasses and earnest demeanor, but he only hefted the books and nodded.

"Great. Can I just take them over there?" Sen tilted his head toward the long tables at the center of the main library space.

"Sure. But don't wander away. We get nervous when these are too far from the circulation desk." He handed Sen a bright red index card with a smiley face sticker on it. "Keep that with you too. It's basically a hall pass, saying one of us let you have the books."

"Got it. Thanks." Sen tucked the card on top of the books and claimed a seat at the back corner table.

Several days after concluding that the cemetery played no role in the strange goings on, Sen decided to get serious about investigating Greycote. Wednesday had come and gone, and he'd cleaned the empty house and traded brief texts with Morgan to update him.

He chose to keep his distance and tried to gain back some balance and perspective.

Sen searched the index, and in minutes he located information on Greycote.

He got out his laptop and ran a general search, then began opening promising links in multiple tabs. The obscure government website gave dry history, the obscure hobby site had pictures of the neighborhood through time, and several real estate database sites pinged with results.

The history of the house was straightforward. Relatively young by New Orleans standards, and it had progressed through a succession of owners of no discernable notoriety. Nothing bad had happened in the house or on the property.

Sen started to write down facts but stopped. He had prepared to hunker down and be in the library all day, but he already had what he needed to know. The house was a dead end, the cemetery wasn't cursed, and no ghosts cohabitated in Greycote.

He sighed. "Just great. Now what?" he asked and earned a glance from an elderly woman reading a stack of magazines.

The findings weren't unexpected. Sen knew the house wasn't haunted. He felt it as surely as he did the draw to Morgan, but he wanted a straw to grasp. A haunting or a curse would give him something tangible.

He was glad they weren't possessed or influenced by something secret and cursed buried in the cellar, but he wasn't exactly relieved. Something indefinable still drew them together and held them in thrall—as mysterious as a haunting and full of similar shadows—but it seemed Morgan held the key.

Or was the cause.

Sen shivered. He hated even the suggestion, but the idea couldn't be denied. His dynamic with Morgan went beyond place. It was proven by their similar histories, their shared Portlands, the signs leading Sen to New Orleans, and how everything there conspired to bring them together. Without thought he quickly drew a familiar pair of eyes, a miniature Greycote, and a line of palm trees.

Then he went cold. Recent updates listed the house as available or pending, and one of them noted it as sold. From owner, Morgan Ballard, to buyer, A. Porter.

"Who's A. Porter?" he asked the computer. He reread the scant information, and then closed the tab.

His search had taken all of twenty minutes. As his findings sunk in, Sen e-mailed his mom and then answered Bharti to say the paintings were coming along and he was pleased they liked the others from the pictures he sent. Then he shut down the computer and packed up again.

"That was fast," cutie librarian said as he took the smiley-face index card. "Did you find what you were looking for, or was it a bust?"

"You do good work." Sen smiled. There was no reason for his bad mood to spill over. "If I ever want to finally master the Dewey Decimal System, I know where to come."

"Tutoring sessions cost extra." He laughed. "I'm glad I could help."

"So am I. Thanks again." Sen handed the books over. "Have a good day."

"You too," cutie said. He smiled but got distracted by another patron who hovered at Sen's elbow.

Since he came to the library to get out of the house and avoid all the not-painting he'd been doing, it wouldn't be much use to go back. So he biked around, treated himself to some downer-mood beignets, and then gave in to his urge to go to Morgan's house. Well, Morgan's once-house.

No For Sale or Sold sign in the yard, which wasn't proof of anything, but neither were random websites. The empty garage emboldened him to go inside and have a last look around, but the key code didn't work. He peeked into Morgan's study window and got a jolt. The bookshelves were bare, and a stack of boxes lined one wall.

He lost his breath and stumbled backward. The cold he felt in the library turned to numbness.

Sen went to stand by the fountain and then rummaged in his bag for his sketchbook and pencil. He ended up walking around the house, capturing impressions in small, quick drawings from various angles. He filled one page with a vista of the lawns and the house small in the distance, and another page with thumbnails of various specific features. He made a rubbing of the carved side door and loose drawings of the stags and rabbits. The turret dominated several sketches, and he drew the third-floor-room view from memory.

He got to the backyard and drew the rolling spread down to the cemetery, the line quality loose and abstract, but he kept returning to and developing the trees where he and Morgan had kissed in dark, heavy strokes. When he finished he held the book at arm's length and grunted in aggravation.

Sen clapped his sketchbook closed and pitched it into the grass. He shut his eyes and breathed—in and out, in and out, in and out. Then his phone rang.

"Yeah?" he asked as he retrieved the sketchbook and sat on the top patio stair.

"Are you cranky because you're up and it's like ten after nine?" Adri snickered. "Look out, you're turning into a morning person."

Sen scoffed. "Hardly." He didn't add not sleeping. Admitting defeat after lying in bed for a few hours to get up and start another day didn't count. Or that turmoil caused his crankiness.

"On the bright side, I'm about to save you from part of that downward spiral."

"Oh?"

"Yes. Ballard called." Adri paused. "On the less bright side, he canceled the service. So you don't have to go tomorrow. But he made pains to say how pleased he was with the work you did and glad that he found me. It's just that he's moving soon. He also said he'd leave my business card behind as a recommendation to whomever buys the place and give several to the realtor." She sounded excited. Losing a steady weekly gig wasn't great, but Morgan's gesture offset it.

Sen's focus slid from the conversation to the shimmer of leaves obscuring and revealing the cemetery as the wind blew. He knew Morgan didn't intend to stay here forever, but none of Morgan's brief notes asking whether he would please organize the study drawers, or his texts to touch base about the illustrations, had even hinted that Morgan had decided to sell.

The shock and sting of betrayal stole Sen's breath.

"That's super. I hope it brings in good leads," he managed to say. "And, awkward segue, but this reminds me I should take you to dinner or drinks, so we can talk."

"So you can tell me you're leaving soon, you mean." Adri paused and then hummed.

Sen sighed. "Yeah, that. Sorry?"

"Nah. It's cool, and I'm cool. You warned me about this when we met." She clucked her tongue. "Don't get me wrong, I'm totally going to buy you drinks and something for that sweet tooth of yours at least twice before you go, but don't worry about it now. I know you have your show and a lot on your mind. When you need to rest your painting genius, buzz me, and I'll drop everything."

Sen swallowed his rising bitterness and said, "You're the best."

"It's a gift and a burden." Adri said something muffled and then came back to the phone. "Phoebe tells me Kenyon is experiencing a scheduling meltdown. Oh, you don't know her. She's my new hire, office-manager-assistant thing. I'm moving up in the world. Anyway, I gotta scoot. We'll talk martini options soon."

"Later, babe." Sen ended the call. So he wasn't needed to clean anymore. "And what does that mean, I wonder."

Once the illustrations were approved by Morgan's bosses, all tangible ties between them would unravel.

He shifted to lie back on the stone patio and crossed his arms over his face. Fatigue settled over him in the warm sunlight and muted the sounds of the quiet neighborhood. Unease pooled in his gut. This could be where his inspiration for the paintings ended, how he and Morgan ended.

He woke with an aching neck and hungry for lunch as the sun started its decline. Sen stopped his bike at the end of the driveway and had a last look.

"Good-bye, Greycote. Take care of yourself—and everyone you shelter."

Sen cut a direct route home as a headache built behind his eyes. He didn't take in anything he passed and wound up at his place on the stair landing, got inside, and dropped everything at the door. He didn't even pretend he would paint.

After a while he roused from standing in a stupor next to the sink, drank his water, and flopped on the bed. He opened a text box, closed it, and then opened it again.

Just touching base re the illustrations, he typed and then reread a dozen times. He had his thumb hovering over Send when the phone chirped. He started, and the phone almost landed on his face.

Illustrations looking great—just wanted you to know. Talk to you soon.

Sen blinked at the message from Morgan and sagged backward. He sent a brief thanks, waited, and after there was no indication of a reply, he gusted out a breath.

Evening fell around him still lying in bed. He got up to eat something and then did the dishes, which turned into scrubbing the kitchen, sweeping, and neatening his studio area.

"I'm not a starving artist. I'm a frustrated cleaner," he said into the purged and reorganized junk drawer.

Sen sorted the hanging files of magazine clippings he used for reference and collages and then curled on the couch with a cup of tea. Exhaustion once again claimed him, and hours later he woke to the rising sun, his headache not quite gone. He dumped the tea, made super-strong coffee, and headed to the park for some fresh air.

He found a good spot under a tree and settled in with a book, but instead he watched the neighborhood start its day and did some breathing exercises to calm his unbalanced state. A dog walker and her charges strutted past and scared a roost of pigeons into scattered flight.

"Sen?"

He looked up to see Morgan walking toward him.

An incandescent spark flared at his center and radiated out and out. Sen viciously thrust it aside and offered a cool nod to Morgan's greeting.

Morgan wore a lightweight shirt and linen trousers, and Sen appreciated every fold and cling of material on his legs and chest. It made him glad he changed from his painting clothes into his favorite unicorn T-shirt and cargos, in colors that brought out his eyes and brightened his hair.

"Hey," Sen said, not quite welcoming, and closed his book. "Why aren't you at work?"

Morgan laughed, and his infuriatingly adorable eye crinkles came out in force. "You always do see right to the heart of the matter. When I'm a retired old crab, I'm going to run into you, and you're still going to ask me that."

"Probably." Sen eyed the basket Morgan carried and couldn't help his curiosity. "What's up?"

"Believe it or not, I'm here to claim some turf and get everything set up to call and ask if you wanted to meet for a 'preshowing up to my house' picnic. I wanted to redirect you from coming over, so we could talk, but here you are."

Sen crossed his legs and took the basket from Morgan. Warmth and the undeniable goodness of just being with Morgan started to crack through his frustration and anger.

"Here I am." Sen turned the basket in his hands and had a peek inside. "I don't remember you owning this."

"I don't. There's a place in town that does custom picnics, complete with basket." Morgan produced a blanket. "You already seem comfy, but do you want me to spread this out?"

"Duh. Otherwise it's not a picnic." Sen tipped out of the way and then rolled onto the blanket. "This from the store too?" he asked, fingering a corner of the pretty gingham and floral pattern.

"Yup." Morgan started laying things out. "Hope breakfast food is okay."

"As an avowed member of Team Breakfast, any meal made from breakfast delights is aces with me." Sen opened a vacuum flask, and the glorious aroma of expensive coffee wafted out. He poured it into the two solid ceramic mugs and sat with his in his lap. "So... talk?"

Morgan gave Sen a fresh fruit cup and a real fork. "I'm so slammed at work the days have become a blur. Last night as I was falling asleep, I actually sat up realizing I hadn't told you I canceled the cleaning. It was too late to call, so I decided I'd catch you this morning and tell you before you found out in an offhand way."

Sen's exhaustion and wariness dissipated. Morgan hadn't cut him out on purpose. Morgan hadn't cut him out at all. His relief and acceptance might be foolish, but he was past being reasonable. Any other defense eroded when Morgan shifted so their knees touched, and heat spread to fill Sen from their point of contact.

"Guilt-provided treats are often the best treats," Sen said and nabbed a biscuit stuffed with goat cheese, a fried egg, arugula, and bacon. He made obscene noises when he took a bite. "Wow, that's good. I'm so glad you forgot until it was too late to call last night."

Morgan gazed from Sen's neck to his mouth and then rested on his chest, right over his heart. Sen visualized a line from Morgan's eyes though his body, to the spot just inside his shoulder blade—*that* spot. Sen flushed and looked away.

"Uh, yeah," Morgan said. "And it's more than cutting you off at the pass so you didn't needlessly clean Greycote today. It's not mine anymore."

"What? As of when?" Sen's skin prickled.

Morgan gestured at Sen with a thick waffle. "Also yesterday. As you might guess, I know people in real estate, and those contacts all knew I would sell the place eventually. I was approached with an offer—never even went on the market. We sign the papers this afternoon, which is how I wrangled getting the whole day off." He looked smug and ate a strawberry to punctuate the victory.

"Excellent work. You should be proud."

"Thanks. And this was way easier than the process can sometimes go, so I'm grateful," Morgan said. "Did you want to swing by the house, have a last look around, and say good-bye?"

"No, that's okay. Greycote and I are at peace. If you don't have a house anymore, where are you staying?"

"A little bed-and-breakfast near the hotel site. It's nicer and more convenient than any of the long-stay suites I found." Morgan frowned. "I kind of miss the house. I'd grown to really like it, and even though it wasn't permanent, I would have enjoyed staying there for the rest of my time in New Orleans. Even if this way is for the best."

"Maybe you can build one of your own someday, when you find wherever it is you're meant to be for a long while." Sen noticed the pain au chocolat. "Is that for me?"

Morgan gave it to Sen.

"Good of you to continue exploiting my weakness like this. I mean that genuinely." Sen had a bite and leaned against the tree to savor it. "Even if it puts me at a disadvantage."

"Hardly." Morgan pulled a wry expression. "But if it'll make you feel better, go ahead and start organizing something. I'll stay right here, rendered defenseless in the face of such majesty."

"Majesty? I like that." Sen licked chocolate from a finger and said, "I also like stargazing, birding, and hiking the trails on the map that are dotted lines because they're harder and not well maintained."

"I can identify buzzards from at least ten yards out. Especially if they're eating roadkill."

"Impressive."

Morgan held a hand up and inclined his head. "Yup. I don't want to intimidate you or seem like I'm issuing a challenge, but I thought you should be aware of my prowess." He breathed in, thought for a moment and then said, "Dad taught me the constellations and how to navigate by them, so fair warning if we ever have a gaze-off. I'm not really comfortable with heights, but I always take the peak trail, because I love the view and the feeling up there. I've never owned a pet, which might be the only thing I haven't forgiven Dad for. I like seeing you with your hair loose, and I can't turn down a lemon shake-up."

Sen smiled. "I'll remember that. All of that."

"What's your favorite star?"

"Betelgeuse—it's the name. That and our sun. How could it not be everyone's favorite?"

"I never thought about it that way." Morgan nodded. "Mine's Deneb."

"So, all the way back to birds."

Morgan arched an eyebrow. "Are you testing me or showing off? Is there a written part of this exam after, where I have to do math and show my work?" He tsked. "Yes, back to birds. And to prove myself, swans to be exact, as Deneb is in Cygnus's tail."

Sen bit his lip. When he caught Morgan's eye, they both burst out laughing.

"I'm going to ask something that always sounds corny and probably sounds strange, at this point, but I think about it whenever we're together. I wanted to ask the first time I saw you." Morgan tucked a leg under and sat forward. "Have we met before?"

Sparks ran along Sen's limbs, and he shivered. "No. At least I don't think so."

"Hmm. Probably not. I just thought, since we each moved around a lot, and I don't usually immediately click with people, it was possible we had. Hung out one long day when our paths converged. Teenager or younger, obviously. I'd recognize adult-you."

"Obviously." Sen racked his brain for any lead but came up empty. "Some years we were in a different place each week. I couldn't begin to narrow it down."

"Okay, then. I'll say where I was, and you can keep a tally sheet." Morgan looked expectant.

"Ah, right." Sen got a pen and notepad, and Morgan rattled off a list of Army bases and nearby towns.

Sen recognized several and knew they'd been there, but their dates never quite matched.

Morgan huffed. "So much for that." He tapped a finger on his chin. "Out of curiosity, where have you lived since leaving home?"

"At eighteen I was fresh off the bus in Sedona, and then I've been here two years, which is a long time for me. In between was San Francisco, Pueblo, Omaha, Charlotte, and Portland—Maine." Sen wrote them down to make sure he got them all. "And a lot of drifting while getting from place to place."

"May I?" Morgan held out his hand for the paper and pen. He made several quick marks and handed them back to Sen. "I did a project in each of those cities, in that order."

Four of the six were circled and he'd numbered them. Sen had lived in each place after Morgan, but hadn't directly followed Morgan's steps.

"Spooky," Sen teased, but his trembling wasn't false. "We're both coffee fiends. Maybe you saw me in line at the local cup of joe a few times."

"Could be. Given the givens, I'm disinclined to rule that out entirely, although that doesn't really satisfy as having met." Morgan ran a knuckle up Sen's shin. "But here, you finally caught me."

"Have I?" Sen closed his eyes. He wanted their friendliness in the moment to be enough. It wasn't. "Another thing I like is you and how easily we get along." He opened his eyes to find Morgan staring at him, hard. "But are we never going to talk about it—everything else?"

Morgan blinked. "What else?"

"You don't remember anything more about—" Sen stopped and raised both hands. He didn't know how to ask. "Even what it was you kept wanting to tell me?"

Sen sighed. His research to learn about Greycote's tortured past had led nowhere, but seeing Morgan's perplexed reaction made him wonder whether he'd missed something. If he had, it might not be about the house.

"There is, and no, I can't remember." Morgan rubbed his forehead. "It's making me crazy. There's this big dark nothing in my mind, and I run into it every time I try to tell you. No. Not a nothing—a wall."

"Maybe it relates to your nightmares," Sen suggested. He watched Morgan start to tense, and he prodded gently, "And something about storms?"

Morgan's eyes snapped to hold Sen's gaze, and they flashed with color. He sneered, but the anger passed quickly, and then he shook his head and seemed lost.

"Storms and bad memories?" Sen guided. He readied a hand to touch Morgan—touching always helped—but he repeated the question.

"Memory?" Morgan asked, his voice low and indistinct, and then his eyes widened.

"Benny. Oh no you don't!"

Something low and rust brown streaked past Sen, circled around, and then returned to snuffle at the picnic leavings. Morgan frowned and sought Sen out with a light hand on his knee.

Morgan patted the intruder—a tubby dachshund—and grinned. "Heya, fella," he greeted and prevented the dog from eating the remaining hunk of waffle.

The dog managed to get his tongue out far enough to lick up a butter pat. Morgan chuckled and rubbed his butt until his whole backside wagged.

Sen swallowed a frustrated curse and let the dog sniff his hand. Morgan plus cute dog equaled dangerous levels of adorableness. He sighed. In moments the dog walker he saw earlier ran over, harness in hand.

"I am so sorry. Benny, come here." She held her palm open and Benny resisted, so she gave him a look. He snuck a last taste of butter and then gave in and trotted back to her. "He's on a diet," she explained and fit him back into the harness. "This is the second time he's given me the slip—which, yay for progress, little man. But time for a tightening, hmm?"

Morgan scratched Benny's doubtful chin. "His rampage was brief."

"At least there's that. Sorry again. You guys have a nice day." She waved and got Benny up to speed walking alongside her.

Sen waved back and shook his head. Benny had on-the-nose timing.

"Whoa. It's going on noon. I have to return this basket and then go to the signing." Morgan exhaled. "We were talking about something important just before Benny stormed the beach."

"It'll keep." Sen cleaned up the picnic. "Or at least it has to. Again."

Morgan gave him a look. "Are you sure? Going on noon doesn't mean I have to race away, right this second." He stacked the cups and plates and set them in the basket.

"I'm sure." Sen stood and folded the blanket. "Thanks so much for breakfast. I hope everything that happens at the signing goes well." He resisted an impulse to offer to walk with Morgan partway to wherever or to take the basket for delivery. "And you know, I'm going to miss Greycote too. It's one of the rare actual houses I've been in that I thought, 'Hunh. I could live here.' It's too big but I like it."

"—it's too big," Morgan said, overlapping Sen's words. "Yeah, that." He took the blanket and shifted his weight from foot to foot. "Next Monday we're having the final walk-through with everyone, including my bosses. It starts at two. You should come—you're invited—and see the illustrations in place."

"I'd like to do that. Thanks." Neither of them moved, so finally Sen grabbed Morgan's wrist and checked the time. "It's after noon. You should go."

"Yes, yes. Okay, then. See you Monday." Morgan caught Sen's hand and gave it a tight squeeze.

Sen nodded and stood rooted as Morgan crossed the park, got in the dorky Volvo, and drove away.

It reassured him that the person he couldn't stop thinking about or quit wanting wasn't an intentional dickhead. But the unintentional lapses were getting to him, wearing him down, and aggravating his already frayed nerves and patience. He could only suffer so much collateral damage, and one day soon he wouldn't have the energy left to keep worrying and trying.

But Lord above, he could get used to something very like their picnic every day instead of as the exception. So fast and so easily. The glimpses of normal and how they could be together, the spice of their constant attraction, their sweet comfortable rapport, Morgan's easygoing charm, and making art while he made money illustrating. Sen did want it—more than anything—but which was the illusion?

To give his thoughts room to percolate, he biked a long section of the levee path and then went home. Conflicted though interactions with Morgan proved to be, it still cleared his pounding headache, and the tightness in his chest and limbs had released.

Sen changed clothes, stared at the blank canvas he'd done nothing with for days, and started to paint.

This portrait developed more slowly than the others. Her face took form in increments, and he needed breaks to walk around, study it, consider the negative spaces, and then paint more. She was cautious and the color of stars—blue, amber, faint yellow, a hint of red, and orange-red—and the background washes were more controlled.

"There you are," he said as he found her eyes, soft and warm and liquid brown. "Hunh," he breathed and sat back.

He knew her, but she didn't have the piercing, stormy eyes. All the other couples started with those as a foundation and cornerstone, but she stood apart. Sen squinted and tried to imagine her with that gaze instead. He couldn't, but inspiration tingled through him, and he grabbed a pen and pad of paper and rough-sketched her partner.

"And there *you* are," he said to the familiar visage as he set it into feminine lines and long hair.

Sen added a last stroke, considered the face, and envisioned its palette in blues and greens, rising like a complementary star. Then he set the pad aside, and the shy girl called him back.

No storms had called her forth, no dramatics with Morgan. He'd thought about leaving and she appeared. When he completed these starry ladies, he'd have four couples, and as a must could include other-Morgan and companion, and be almost finished. Finding the last two portraits might not require Morgan at all—or might be good-bye.

Sen didn't know whether that was a sign, but he couldn't ignore the possibility.

CHAPTER FOURTEEN

IN THE formless days leading into Monday, Sen finished the fifth couple. He worked in fits and starts, but that got him there. He hung the women on the wall with the other portraits and considered their fit. They had a similar bearing and positioning on the canvas, tawny-complected and their flowing hair merging into the background. From a distance they appeared to be different angles of the same person. But upon study, one stared out with Morgan's eyes and the other showed half her hazel gaze. He painted sigils and landscapes to play hide and seek in the color washes, and on each portrait he hid a constellation deep in the folds of color.

He researched and tried to identify the time periods or places evoked by the impressions of the paintings. Other-Morgan and his companion could have walked out of a Merchant Ivory film, and he thought the high collars, colors and tones, and rigid posture belonged to Georgian society in England.

The others were harder to pin down.

Sen decided ancient Persia came closest to defining earthy girl and her mate's flowing robes, darker features, intricate trim and patterning, and rich colors. The woman with the pearl matched it in complexion, and her companion's collar and both their bearings could have been a subject for any number of Renaissance painters. Probably courtly or at least wealthy merchant class.

He could tell the least about the angry couple. The storm surrounded and obscured them from view, but the blunt violence of the pieces and their features, pale coloring, and bright hair had him thinking Vikings. Maybe Saxons.

The starry girls' sigils and landscape hid the band of a river. Abstract horses and endless grass giving way to plateaus and buttes. They had high brows and prominent noses, and turquoise and jasper beads in their long, dark, flowing hair. Sen couldn't begin to name a tribe, but he knew they were indigenous Americans, from where the plains met the southwest.

Knowing that connected him even more strongly to the portraits and their personalities, but it didn't help him get any bright ideas for what to paint next.

Sen had just under enough time to complete the final couple and get ready for his show.

"Might just make it," he said and secured his bike near the hotel. He wondered what seeing Morgan would bring.

When he was with Morgan, the questions ceased and his mind—his very person—was at rest. He raced from uncertainty to uncertainty when they were apart. Morgan didn't have control over him, and Sen laughed at the idea he couldn't assert his independence or that he feared Morgan. What they had and what he felt wasn't fear. It was belonging and rightness powerful enough to overcome any doubts—until he started doubting again.

Cars crowded the circular drive and people milled around the entrance. Sen had dressed up—or his version of dressed up—in dark corduroys, a cotton dress shirt with a vintage pinstripe suit vest over it, and ranch boots instead of his Chucks. Having moved so often required he make overtures and acquaintances time and again, and he approached the hotel without apprehension.

With one foot in the wide double doors, he spied Morgan. As if tugged on a towline, he cut across the lobby, and Morgan extricated from a conversation to meet him in the middle.

"I didn't expect all this," Sen said. "It's more like a reception than a business meeting."

Morgan wore a beige summer suit and the pearl cufflinks Sen had admired.

"You look… more than I expected too." Sen licked the corner of his mouth. Good enough to eat or climb-you-like-a-tree good was what he meant and almost said, and he hoped Morgan didn't notice his awkward recovery.

"Well, thank you." Morgan preened and mock-straightened his tie. "We prefer making these more like mixers than meetings, because why wouldn't we? There's food and cocktails in the lounge, and no formal itinerary. So mingle and eat a lot of meatballs and peek into some of the rooms."

Sen nodded. "I can get behind this."

"You're among the lucky few—you saw the whole place and had it to yourself—but the tour is limited to save foot traffic wear and so no one gets lost." Morgan reached around and fingered the leather cord holding Sen's ponytail. "Is it up because this is a work event?"

"Because I tell myself kempt hair is formal wear." Sen smiled at Morgan's smile and relaxing posture. "How did the closing go?"

"No hiccups, thankfully. Signed, sealed, delivered, and most of the furniture to boot. A lovely couple with three lovely kids are the proud new owners." Morgan looped Sen's hair over a finger and then let it escape a few times. "I hope they like it."

"How could they not? Of course they will. It's a wonderful setting and a lovely place. Plus you renovated it so well. A blank canvas that's welcoming to the owner's imprint." Sen shivered as Morgan ran his thumb along his neck, and he flinched away. "Meatballs, you said?"

Morgan's expression clouded momentarily. "I did. But first come see your illustrations." He cupped Sen's elbow and guided them through the crowd. "They're the crowning jewel. Everyone I've talked to has effused over them."

The illustrations were hung salon-style behind the reception desk, creating a visceral impact. All the elements encouraged the eye to keep moving from one illustration to the next—Sen's flowing black-and-white line work, the pause at the black mat, the wide, white resting place, and the dancing explosion of gold ornamentation to the edge and back in again.

"That's precisely as I envisioned." Sen smiled and leaned into Morgan. "The layered matting and just over-the-top cake-frosting frames. I like how the gilding is dusted on the ivory undercoat. It really highlights the reliefs and decorations, but it has a richness that just being dipped would lack. Whoever framed them did nice work."

"Thank you." Morgan shifted his hold to the small of Sen's back. At Sen's look he said, "I had to learn to build things and be handy in school. It's not all drafting and applied physics. And I was decent at it, so I like to keep up the skills."

"More than adequately." Sen studied the mitered corners and couldn't find any seams or mismatches, even minor. Knowing Morgan did them, and with such skill, activated his competency kink. Sen imagined Morgan wielding power tools and smelling of sawdust. His imagination provided an image of Morgan in a tool belt, and he cleared his throat. "Hidden depths," he said, tone husky and leading when he had only tried to tease.

Morgan swallowed. "Glad you approve the frame choice. I almost called, but when I saw that one, I knew it was right."

"It is."

"Good. I'm glad." Morgan rubbed circles on Sen's back and briefly touched his forehead to Sen's. Then he straightened and pointedly withdrew. "You go for the meatballs. I'm afraid I have to keep circulating. We had books printed of the whole restoration process, so be sure to get one."

"Cool. Will do." Sen turned away and then went to tap Morgan's shoulder as Morgan caught his arm. They paused and waited and Sen laughed. "You go."

"I wanted to say see you soon."

Sen's laugh faded and he said, "Me too. See you soon."

He nearly followed Morgan, but then he corrected and ducked into the lounge.

"There I go again," he muttered.

He nodded and smiled, drank one mimosa as he stood by the bar, and took a second with him. The meatballs were delicious, so he left the room before he could eat another dozen.

Not much had changed since his tour and subsequent visits to draw the exteriors and make reference checks. He knew his way around the niches to stand out of the way and observe, feeling like an insider. Awareness of Morgan thrummed with every breath, as though they were standing together, and he could find Morgan in a heartbeat. Whenever he did, Morgan was staring back at him.

Sen looked in on the second-floor room they'd used as a workspace and found it transformed into a general impression of silver and gray tones, dark wood, mingled seating groups, and quiet nooks surrounding a grand piano and an enormous planter filled with palms and exotic flowers.

"Sen." Nicole beckoned him to the piano, where she stood handing out the booklets Morgan mentioned. "Good to see you. This room's a bit different since you last saw it, yeah? What do you think? It's all mine—an old-style salon. Afternoon tea will be served in here, and the furniture can be moved to host evening concerts, readings, and such." She leaned in and whispered, "We finished it yesterday. Late."

"No one would ever know," he confided back. "And I think it's stunning. Awesome concept too. I'll have to come back for tea sometime."

Nicole winked and addressed the larger group. "Everyone, meet our artist, Mr. Sebastian Holt. He did the illustrations in the lobby for us," she said and showed off the back cover of a booklet featuring his drawing of the formal gardens.

"Thank you," he said and acknowledged the murmurs of appreciation. Then he turned on the charm. "They were a lot of fun and a fun challenge. I'll also make a shameless plug and invite you to my solo painting exhibit at Gallery Paon."

People passed pleasantries for a bit, and the group shifted. Sen took a booklet and flipped through it. Several of his drawings were featured among copy and photographs.

"Can I have a few of these?"

Nicole pointed under the piano. "Take a box."

"Ooh, upgrade." He hefted one. "If you're still in town, please come to the opening. I'm inviting you for real and directly, not just as polite banter."

"I should be around. A solo show? How exciting." She slid a business card to him. "E-mail me the details."

Sen pocketed the card and wandered back to the hall. He took position at the top of the stairs and scanned the lobby. Then he moved to join Morgan before he quite made the decision to do so. He was halfway there when Jerry waylaid him.

"Hey, Sen. Good to see you here." Jerry offered his hand, and they shook. He gestured at the trio to his left. "Sen Holt—the artist you asked after—meet Ken Thorpe, new owner of this hotel, and then Greg and Nina Frost. My bosses."

Sen shook everyone's hand in turn and then they stood and nodded at each other. The Frosts matched their name. They were a handsome couple in their forties, both tall and angular, friendly but keen. Thorpe looked fifty-something, wore a full gray mustache and trim beard. He was built like a portly fireplug, and under his bushy brows were shrewd eyes.

Greg patted Sen's shoulder. "Your illustrations are everything I hope for in a commission, Sen. I'm so glad we found you."

"Hmm," Sen agreed and resisted the urge to correct that Morgan found him. He gestured to encompass the hotel. "Congratulations on the renovation. Mr. Thorpe, you own quite a sumptuous piece of history, and the Frosts have graciously ushered it back to beautiful life."

"Such pretty small talk," Morgan whispered in Sen's ear from behind and to his right.

Sen broke out in goose bumps and reflexively scratched his neck where the hickey had bruised for so long. He hissed and dropped his hand and then curled it into a fist and made an agreeing noise to whatever Nina was saying. When it began to register, he straightened.

"How many?" Sen asked.

"I think three would be perfect. Greg?"

"Let's talk him into five. Three for prints and then an original for Ken and us," Greg said in that conversational yet commanding tone people employed when they were accustomed to only hearing yes.

Nina smiled in anticipation. "Perfect-er. Yes, I'd love to have one of your originals. Do be talked into five, Sen dear."

"Pay double the rate for the original illustrations, and he might consider it," Morgan cut in with a laugh. "With apologies, can I borrow Sen a moment?"

"Yes, yes. I think we're due another mingling round anyway. Good to meet you, Holt. Hit me up for a weekend discount sometime." Thorpe narrowed his eyes and thumped Sen's arm. "Charge them triple."

It got a good chuckle, but Sen could tell he was serious.

"What am I being talked into?" he asked as they walked.

"Drawing five more illustrations. Three to make into prints and use on swag, and then two as gifts. One for Thorpe, one for themselves." Morgan's lips flattened. "They want them before they leave New Orleans in a week. Entirely up to you. But Thorpe is right—charge them a lot."

Sen pinched the bridge of his nose and weighed the pros and cons. The frames he wanted for his paintings weren't cheap. If he sold anything, he'd recoup, but if nothing moved, he'd take a hit, and the bargain option just didn't compare. More commission money would make a huge difference in that, and add to his "leaving NOLA to roam" fund. He only had two more paintings— four, depending on his decision about other-Morgan—but zero ideas about what they were going to be and dwindling time to paint them in. Knocking out the illustrations would take three, four days. Add in drying time so they could be handled and framed, and that left a small window to make or break on the twelve portraits and have them delivered to the gallery on time.

"Will it make you look bad if I say no?" Sen turned into Morgan's space.

"Nope." Morgan stroked Sen's side with his knuckles. "Turn them down flat, if you want, as far as I'm concerned."

He should. He had every good reason to and wasn't beholden to them. He couldn't really think strategy with his whole body buzzing and alive from Morgan's touch. Sen leaned away and tried to look serious.

"They're quite connected in the art scene, if that's any incentive. But no one will have hard feelings if it's not." Morgan noticed Sen leaning, curled his hand into a fist, and pulled it against his hip. The faintest blush dusted his cheeks. "I have to stay through June to oversee a smooth transition to Thorpe taking ownership. So I'll be around and can help with your painting stuff? If you need?"

Sen needed Morgan around more than anything else.

"Could you frame the canvases for me?" Sen reached out and twiddled Morgan's cufflink, realized he was doing it, and moved back a step. "I can manage all the rest, if you do that. Especially if I charge triple."

"Then charge triple."

"Yeah?" Sen sounded surprised, but the lift in his voice was happiness.

"Yes." Morgan pulled Sen back to him and flattened his hand on Sen's waist. "Of course yes." He smiled and moved in as though to kiss Sen. Then he swallowed and worked his jaw. "Let's go tell them the good news and negotiate triple and a half."

Disappointment at the unfulfilled kiss crashed around in Sen's chest. That gravity—that pull—always got the better of him. He'd forgotten where they were as Morgan held him and demanded more from him. Morgan might finally remember doing so, but this wasn't exactly the ideal place to step beyond their strange dynamic.

"If they agree to my price, that'll really help." Sen said the first thing that came to mind as the kiss-me-please haze cleared.

"Help what?"

"Oh, extra expenses and such. You know." Sen waved his hand in vague loops. "My show and my folks visiting for it and padding my moving-on fund."

"Moving on?" Morgan's focus drew on Sen like a bead. "Of course. You mean from New Orleans. After all, you're a vagabond, like me." He smiled tightly and the quality of his gaze changed. "Not like we ever talked about your plans."

"Not like I haven't tried," Sen said with a flare of annoyance, and felt something shift in Morgan's mood.

"You go tell them, but feel free to wave me over if you need." Morgan frowned and seemed to try to shake something off. Then he tilted his head to indicate a spot behind him. "I've avoided that person currently circling like a shark for too long and should say hello before it gets ugly. Then I'm free of obligation."

"That sounds smart. And promising," Sen added, but Morgan strode away as he spoke. A chill went down Sen's spine in an unsettling premonition.

It didn't take long to find Nina. She was looking for him.

"Well?" Nina asked lightly, her voice threaded with steel.

"I'm interested in the work. Fifteen hundred for each, considering the deadline and factors involved." Sen didn't hesitate or apologize.

"Hmm." Nina clinked the glass with her nails. "I want them, but Greg will kill me if I just agree to that. Seven fifty?"

"And I can't just agree to that. Twelve hundred," he countered.

Nina clicked her tongue. "One thousand?"

Sen almost said yes, but he decided it wasn't enough. "I'm afraid it's twelve hundred or not at all."

"Terrible man," Nina admonished and then kissed his cheek. "Then twelve hundred it is, because not at all would be impossible. Good. I'm so pleased."

"I think I could say the same." Sen glanced around for Morgan. "I'll get started right away."

"Thank you, darling. I'm going to just love them, and it'll be worth every penny." Nina patted his arm, and her lips curled with mischief. "Now to get some bourbon and get that into Greg. Then I'll tell him the good news. We'll talk soon."

Sen nodded and went in search of Morgan. He wandered past the bar, through the main rooms, and peeked at the outside patios and terraces. No sign, so he went upstairs, bypassing the ballroom and suites on display to stand on the balcony. Still nothing except the feeling that he should continue up and up, until he stood in the dark, narrow sixth-floor hallway.

The walls were painted and the rooms finished. Sen walked to the far end of the hall, where he could look out the window. Moonlight painted long slats across the floor, and his footfalls echoed louder than the muffled sounds from the party.

He peered out at the silver landscape. The damp Spanish moss sparkled as it swayed, and he searched the horizon for dark clouds.

"What are you doing here?"

Startled, Sen hit his head on the window. He groaned and turned, rubbing his forehead, and Morgan loomed from the shadows.

"Looking for you?" Sen patted the owie. Then he let go and frowned. Apprehension flushed heat to his neck and chest. "See if you wanted some of those meatballs?" he tried.

Morgan dismissed that with a short noise. "You should not be here."

"The upstairs? I'm sorry if it's closed for the party, but I didn't think anyone would really notice or mind." He pitched his voice to be light and conversational.

"The party is exactly the problem. Do you believe we are unobserved?" Morgan's lips compressed. "Just go."

Sen straightened. "Come with me." He held out a hand.

Morgan looked at it and wavered. Then his mouth compressed. "Never." He glared at Sen and turned away. "You want too much and push too hard, and it is more than I will give. Do not continue to make a fool of yourself."

Sen burned with humiliation, even as he clamored to deny Morgan's behavior and words.

"Morgan," he said, and splayed his hand over his heart. "It's me. Look at *me*. Don't push me away." Sen took a step, then a second, as Morgan retreated. He thought of Morgan's reaction to other questions. "Don't push your memories away."

He started to speak without having a clue what to say, but Morgan cut him off.

"Memories are all I have." Morgan shook his head and made a confused noise. Then he slashed a hand through the air. "No. Enough of this. I do remember. I know what we have done. So do not think to remind and soften me." His shoulders tightened, and he pushed past to trade places with Sen and gaze out the window. "Just go. Finish what you are here to do and then leave and do not look back or look to me to follow."

Sen heard the rumble of thunder. Dark clouds gathered and rushed toward the hotel.

"Stop this," he begged and put his hand on Morgan's arm.

Morgan didn't react, not even to flinch. He stood ramrod straight, and he shook.

The clouds blanketed the yard, boiled into the window, and surrounded them in darkness. Sen tried to hold on to Morgan's arm, but the clouds swirled and tightened around him. The darkness filled his eyes and nose. He coughed, and it pulled him down to his knees.

"Morgan? Hey. You up here?"

Someone's voice penetrated the black and started Morgan into motion, but Sen couldn't escape.

"Morgan?" Jerry appeared from around the corner and waved. "There you are. People are asking for you."

Morgan blinked and scrubbed his face with a hand. "Yeah, sorry. Just taking a breather."

"Party's almost over, buddy. You've almost made it." Jerry waited for Morgan to join him, and they started down the hall.

They left Sen as if he were invisible, and Jerry didn't react to the tendrils of black clouds still clinging to Morgan as they trailed behind and slithered apart while they walked.

Sen panted and gathered strength. Then he clambered to his feet and looked outside. The silvered landscape and sparkling Spanish moss twinkled in the moonlight. Partygoers roamed the gardens, and music drifted on the air.

He leaned on the windowsill and caught his breath, but the sinister apparition remained, dirty on his skin and down in his lungs. The threat had always been *to* Morgan, not *from* him, and Sen's fear and anxiety spiked. He followed the maze of halls to the stairs, gaining speed as he went, until he nearly ran through the lobby and burst out the front entrance and into the night.

CHAPTER FIFTEEN

SEN LOOKED over the finished illustrations and rubbed the crust from his eyes. He walked the length of the portrait wall and stopped in front of other-Morgan.

"I'm done. And I'm out of time."

He had five illustrations, as promised, and scant days until his solo show, with no clue how to bridge or mend the last of whatever kept Morgan under its thrall and him and Morgan apart.

"Any ideas?"

Everyone stayed silent and he threw his hands up at them.

"Naturally. Thanks."

Sen glanced at his phone on the kitchen windowsill, but didn't retrieve it. He'd turned it off a while earlier, needing to buckle down and finish and not reread the texts from Morgan asking why he left the reception without saying good-bye, how was he doing, and did he need anything.

He couldn't shake memories from the hotel reception—Morgan's cold anger or the freaky storm had invaded and possessed a place he considered neutral. He also couldn't escape the certainty that the storm meant everything was boiling to the surface. But what would it bring, and could he pull the real Morgan out of it?

Sen flipped through the illustrations. Each drawing ate up an entire day, and nothing he did sped the process. If he stayed up late to work, with the intention of napping and continuing on in a few hours, he slept through his alarm, woke at relatively the same time as usual, and went to bed early. He sat in front of the paper with pen in hand, and drew in fits and starts.

Creativity was a force unto itself, and he'd learned to accept it and ride out the pitches and rolls. Plus stubbornness. Stubbornness helped too.

"All that angst doesn't show," he mused, glad the quality was up to his standards and the works would blend in with the others.

They were due for delivery.

"Shit," Sen muttered and went for his phone.

He turned it on and carried it back to the center island, which he had scrubbed and cleared. As he packed the drawings in a flat, protective portfolio, his phone chirped a nonstop chorus of notifications.

Sen zipped the portfolio closed and scanned his messages. One was from Adri, excited about attending the opening for his show. Some were from his mother, checking in and updating him on their travels en route to New Orleans. Several were from Morgan, and Sen zeroed in on a few.

Just saying hi.

Thought I'd come by with takeout—y/y?

I know you're working. I'll buzz when the frames are done.

Sen massaged his neck and couldn't decide between annoyance at Morgan for being so cute or guilt at himself for missing his messages. He thought about how to answer without getting apologetic or gleeful, and then his phone chirped.

Frames for paintings are finished. This a good time to bring them by?

Sen sagged to thump his forehead on the counter, chided his heart's happy flip-flop, and sucked in a breath and replied.

Could you meet me out front?

Be there in 20, Morgan shot back.

He grabbed the portfolio on his way out, settled on the concrete planter, and soon enough was doing that "grinning without being able to stop" thing that happened whenever Morgan came into view.

Conflicted apprehension quickly eclipsed his grin, and he stood but didn't walk over to the car.

"Hi," Morgan said through the open window. He got out of the car and came around to the sidewalk. "You okay?"

"I'm tired."

Morgan frowned and stepped closer. "Sorry." He fidgeted and reached for Sen but corrected himself and pulled back.

"It's fine. Price paid for getting these done on deadline." Sen pointed to the portfolio. "I was just thinking about you."

"Were you? Hearing that was worth driving over here." Morgan's eyes gleamed. "All good things, I presume."

"Oh." Sen shrugged. "Nothing over the top."

Morgan leaned closer, as though anticipating more.

Sen lowered his lashes and tried to resist, but his resolve crumbled. "I'm hoping to talk you into running me to the office so I can get these delivered."

Morgan nodded and popped open the rear door. "Of course. Let's do that now. Then I'll run you back, and we can unload the frames. And get your final approval on them."

"Thanks." Sen stashed the portfolio and got in. "I'm sure they'll be great."

"I assumed, from your radio silence, that you were busy toiling away at artsy stuff. Are you just finishing the illustrations, or is this just when you had a chance to peel yourself away from a painting fever dream?" Morgan slid into the car and eased it into motion. He handed Sen a to-go cup of coffee.

"Oh, I needed this." Sen had a deep swallow of coffee—exactly as he liked it—and hummed in appreciation. "Just finishing. And I really wish it were the latter, but nope. I'm kinda stumped about what to paint next."

"Did this added work trip you up?" Morgan glanced at Sen with concern in his eyes.

Sen smiled. "No—I wasn't in the painting groove before I agreed to do them. Drawing them didn't change that. A lot of times, I find when you're supposed to be working on one thing, the thing second or third in line that you've happily ignored for months is suddenly a demanding wellspring of inspiration." He harrumphed. "This time everything decided to run dry."

"Ahhh." Morgan put a hand over his heart. "How completely and viscerally I understand that pain. The number of times I've been toiling over preliminary blueprints while battling conceptual ideas for footbridges and some random design competition for historic downtown building revitalizations I hadn't given much thought until that very moment." He shook his head. "Do you think with the illustrations out of the way you'll find the painting muse again?"

"I damn sure better." Sen spread his hands. "Or figure a way to fake it. I only have two left—which sounds so reasonable because, you know, the words *only* and *two*. But, yeah."

Morgan made sympathetic noises and tapped the steering wheel. "I can take the others to the gallery and get them framed there. Then I'm not in your way, you'll get a boost from knowing those at least are finished and handled, and it buys you some goodwill time with Lars and Bharti."

"You can? You'd do that?"

"I definitely can and definitely will." Morgan shrugged. "The hotel doesn't require my attention anymore—I'm really here as a formality at this point—and I'm glad to help."

Sen stayed his excitement. Morgan's willingness made his spirit dance, but he couldn't accept. There were too many complications. Sen's desperation for more of that Morgan, even-keeled and great and amazing, gnawed at his insides. But he couldn't trust which Morgan he'd get. And he didn't have the luxury of time to risk it.

"I'm not sure."

They pulled up to the hotel, and Morgan cut the engine and looked at Sen. "Well, think about it and let me know."

"I will." Sen got out and reached into the back for the portfolio. Then some impulse made him ask, "Come on inside with me. Please."

Morgan nodded. "Happy to." He went ahead to hold the side office door open while he got the portfolio. "Not quite as grand, is it?" he said as they passed from the vestibule to a reception room.

"No. But obviously just as considered. It's a practical space, so it might not be dripping in crystals and cherubs and brocade wallpaper, but it's nice." Crown molding topped warm putty-colored walls and a floor in gleaming bamboo, and the fixtures were subdued. "I could work here."

At Morgan's raised eyebrow, Sen conceded, "If I could work in an office."

He smiled at the people bustling behind the main desk. A guy wearing a "Laird" name tag looked past him to Morgan and then glanced at his enormous portfolio bag.

"Are you Mr. Holt? Here with the illustrations?"

"One and the same." Sen noticed Fran—the other name-tagged busy beaver—eyeing Morgan with appreciation. He didn't blame her.

Laird tucked the office phone under an ear. "Let me just buzz back there and let everyone know you're here. It shouldn't be long."

Sen nodded and then found himself eyeing Morgan too. Their glances met, and he waggled his brows. That made Morgan smile, which made Sen grin.

"Okay. Mr. Holt, right this way." Laird opened a connecting door and then paused. "Mr. Ballard, did you need anything?"

"He's with me," Sen said and glanced at Fran before he could stop himself. "I mean, he hired me in the first place, and so he's welcome to join me in presenting these, if he wants."

Morgan, already behind Sen by a step, put a hand on Sen's back and said, "Duh, he wants." He ushered them through the door.

Laird led them into a conference room. "Coffee? Water? Do you need a display board wheeled in or anything?"

"No thanks, I'm good." Sen waved at the table. "I'd like to lay things out here, if that's fine."

"Anywhere that works for you." Laird looked to Morgan. "Anything?"

"I'm good too, but I appreciate it. How's it all going?"

Morgan stayed back to chat with Laird as Sen started to undo the careful portfolio layers. He had them spread on the table and the portfolio tucked away when Thorpe, Greg, and Nina joined them.

"Ah, here we all are." Laird smiled at the room and then addressed Greg. "And anything for the new arrivals?"

Greg shook his head. "No, no. This shouldn't take long, anyway. Thank you, Laird."

"Sen, these are outstanding. I'm thrilled you could do these." Nina gave him a large manila envelope. "Payment, invoice, and other such paperwork."

"Handsomely drawn, and a fine gift, Nina, Greg." Thorpe leaned over the picture he had requested—a view of the lobby from the main staircase. "I planned on hanging this in my office, but I'm thinking I'll take it home. Get it over my mantle."

"Now that is a true compliment and an honor. I hope it inspires you to lead this hotel into greatness," Sen said, and Thorpe's eyes twinkled as they shared a look of mutual respect.

"Don't want the frou-frou, though, I'm a straightforward black walnut or even pine kinda guy. But I think Nina is framing hers that way. Eh, Nina?" Thorpe smoothed his mustache and grunted.

"Yes, and we're sending it to our place in Jackson Hole." Nina admired her drawing, a detail of the fruit and bird motif carvings above the bar in the lounge. "It will look perfectly at home there, with our other treasures."

"You go for a view of the Tetons or get on the Snake River?" Thorpe asked.

"Both." Greg nodded.

Any qualms Sen still held about quoting so much for the illustrations went up in smoke.

Greg separated the three drawings for the firm's use—a three-quarter angle of the front, the tea salon, and the ballroom—then straightened and came toward Sen.

"As discussed, we're going to use these as promotion for the hotel, but also the business, swag, limited prints, and such. There's a rider allowing the use for the prints, and compensation, but there are also stipulations for further compensation if we go over and above the agreed use."

Sen shook Greg's offered hand. "Fantastic. Thank you. I'll read everything, and if I have questions, I'll get in contact. Otherwise, I feel we're in a real good place here."

Greg's efficient demeanor melted, and he smiled. "Real good. You do impressive work, and in a time crunch. Nina and I talked about it, and we're very interested in working with you in the future on other projects."

When Sen started to answer, Nina pressed her hands in the air to cut him off.

"Think about it, is all. We're not looking for a contract or agreement." She squeezed his arm. "Our interest is genuine, and so is the offer. We'll make it again formally once the next project is underway. Until then just keep the notion pinned somewhere safe and give it some thought."

Sen glanced at Morgan. His intense expression of hopeful speculation knocked Sen momentarily silent.

"I most certainly will," he said, and he patted Nina's hands. "And your interest and belief in my work means a lot to me. I just can't say for sure where

I'll be or what I'll be doing by the time you're investing in a new renovation. However, I promise the offer is pinned somewhere quite safe."

"All we can ask," Nina said. "We're so fortunate Morgan found you."

"Yes," Sen said. He stared at Morgan a second too long and then cleared his throat.

"And what's this I hear about a show something-or-another happening?" Thorpe pumped Sen's hand and waited.

"It's an upcoming solo exhibit of my paintings at Gallery Paon. Everyone is welcome, and I hope you can come." Sen chuckled. "Only a few days away, so we should all remember. Right?"

Morgan retrieved Sen's portfolio. "Since I'm here, have there been any issues? Anyone have questions as our end of the project winds down?"

"I figure whatever it is in this stack of beautiful bricks that's going to go sideways is waiting until you all leave. Like a bad engine that just won't knock once you're at the garage." Thorpe winked. "Meaning no, but thanks."

The three of them accompanied Sen and Morgan down the hall, said another good-bye, and left them with Laird, who delivered them across the short reception area and outside.

"Have a great day," Laird called as he held the door.

Sen waved and then looked at Morgan. "That went well. Yeah?"

"Very yeah." Morgan opened the passenger door for Sen and then stashed the portfolio. "You delivered on your end, so that alone made them glad to meet theirs. But they'd never ask you to do anything else if they didn't, one, really mean it, and two, want you to accept." He started the car and leveled Sen with a serious look. "That wasn't professional courtesy or hot air in there."

"Good to know." Sen sat back and nodded once. "I surmised as much. That's how they seem—the genuine parts and the business parts—but it's nice to get confirmation."

Morgan smiled. "Don't you worry. They love your stuff. I hope—it's a good opportunity if you ever decide to pursue working for them again." He exited the hotel parking lot and pointed at the envelope Sen held. "Do you want to swing by the bank?"

"Uh, yes, actually." Sen directed Morgan to the bank, and Morgan let him out at the curb. Sen leaned into the car and said, "Okay. Back in a jiffy." Then he leaned farther in, kissed Morgan without thinking, and pulled away so fast he hit his head on the roof. "Sorry."

"I'll be right here." Morgan didn't acknowledge the kiss but didn't seem bothered by it either. The corners of his mouth tipped up, and his eye crinkles started to crinkle their worst.

Sen pushed away from the car. "Uncool, uncool, so not cool," he repeated as he walked into the bank.

It did take only a jiffy, and Morgan stood outside and took his elbow as he exited the bank. Sen glanced around for the Volvo.

"Celebratory lunch? There's a Cajun hole-in-the-wall nearby that's good."

Sen should definitely not go to lunch. He should definitely go home and paint and not think about Morgan for a while.

"Sounds perfect," he said and let Morgan guide him along.

Morgan beamed. "I missed you."

"I wasn't in the bank that long," Sen deadpanned.

"Pfft. I meant this past week."

Sen didn't answer, but he didn't move away from Morgan's hold on his arm, and they walked in step.

The open air restaurant would hold maybe fifteen diners at mismatched tables with mismatched checked tablecloths. Its walls were covered in Louisiana license plates and an old-fashioned chest drink cooler planted in the corner. They were the sole patrons.

The food smelled incredible. It didn't take them long to read the handwritten menu above the counter and agree on what to get. Morgan held a chair out for Sen, squeezed his shoulder, and then went to order.

"Kiesha said they're just frying a fresh catch of catfish, so I tacked on a basket to our order." Morgan set two huge plastic cups of iced tea on the tiny table and sat. The cramped restaurant and small two top they crowded over emphasized his height, his wide shoulders, and their ratio to his lean hips.

Sen leaned way out and checked the cane chair Morgan sat on. "Think it'll hold? I'm not sure, but I'd wager your chest has more dining space than this table." He pulled his hands apart from a center point like he was taking measurements and laughed when Morgan blushed.

Morgan huffed and shifted and their knees came together under the table. He pushed closer, more pointedly, and made Sen blush.

Their food arrived quickly and piping hot. Kiesha made room for everything on the table with masterful precision, and not an inch of blue check showed after she unloaded. Shrimp po'boy sandwiches, smothered vegetables, cornbread—because they'd agreed one should always get cornbread—and then the catfish.

Sen singed his tongue on the catfish and kept eating. He grumbled when Morgan nudged his iced tea closer but still picked it up and had a drink. After they put a respectable dent in everything, he straightened and paused to breathe.

"Glad you like it," Morgan said.

"It's okay." Sen waved an imperious hand. "Give me another ten minutes, and I'll have the flowers licked off the plate."

Morgan laughed, but then sobered and stacked some dishes and leaned forward as Sen's chuckles quieted.

"I haven't forgotten—the thing I still can't remember." Morgan briefly closed his eyes. When they opened again, they were still clear. "You'd think I could let it go by now, but nope, hamster's still on the wheel."

Sen rested a hand on the table so it just touched Morgan's. "You said before it was something you wanted to tell me."

"Yeah, that's part of it." Morgan rubbed his mouth and sighed. "It's so damn weird. And damnable. Like there's a block or blank spots in my memory, but not enough to make me forget entirely. I even got a teacup at the junk shop when I bought that teapot, so I could have one to turn over. Didn't work."

"Not even a hint?" Sen tapped Morgan's fingertip with his. "Maybe your head's messed up from not sleeping well for so long." He pushed a bit. "Or maybe you're afraid of the memory, and that's why you're blocking it."

Morgan flinched at "memory" but nodded. "Maybe."

Sen pushed a bit more. "What if the memory is about a storm? You did say storms bothered you lately, but they never had before."

Approaching thunder rumbled lowly, and the stacked dishes rattled. Morgan reacted—in-the-moment Morgan.

"That sounded close." Morgan shifted the bowls to stop them vibrating and glanced outside. "As if on cue."

"And is it bothering you?"

"Not at the moment." Morgan covered Sen's hand with his. "I'm sorry I can't just remember, or at least explain it better. And I'm sorry for whatever it is, because I can remember the tension it caused with us. Does cause—it's still there, under the surface—for all that it seems not to matter whenever we're together."

Sen nodded as Morgan spoke. He certainly hadn't made headway untangling the knots in his mind about whatever was going on with Morgan. But having Morgan come back to that point—seeking and wanting to understand and make amends—loosened the bindings he'd ached within since they met.

Sen flipped his hand, and Morgan's thumb slid into his palm in their perfect-fit way.

"When are you leaving?"

"The first week of July." Sen didn't pretend not to understand.

Morgan tightened his grip and nodded.

"Why?"

"I hoped we'd have enough time." Morgan's smile didn't reach his eyes and didn't make the adorable crinkles. He looked away and withdrew.

To figure things out. Sen knew without having to hear anything else.

"When are you leaving? You said you'd be here through June." Sen's voice wobbled, and he picked at his shrimp as a distraction.

"Soon." Morgan checked his watch. "I'm keeping you from painting, and they close up to get ready for dinner service, anyway. The bill's paid—done when I ordered."

Sen reached for his wallet, but Morgan shooed away the gesture.

"I'll leave the tip," Sen insisted and went to the counter. He stuffed a twenty in the slotted coffee can—the Frosts had been generous, above and beyond his added commission—and Kiesha emerged from the kitchen.

"You boys should get a move on. Storm's nearly on us."

Good to her word, a gust of wind rattled the small building, carrying with it wet and a waft of ozone. She hustled to the front and started to stack the tables and chairs out on the sidewalk and move them into the restaurant. Without discussion, Sen and Morgan pitched in. Sen kicked the brick away from the propped-open door, and Morgan reeled the double awnings down. They tied them, shut the wide swinging double doors, and stood in the even more cramped, dark restaurant.

Kiesha darted behind the counter and returned with a large takeout box. "Thank you. Get home safe, now."

"No, thank you. Everything was superb." Morgan went out, looked up, and then grimaced at them.

"Superb and then some." Sen took the box and hurried after Morgan.

The sky roiled with thick, gray-green clouds that seemed poised to swallow the ground. Sen scanned the mass for the telling squall line and then followed the undulations back into its center mass.

"I think the world's about to split apart," he said. They shared a look, and then they ran to Morgan's car.

CHAPTER SIXTEEN

As THEY sped to Sen's apartment, the world didn't split, but the sky broke open. Wind powerful enough to shake the car pushed heavy drops of rain in sprays and spatters. Morgan parked on the street, grabbed the empty portfolio, and then followed Sen around back, up the stairs, and inside. The hard rain soaked them during their brief, mad dash.

The wind followed too. It rattled and groaned through the carriage house and scattered the recycling bins in the alley. They stood panting and dripping as the storm built. Lightning lit up the windows, and for a second, the room looked like a photo negative. Sen flipped on the dim light over the sink and put the takeout box down.

Morgan's drenched state left nothing to the imagination. His polo and jeans clung like a second skin—every bulge wet and defined—and moved in time with his labored breath. His honey blond hair looked darker and untamed.

Sen tore his gaze away. He toed off his shoes and eased past Morgan to get towels.

They made contact as he squeezed by. The air snapped around them like the moment that presages lightning. Morgan growled a low, throaty noise, then gripped Sen's waist and jaw. Sen pressed the small of his back to the counter as Morgan crowded in, and he tugged Morgan's shirt to get them closer.

Sen shivered. Every nerve thrummed with anticipation. Morgan leaned in and cradled their faces together. Their noses aligned, their breath intermingled, and Morgan stroked Sen's lips with featherlight touches of his own.

"Morgan?"

"Right here," Morgan whispered.

Tears choked Sen's throat and heated his eyes. He gripped Morgan's soaked shirt and invited the kiss. Morgan's kiss. He lapped at Morgan's mouth. Morgan kissed him tenderly—not passionately and darkly and demanding—and pulled back.

Frustration and confusion rioted through Sen, and he tried to read Morgan's expression.

"These are your paintings for the show?" Morgan kissed Sen's temple and then, as if drawn by an unseen force, went to stand in front of the far wall.

Sen could have screamed or bitten his tongue out. Instead he made good on getting them towels and hid under one to dry his hair and neck and to chase errant tingles away. The storm settled in and gave no quarter, lashing the windows and shaking the heavens. But Sen's attention was on Morgan, and Morgan's was riveted on his paintings.

"Yes. The majority, at least. I still have two more to paint." Sen pointed at other-Morgan and the young man companion. "And I'm just not sure I want to include those two, although it's looking like I'll have to. They were the first I did—the breakthrough for this series and a creative block—but they're the ones I'm least sure about." He crossed his arms. "Or the ones I'm unsure about sharing with anyone else."

"Do you mind me being here, seeing these? Sorry. I just barged in." Morgan's hair was spikey and his face pink from being towel-dried. It should have looked ridiculous but instead looked ridiculously sexy. And endearing.

"No. I don't mind that you're here." Sen glanced outside. "Do you mind the storm?"

"Actually, no." He kissed Sen then pulled back. "Think that's why," he said, and he returned to the portrait of other-Morgan.

For Sen the effect was like looking in a dark mirror. Errant shivers skittered beneath his skin as he watched Morgan study that piercing gaze, and how their faces had such similarity of expression.

Morgan stayed deep in contemplation for several minutes. Then he moved on to study each successive couple and portrait with equal focus.

Sen watched his reactions—smiling at earthy girl and her young man, a pained flinch at the couple in opposition, and an abortive reach to touch the starry women—and listened to the storm. He wanted to ask for reactions as Morgan went on, but held back so Morgan could proceed and absorb everything without comment. A strange and wonderful prescient awareness seeped into the room, gathering and building, connecting them.

Morgan finished and then went back the opposite way, faster but no less intently. "When did you start painting these?" he asked, standing again before other-Morgan.

"The first day I cleaned Greycote." Sen's nerves stood on end.

Morgan covered his mouth with a hand and went still. He appeared to be processing something. Then he shook his head and let out a sharp breath. "Why did you paint me—us—again and again?"

Sen's mouth flooded with saliva and his pulse jumped. "What?" He looked at the paintings—every one unique—and opened his arms. "What?" he repeated.

"And how did you know to paint me if you started before we met but did this one first?" Morgan asked, pointing at other-Morgan. Their faces blended, both Morgan's eyes and those in the painting conflicted with storm and shadows.

"I didn't," Sen said, incredulous. "I couldn't know, and I didn't paint you." He looked from Morgan to the painting, and his resolve wavered. "I mean. Not knowingly." His tone begged forgiveness and belief.

"You didn't? But that's exactly what this is… who these people are." Morgan seemed almost to accuse him, and his expression swirled with wonder and doubt.

"No, and clearly not. Look at them and then look at us. Which—what do you mean *us*?" Sen challenged. "What do you mean I painted us?"

Morgan threw up his hands.

"How can you not see? You're this beautiful young man," he said of other-Morgan's companion. "And this earthy woman's mate," he described, in the very words Sen used. "The angry one on the left of the fighting couple and the gorgeous pearl-wearing woman." He pointed at the veiled star girl. "And the shy, sweet creature, hiding but waiting for the right person just behind the heavens. That may be most like you now." Morgan tilted his head and seemed lost in thought.

Sen wanted to dismiss it outright as ludicrous and as Morgan seeing things, but he couldn't. Each of them had his hazel eyes, delicate brows, and high cheekbones, and they all seemed familiar in a way he couldn't explain as recognition. Their counterparts all resembled Morgan.

"Tell me I'm wrong." Morgan retraced his steps and stabbed at each painting as he walked and said, "Me, you. Me, you. Me, you. Me, you. Me, you. Tell me I'm wrong."

Sen scrubbed his face with both hands. Lightning flashed, and Morgan tensed. The room distorted, and then a thunderclap heaved. Sen felt distorted too, shifting in and out, trying to grasp something just out of reach. Morgan's accusations and insistence stirred something to life inside. He pressed the heels of his hands to his forehead and looked at Morgan, bewildered and unable to answer Morgan's demands.

"I can't." Sen shook his head and made a helpless gesture.

He had sworn he'd painted Morgan without ever meeting him and then dismissed that as unreasonable. Crazy. Too much to be believed.

Sen staggered as the tumblers all began clicking into place.

The more he studied the portraits, the more his and Morgan's energies shimmered beneath the surface, an essence as foundation for all of the faces. But each portrait relied on its pair for its identity, for its nuances and full impact to be seen.

Shock, awareness, and sudden *knowing* crashed through Sen and overwhelmed him.

"I did paint us," he whispered and then said louder, "I did."

Morgan didn't hear him. He was lost in study of the young man, his gaze hooded and searching, and a tear ran down his cheek. His stance and mood and the very real storm sparked something in Sen.

His first vision from the turret room roared back, and dark clouds filled the room to obscure everything, transporting him back to where it all began. Smoke, hatred, and fear reeked on the air, and distant shouting got louder and louder.

Sen remembered going to Morgan in the dark of night. His heart thrummed with the anticipation of being in Morgan's arms and seeing Morgan's surprise. But things went wrong. Horribly wrong. His secret had been revealed somehow—their secret—and he'd paid the price. Sen remembered the men who'd surrounded him in the circle of trees, the weight of their angry fists and blows with sticks, and then the sharp jabbing pain in his side.

"Oh God," Sen gasped and blinked back into the present.

Through the haze he saw Morgan, still caught in the painting. Caught in the tortured memories of that night.

"A storm is when I lost you," Morgan said, in that formal, lilting way Sen had come to recognize and dread. "I told you to be safe, to stay safe, but you were bold and brave and didn't think harm could come to…." His voice cracked. "But harm did come, and there was nothing I could do. I failed to protect you, despite my every wish and warning. Our overheard plans to be together brought this about. After we were so careful, after we paid off the whisperers and paid others to whisper differently."

Morgan touched the painting, and Sen felt it on his cheek.

"I couldn't even claim you or mourn," Morgan continued, held in his fugue state.

The rest of Sen's other memories returned, clicking into place, fitting with memories from his current life and making sense of the past. Morgan had been a wealthy noble in that life. He was spared but exiled from society—more by choice, after what *society* did to his young lover—Sen—when they were discovered, than by necessity. Sen was the expendable one, and other-Morgan learned a terrible lesson.

"You were simply gone, and in most ways, I followed." Morgan curled his hand into a fist and turned. "You haunt me, and I am incomplete, and I suffer it most acutely with every storm."

With every storm.

Sen lurched and the room spun around, so he grabbed his knees and hunkered forward. With every storm.

The words echoed in Sen's mind as his and Morgan's present-day encounters replayed in a montage as though he were watching from afar. The

palpable connection that had drawn them together from the first moment—
Morgan's quick kiss in the hallway, how they gravitated to each other and
were always touching, their instant rapport, and the urge to paint that Morgan
inspired.

So Sen painted their memories, compelled to channel the visions and his
confusion of emotions onto canvas. But storms seemed to trigger and drive
Morgan.

Morgan too got caught in memories not of this lifetime, but he remained
stuck in the one from Sen's vision in the turret room. Painting provided Sen
a way to exorcise the flood of emotions and memories, an outlet to channel
everything into. Morgan had no such escape and got stuck in the loop of their
one tragedy.

He wished one of their happier lives, lived fully and together, had found
its voice across their connection for Morgan to remember instead. But he
understood just how powerful and consuming the reverberations of trauma and
loss could be.

Sen wiped his eyes clean of tears and watched the dark clouds thin, recoil,
and retreat from the room.

He went to Morgan and wrapped both hands around Morgan's arms. "I'm
here. Morgan? I'm right here. The storm is over."

Morgan started at the sound of Sen's voice and turned to face him. His
eyes were clouded with sorrow and confusion, and thunder shook the room.
Lightning forked, vivid and bright blue-white, and he gasped. His hand shook
as he touched Sen's cheek with the same light caress as he had the portrait.

"Sebastian?" Morgan blinked. His expression began to clear as his hand
steadied. "I lost you. Over and over." He made a trembling fist, seemingly to
keep from touching Sen. Tears escaped his shimmering eyes, and he choked
back a harsh breath. "I lived so long without you."

"But we lived before, and then lived again, and found one another again,
and I'm here." Sen gentled Morgan's hand onto his chest and let Morgan feel
his heartbeat and warmth. "I'm here. See?"

Morgan bit his lip and nodded. "You did paint us, didn't you? I'm not
imagining things? Not going crazy?"

"No, you aren't." Sen edged closer until their toes bumped and their thighs
touched. "I did paint us, in all those lives we've shared. You just recognized
it first. But I see it—see us. I believe." He shook his head and let out a watery
laugh. "I was supposed to figure it out and save you."

Morgan's watery smile matched Sen's laugh. "You did. I couldn't have
known without seeing your paintings, and you couldn't paint without knowing
me. Us." Morgan took hold of Sen's arm. "You needed me to fill in that last

blank—like I needed to see them—and then show me how to get free of the storm." Morgan loosed a long, cleansing exhale. "I remember."

"Me too." Sen did—far back and far forward. There wasn't a timeline and they weren't separate stories. It was a continuum. Twin colors of light and heat stretched in both directions, bending and coiling, but always joined.

"Have we met before?" Morgan asked roughly. "Do I know you?" he breathed.

"Yes," Sen answered. "Yes."

Morgan surged, and Sen met his demanding kiss with equal measure. Thunder rumbled through the room. They staggered, and Sen almost fell over, but Morgan caught him. Kissing and ripping at clothing, they bumped into furniture as Morgan walked them to the wall, shoved Sen up against a support post, and finally onto Sen's bed.

His twin mattress and box spring on the floor barely held them, no space to move without touching or crowding each other. It was just right.

Sen curled his thumbs in his waistband and pulled. He hissed with frustration as the wet material resisted.

Morgan boosted to his knees, took hold of the waistband, and yanked. He pulled Sen into his lap, wrestled his jeans off, and tossed them behind him. He stared at Sen's nakedness with raw desire and appreciation and dusted his knuckles up and down Sen's legs. The lightning showed him in warping shadow and relief. Then he peeled Sen's socks off and tickled until Sen squirmed and kicked. He held Sen's ankle, pushed Sen's legs open, and proceeded to kiss Sen from navel to neck.

"Before it all connected I imagined doing this—and so many other things—with you. I dreamed about it and daydreamed and wondered what to do. I was nervous, excited, confused. You were a fever in me," Morgan confessed between kisses. He pushed up to see Sen. "It was love at first sight, but I didn't know that. I do know the love I came to have for you was only for you—dorky, sweet, shy, talented and sensitive and beautiful Sebastian. And now for everything."

Sen stammered and cried and grinned. Then he said, "I love you too. So much. And I mean—"

"I know," Morgan cut him off with a kiss.

Sen nodded. They always would.

"I've never been with a guy. I mean as only me." Morgan explored, kissing and tasting Sen's throat and chest. "I've looked and wondered, and wasn't bothered that I looked and wondered, but I was unsure enough to never make any moves. Unsure of what I wanted—who I wanted." He bit behind Sen's ear then pulled back and smiled. "I can remember what we've done together, and the memories are good. I'm glad for them too, in case you worried."

He kissed Sen again, conveying his gladness and surety and an eagerness Sen would have been able to pick up on even without their connection. Sen kissed Morgan back, full of relief and release, and just as eager.

Morgan nibbled Sen's lips and then withdrew and fanned his hands on Sen's chest. "But it feels like just that—only memories, and some are hazy. So I still haven't really been with a guy, but I'm not nervous or the least bit confused."

Sen dragged his fingernails up Morgan's back and grinned when Morgan growled. "Which leaves excited?"

"Very." Morgan shuddered when Sen scratched him again. "So much that I'm going to come if you don't stop that. Even then, no promises." He widened his eyes in warning and then manacled Sen's wrists to the bed with his hands.

"What else did you imagine?" Sen whispered as he ran his toes along Morgan's legs and sucked at Morgan's earlobe.

Morgan growled. "Not coming in my shorts while you were a merciless tease. At least not for our first time."

Sen's mind reeled at everything Morgan shared in that blunt phrase. He swallowed and then pressed his hips to the bed, almost overwhelmed. Morgan laughed knowingly, so Sen nipped at the jut of Morgan's jaw in retaliation, and Morgan let his hands go. They lay awhile under the storm, with their hips grinding and their hands exploring, trading kisses and soft caresses.

"I don't know where to start," Morgan admitted at last.

"I do." Sen rose onto his elbows and spread his legs wider. "Get up, get out of those boxers, and fuck me."

Morgan cursed and stumbled off the bed. He stripped his boxers when he stood. "What about… everything?" he asked as he knelt on the bed and got close again.

Sen needed his own moment of appreciation. His gaze lingered on Morgan's muscular thighs and the gorgeous cock straining toward taut abs. Morgan was big without being huge, and it would hurt a bit and feel so good. He twisted and searched under the pillows, then felt on the floor, and finally grabbed the lube from where it had escaped and gotten wedged next to the wall.

He huffed in triumph and promptly dropped the bottle when Morgan palmed his ass, lowered over him, and bit the hot spot at his shoulder blade.

Sen shuddered as Morgan licked and sucked his hot spot and then down.

Morgan pulled back to admire his handwork. He rolled the thin skin along Sen's spine, massaged Sen's back in long, sweeping strokes, and then he went back to that spot and continued.

Sen ground against the mattress and groaned. "Coming like this is fine with me, but you'll have to understand I'm just gonna lay here after and let you just do whatever."

Morgan's teeth snapped, and he pushed his forehead to Sen's shoulder. "Something else we should definitely explore—later." He pulled away. "Should we... like this? Or...."

"Or this," Sen said and rolled over. "Wanna see you." He tugged Morgan and they kissed.

"I haven't done this in a while. A long while." Morgan kissed Sen's chin and behind an ear. Then he went back onto his heels. He clenched his jaw and lifted Sen's hand to his mouth. "I am so not going to last."

Sen vibrated all over, and he felt Morgan's answering tremble. He flipped the cap on the lube and poured some into the crease of his hip. Then he rubbed it around, lower and lower, as he worked his legs higher.

"We have forever to do it again," Sen said, matter-of-factly. He grunted as his index finger slid inside his hole.

Morgan grinned, kissed Sen's palm, and then nodded and scooched back. His heated gaze darted between Sen's expression, cock, and hand. He gripped behind Sen's knee and tilted Sen's leg.

"Have you ever been with another man? Before all this?" Morgan's question was warm and curious, not guarded or jealous.

"Casual dating. Nothing like this." Sen bit his lip and concentrated. "And even then, there haven't been many." He let out a noise and shuddered when Morgan's long fingers joined his, gentle and sure and finding his sweet spot in moments. "Never anywhere long enough to trust giving more—didn't want more from anyone else. Never had a reason until I found you."

Morgan kissed him, hard and possessive. He scraped his teeth along Sen's jaw. "Same."

Sen moaned and tensed as Morgan massaged inside him, sparking light and heat so that Sen's every nerve hummed. Morgan's touch was insistent and absorbed in him entirely. Sen's toes clenched, and he lost his breath, so overstimulated he had to bat at Morgan and twist away.

Morgan resituated over Sen with the heels of his hands at the line of Sen's hips and his knees nudging under Sen's ass.

"Do we need protection?" Morgan sounded hoarse and struggled to focus and hold Sen's gaze. "It's okay if you want."

Sen shook his head. "It's been a while, and longer, for me too." He bit his lip and raised his hips in invitation.

Morgan didn't need more than that. He entered Sen slowly, mindful of Sen's noises and reactions. He checked for Sen to nod and paused at Sen's intake of breath. When he was fully in, with his hips against the curve of Sen's thighs, he pressed harder and tucked his face toward Sen's neck.

"I missed you," Morgan whispered. "I love you so much."

Sen tangled his hands in Morgan's hair and braced his heels at the small of Morgan's back. He began to rock with a slow build, and then guided Morgan's mouth to his.

"I love you so much," Sen repeated between kisses, and their words reverberated in his mind and his heart, and their completion within each other.

Every move and touch was a feedback loop. Sen experienced Morgan's pleasure along with his own, and when his pleasure spiked, he saw it in Morgan's responses. They spiraled together in a tight rhythm of thrusts and withdrawals, wet with sweat and tears, their hands clinging and their mouths tasting. Sen couldn't tell where he ended and Morgan began.

Morgan lifted up and hitched Sen's legs higher to change the angle and fit more deeply. Sen groaned and clawed at Morgan, and his vision went white at the edges.

"I'm close… so close," Morgan chattered. "Can't last."

Sen rubbed his thumbs over Morgan's nipples, swept his hands down to where they were joined, and pulled at Morgan's hips.

"So give in," Sen begged with his mouth and hands when Morgan tensed.

Morgan made a broken and exultant noise, and his movements became rough and wild. He grabbed and pinned Sen's hands to the bed and then shifted his grip to Sen's waist.

"Then come with me," Morgan charged and bit at Sen's neck.

Sen found it almost impossible to distinguish between his shuddering completion and Morgan's. He threw his head back and panted, dizzy and tingling from every pore. Sen knew Morgan was the same. There was a throbbing, physical point of contact buried in each of them, but it went beyond that tangible connection and suffused them in each other.

Thunder cracked, and the house shuddered.

"Me too," Morgan said. He whuffed against Sen's neck and kissed a trail to the rise of his cheek. Then he held Sen there and tenderly kissed the cup of bone that sheltered Sen's eye.

"Beautiful hazel—like tiger's eye and opals—there in each painting. I recognized you immediately." Morgan smiled. "Too bad I didn't *know*-know it as instantaneously when we met."

Sen shrugged. "I'm okay with this version. But then I don't think I'm going to have many complaints, period, so long as we're together."

"Fair. And agreed."

Morgan settled back into Sen, and they stayed there, kissing, dozing, and whispering secrets as they reunited. Sen's lungs at last pinched, and he shifted to the side. Morgan swept his gaze up and down Sen's nakedness.

"Roll over," Morgan said, and he moved so Sen could. He propped his chin on one hand and drew circles on the stretch of skin along Sen's shoulder blade until Sen trembled. Then he leaned down, kissed that special spot, and settled there with his ear pressed to Sen's back.

"What are you doing?" Sen eventually asked. He felt Morgan smile.

"Listening." Morgan stretched and took Sen's hand. "Here." He turned his wrist into Sen's hold and waited.

Sen tightened his grip to find Morgan's pulse but couldn't, at first. His own pulse drummed in his ears and chest, louder from being pressed into the pillows and from supporting Morgan's weight. He breathed in and out, in and out, and concentrated on his fingertips. When he found it, he stilled.

Morgan laughed when Sen shoved up and turned over, moving out of the way and then lowering over him again. Sen kissed Morgan, openly and entirely, so he could feel their matching heartbeats in his mouth and in his seeking hands and everywhere they touched. He cupped Morgan's face and moved them apart to affirm what he already knew. Morgan's look of satisfaction and utter devotion made him helpless and happy.

He reveled in everything—the scent, their shared heat, the texture of Morgan's hair and stubble, the curves of Morgan's cheeks and collarbone. Then he rolled back over, and they shifted and settled. Morgan returned to rest on Sen's back, over his heart.

Lightning lit the room, and thunder followed, slower on its heels as the storm moved away. Sen rested but didn't sleep. He didn't need to. Luxuriating in the sensations of Morgan's deep sleep calmed and refreshed him. He lay listening to their heartbeats and the rain and marveled that the signs he'd followed his entire life had brought him this.

Colors began to whisper and drag around in his mind's eye, and Sen saw his next painting. He eased from under Morgan, and when Morgan protested, Sen stuffed a pillow close to take his place. Morgan's brow furrowed but Sen smoothed it with a light kiss. Then he found a T-shirt and ratty jeans to wear, snapped on the work light over the easel, and loaded his palette.

He built the ground thicker than the other portraits, because he wanted more immediate saturation and physical presence from the paint. Sen scraped and cut with his knife, creating furrows and lines to catch thin washes of ochre, ivory, and verdigris.

Sen got lost in the meditation of mixing color, adding solvents, and applying layer after layer. His breathing became a slow, deep constant, and his inspiration was a continuous flow, not a burst or stop-start of energy.

"Can you paint while sitting down?" Morgan asked when he rose from bed.

Sen turned around. "Probably. Why?" He devoured the visual feast of Morgan stretching, and he waggled his brows.

Morgan grinned and stepped into his jeans. He dragged a battered ottoman over, sat on it, and pulled Sen to sit between his legs.

"Answers that question." Sen adjusted the easel to lower the paint tray.

"I just slept great. And safe to say, I absolutely adore storms again." Morgan flattened his hand on Sen's chest.

Sen nodded. He relaxed into Morgan, sighed, and continued to paint.

Morgan propped his chin on Sen's shoulder and watched the drips and the solvent spread as layers brought his own portrait to life.

"Perfect." Morgan tickled behind Sen's ear. "You make me look good."

"Right? It's a gift." Sen blurred the delineation of Morgan's cheek against the darker background. "What else could I paint as the final pair? Do you mind?"

"I'd mind if you painted someone else. Even another of me. You know." Morgan snickered. "I know you get it, but it's still weird. Amazing and great, but weird."

"Best kind of weird."

Morgan groaned and hid in Sen's neck. "You must have thought I was off my rocker. Hey, nice to meet you. I'm just your friendly, likable, amnesiac guy who goes in for the sex tackle now and again."

"Sex tackle. I enjoy this concept. Let's revisit that idea at some point. Points. With frequency." Satisfaction filled Sen down to his marrow, so much so that Morgan's past actions were insignificant, and the reasons for them were clear. Hardly logical by normal standards, but it made perfect sense for them.

He considered and then said, "I thought a lot of things. That maybe you had a nefarious—and amorous—doppelganger. That I was the one losing it." He shuttled the paintbrush in a jar of turpentine and twisted around so they could see each other. "But I was never afraid or unwilling. Confused? Hell yes. Wondering if we were in some kind of strange heat and mating ritual? It seemed possible. But never afraid. Okay?"

"Okay. For the record, that goes for me too." Morgan kissed Sen and smiled. "Good. And thank God. Anyone else and there might be a restraining order with my name on it."

"Anyone else and it wouldn't have happened. Like, literally." Sen straightened and then flattened Morgan's hand on his chest. "We're meant to be together. I think such a heady destiny allows us a little latitude as we stumble through figuring it out."

"Well said." Morgan rested against Sen and watched him paint. "Do you think there'll be more?"

"I've unlocked the secret of where they came from, but does that mean the floodgates will open or they'll dry up? I honestly don't know. I mean, there's definitely some gaps to fill between the dawn of time and today, but so far, nothing's hit me." Sen dragged the brush to leave a trail of solvents and regarded the effect. "I hope so."

"Maybe someday. Maybe never. I hope so too, but if never, that's okay. I'm just glad you painted these." Morgan lifted his fingers toward the wall of portraits. "Later I'll bring in the frames and work on the finished pieces. I should get out of your way and frame them at the gallery, but I don't want to leave."

Sen squeezed Morgan's leg. "How could you ever be in my way? And who says I'd let you leave?" He added a layer of eggshell blue to portrait-Morgan's left and burnt orange to the right, meeting them to muddle over Morgan's crown. As he built more layers, the tension created by the two colors underneath would make the whole thing dance. "When we met, you were in a business suit. I thought of that as your colors—power black with pinstripes and the bright pop of your orange pocket square—and assumed you were a workaholic."

"I wanted to learn everything about you and that scared me. Including calling Adriane to ensure you stayed on the job after the first day. And it was more than marveling over the amazing linen closet transformation and wanting you to work that magic elsewhere. But I told myself it was all about maintaining the house." Morgan waited for Sen to lift his brush, and then he started to rock them. "The flash drive not working was real, but the weekend off was a stretch. We were given Friday, but I asked for it to be extended to Wednesday so I could be home when you were there. Since I usually don't even stop for lunch, Greg didn't argue it."

"You tricksy minx—I'm scandalized," Sen ribbed Morgan and put the brush down. He lifted his leg to shift onto the ottoman and then curled up against Morgan's chest. "There was every reason I shouldn't have taken the illustration job. Oh, I justified it in all sorts of smart ways, and the cash was nice. But yeah. I just wanted a reason to keep seeing you."

Morgan rumbled low laughter. "I know. Or at least that's what I hoped. There was a space for your use at the hotel."

"But you made a studio for me at the house." Sen snicker-snorted. "We're so awesome."

"I guess after searching for you my whole life, finding any reason to keep you with me seemed not only logical, but necessary. Which makes total sense to me now, but then? I only knew I couldn't let you get away. The very idea of you lived in me and drove me... a compulsion I couldn't resist." Morgan kissed Sen's brow. "But your illustrations really are wonderful. I lucked out, because I was going to hire you even if all you could draw were stick figures and lopsided boxes."

"With off-center triangle roofs?"

"Naturally. That would make quite a statement hanging in the lobby."

Sen's stomach growled. Morgan nuzzled his nape, held on to his shoulders a beat, and then went to the kitchen and rooted around.

"Looking for anything specific?" He glanced over then started painting.

"Just foraging, for the moment." Morgan got out a pan, found the butter, and assembled a random assortment of canned goods, yesterday's lunch, and the pack of breakfast sausage Sen had forgotten about. "Gonna make dinner. Or whatever meal we're at."

Sen paused his brush. "You cook?"

"Yeah. I'm a very good cook, even. I just wasn't going to cook in that house when I spent a fortune on industrial gourmet appliances for resale value." Morgan dove into a side cabinet and emerged with a bowl and a small bag of flour. "Might seem contrary, but—"

"But you were only there a few months. Amazing cooking could wait while you pushed to get the project done, and it's entirely practical all around." Sen resumed painting. "I get it."

Morgan whistled, and Sen looked up and caught a multigrain roll flying toward him.

"Something to tide you over. Now keep painting. You're on a deadline." Morgan hummed and began to mix things into the bowl.

Sen shot Morgan a look. "Really. Suddenly you're all taskmaster on me. After hiring me to do illustrations, then more illustrations, then distracting me with reception and lunch invites, and then remembering we're soul mates and fucking me senseless? Suddenly I gotta buckle down and paint."

Morgan stopped to blaze a heated glance at Sen when he said "soul mates," and his mouth went lax at "fucking me senseless."

"Maybe I'm reminding myself to stay over here and be good." Morgan turned to fill a measuring cup with water. "So that's what I'm doing. Staying over here. Being good. While you paint."

"A most noble sacrifice," Sen conceded.

The storm had passed—Sen didn't miss the metaphor—leaving behind a steady, gentle rain. The pattering rhythm made soothing and suitable accompaniment to his and Morgan's contentment. Morgan cooked with confidence and didn't have to search for anything. He opened cabinets and drawers to put his hand on whatever it seemed he wanted. That the weather no longer distressed Morgan or threaded them with undercurrents of anxiety didn't escape Sen either.

Sen tore himself away from watching Morgan putter and studied his canvas. He stood and adjusted the easel, propped it on the ledge he'd screwed into the wall for that purpose, and changed to the remaining blank canvas. Sen needed to work them in overlapping tandem, and he had to wait for the foundation layers to dry. He attacked the canvas without hesitation. He finally knew everything about who he was, painting a self-portrait would be easy.

CHAPTER SEVENTEEN

"I WANT to build a freestanding temporary wall, here," Bharti said, sketching the idea with her hands. "It will be the entry and focal point for the show, really focus everyone and set the narrative before they dive into the rest of the pieces."

"Yes. Some dramatic lighting, and we'll paint it a different color from everything else. Maybe put your artist's statement on it?" Lars mused.

The faux wall would face the gallery's front door and be wide enough for two portraits, separating the rest of the gallery space from immediate view.

Sen surveyed the empty gallery and nodded. "I really like that idea, but with the statement hung around the corner on the width of the wall. The portraits have the most clarity when allowed to speak on their own." He looked toward the door. "Can I choose the color?"

"Sure, as long as I like it." Bharti laughed. "We'll get the wall built today. It's last minute, because I just thought of it when I saw you and the framed pieces. But our carpenter can get it banged out and painted so it's dry by tomorrow and then ready for the opening. Exciting."

Lars clapped. "Quite. People are already abuzz based on the strength of the promo materials and first glimpses of your work, Sen. I have such a good feeling about this show." He looked around. "We're going to clear the space of any noise. Greeting desk, minimal signage on the front windows, and scrims over the back brick wall."

"Hmm." Sen considered the brick and the offset L shape of the gallery. "I think it's fine. There's a lot of earth tones and grounded qualities in the portraits. Four portraits can be on the long neutral wall, four on the back of the freestanding wall, and the brick can highlight another pair. Like this."

Sen distributed the paintings in moments. He already knew where they should go and how they'd interact with the space, the walls, and each other.

Bharti turned a slow circle. "Yes. Yeah. I really feel this. This is good." She pointed to the two Sen had left by the door. "And those on the greeting wall?"

"Yep." Sen looked at the first two paintings he'd done and felt no more reluctance to show them. With the answers unlocked and Morgan making him whole, he was eager to share them with the world.

"Perfect." Bharti retrieved a notebook and jotted some things down. "I'll call Otis to get over here and start building."

Heat ran up Sen's spine and tingles cascaded down his scalp. He couldn't keep from grinning, so he rolled his lower lip between his fingers as if in thought and walked through the gallery space. Moments later the front door opened and Lars greeted Morgan.

"Hello, hello," Morgan said, eyes on Sen. Sen grinned back, and Morgan's crinkles came out in force.

Sen couldn't believe he'd ever not known who Morgan was to him. Part of him had from the start, and that part proved strong enough to hold fast until the rest of him caught on. At least he didn't have to imagine not knowing Morgan from then on.

"We're just finishing here. Tomorrow we hang everything, if you'd like to be here for that, Sen." Lars walked a circle to examine the paintings. "These here? Are you sure? Not traded with those two?"

"I'm sure," Sen answered without looking. "And yes, I would like to be here tomorrow, thank you."

"Excellent. We're starting bright and early at one." Bharti waved her phone. "Otis is on his way. Any ideas on the paint color you want?"

Sen nodded. "I can run and get it instead of trying to describe or pick a color to match. Figure a quart is enough?"

Lars held up a finger. "Wait, wait, here." He crossed to the desk and pulled out a drawer. "Take some petty cash and just bring back the receipt, please."

"I won't go overboard or buy too extravagant a lunch with this." Sen took the folded notes and stuck them in his pocket. "Isn't there a little hardware store a few blocks away? I'd rather use them than a big box store. Plus that means no driving."

Morgan said, "I can take you."

"You still can." Sen beamed.

Bharti treated them to a speculative look but didn't comment. Her smug, pleased smile spoke volumes.

"There is." Lars showed them onto the sidewalk and pointed the way. "Down two blocks, over three, down another two, and it's around the corner."

"Great. Won't be too long."

Sen started in the direction Lars indicated, but Morgan took his arm and turned them around.

"Going this way detours us through the park."

"Then we're definitely going this way." Sen hipped into Morgan and they walked several blocks without speaking, basking in each other's presence and the growing strength of their connection.

Sen noticed he felt different with Morgan near. It wasn't mind reading and definitely not intrusive—more a persistent sense of wellbeing. As he painted, he could tell when Morgan dozed off, woke again, or got lost in a book. Morgan brought him glasses of water and mugs of coffee moments before he about gave in and got them himself, and waited for him to look up so they could make eye contact, blush, and smile.

They bickered and teased, and while Sen didn't think they'd never fight or have problems, he'd take that too. Belonging to someone was incredible, and he wanted every part of it, whole cloth.

Morgan draped his arm across Sen's shoulders as they entered the park, and Sen was grateful for the milder temps and steady breeze. The powerful storm had cleared the slurry humidity from the city, and the sun had dropped low to lengthen the shadows and allow the world to cool into evening. They went across a bow bridge, threaded through huge live oaks, and then skirted around a fountain.

"I heard from my mom this morning. My folks and younger brother are almost to New Orleans. They'll be here tomorrow and will probably visit a few days afterward." Sen was happy they were coming and thrilled to introduce them to Morgan.

"Nice. I'm looking forward to meeting them." Morgan sounded right but he looked a bit worried.

Sen laughed. "Don't worry. They're gonna love you. They already know I'm pretty much gone on you forever, so." He shrugged. "You treating me great is enough for them to welcome you as part of the family."

Morgan smiled. "I'll take it." His eyes got faraway, and Sen made a prompting noise. "Just thinking about how I'd mentioned my dad was stationed in Hawaii, and that you should visit, and now I'm meeting your parents. Meaning, then it'll be your turn."

"Beaches and ocean and volcanoes. We can watch new land being formed! Ugh, just the idea of that, right?" Sen beamed and knew Morgan understood exactly what he meant and shared his enthusiasm. "I'm excited." He licked his lips and then confessed, "When you mentioned I should go see Hawaii, I was so close to saying, 'You can show me around.'"

"Well, I'd just tripped over not saying, 'When I take you there to show you around,' so we're even."

"I like when we're even."

"Me too." Morgan ran his fingertips up and down Sen's arm. "Question."

Sen shivered and nodded. "Answer."

Morgan covered a snicker with a cough. "I'm not going to acknowledge that."

"You just did." Sen pulled away to find Morgan pouting and avoiding his gaze. He pinched Morgan's side. "Seriously, what? What's your question?"

"Hmmph."

Morgan fought a smile, so Sen pinched him again. Then Morgan pinched him back, and Sen retaliated by tripping Morgan. Then Morgan went low and shouldered into his midsection, and Sen found himself backed behind a monument.

"Answer this," Morgan said in a low, husky voice. He cupped Sen's face and then tipped them into a demanding kiss.

Sen gave readily. He braced his back on the monument and tugged Morgan after him. Morgan hummed and hooked Sen's waist to drag his hips out and push their groins together. The park noises and evening sounds gave way to the heartbeat thrum Sen heard and felt whenever they were intimate, Sen's awareness consumed by Morgan to the exclusion of all else.

When Morgan pulled back, Sen grunted and kept hold of Morgan's shirt. He laughed when Morgan dove back in for another kiss. A woman's voice from the other side of the monument guiding her children into place for the perfect photograph cut through, and Sen managed to loosen his grip on Morgan.

"Okay," Morgan breathed. He rubbed his thumbs at the corners of Sen's mouth and then stepped back. "Okay. We'll get popped for indecency if we don't stop."

"Right. Okay." Sen straightened and started walking without waiting for Morgan. "Any idea where the store is from here?"

Morgan said, "This way?" and pointed in the other direction. When Sen turned, he added, "Or that way? Maybe."

"So you don't. Great." Sen backtracked, tucked his arm in Morgan's, dragged them to the edge of the park, and gestured into the neighborhood. "Behind us is the way we came. Two blocks, over three, down two more should be over there someplace. Let's give it a go."

One large loop and two stops to ask for directions later, and they had the quart of paint.

"But the detour through the park was worth it, wasn't it? It's a really nice park." Morgan had his hands in his pockets and an easy stroll going.

Long-suffering Sen ignored Morgan as he tried to charm him into agreeing. He wanted to duck behind something solid enough to conceal them and pick up where they left off by the monument. Morgan snickered and tugged his hair.

They returned to the gallery and its newly finished freestanding wall.

"You make quick work, Otis," Sen said and grinned at the carpenter. "Paint, change, and receipt."

"That, and you gents were gone quite a while." Lars accepted the items.

Morgan rubbed his neck. "We got a little lost. But managed."

"Handily, I'd say." Bharti smiled. "We moved the paintings to the back while Otis works. There's nothing else we need until tomorrow's setup, so see you then?"

"I'll be here at one," Sen confirmed. "Until tomorrow, everyone."

Morgan waited until they were outside to ask, "Want to grab lunch?"

Sen shook his head. "No. I want to go take a nap." As he said the word, he yawned with his full body. Accumulated fatigue hit him all at once, and he went fuzzy around the edges. "I'm wiped out from… well, everything."

"Then to your apartment, and a nap it is." Morgan yawned too. "I'm parked nearby."

"No detours?"

"No detours."

Sen dozed during the short drive to his place, and then they were up the back stairs. He stumbled inside and shed shoes and clothes as he went, Morgan on his heels and sliding into bed behind him. Morgan spooned them together in a tight hold, but something kept him from falling asleep, despite being past halfway there.

"Hey." He squeezed Morgan's arm. "You had a question."

"Hmmph?" Morgan drew the blanket up and cuddled further into Sen's neck.

Sen raised his shoulder to rouse Morgan. "In the park, you had a question for me."

"Wanted to ask about staying with you until your show ends." Morgan got his hand under Sen's T-shirt and flattened it on Sen's sternum. "Give up my room at the B and B."

"It's so adorable you're asking that. Aww." Sen snuggled back into Morgan. "You're so nice. Of course, and how about you just never leave, no matter where I am."

Morgan patted Sen. "You're nice too. Sleep now."

Sen yawned again and gave in. He slept through the night and past eleven, expecting to wake and enjoy Morgan, but found only a note and a plate of fruit with one pain au chocolat.

Morgan had gone to settle his room bill and run some errands and would see Sen at the opening, but he wanted Sen to please text if he needed anything.

"A good-morning kiss?" Sen asked while he ate his pastry. He went to find his phone.

Morgan sent a kissy-face emoticon, as though prompted by Sen talking to himself. Sen sent a heart and a frowny face. Their messages overlapped, and Sen wrote back *haha* paired with another heart. He had a quick shower, packed a bag with something to wear that night in case prep ran long, got some coffee on the go, and biked to the gallery.

"There he is. Man of the hour." Lars led Sen to a folding table set up in the middle of the gallery. "Have some nibbles, choose your weapons, and Otis is here to help, so whatever you need, make use of it. Do you need anything else?"

Sen spun a Phillips-head screwdriver. "Nope, looks like a good start to me. But I'll let you know."

"I can stay and assist, or you can opt to be left the hell alone. I'm amenable either way. If the latter I'll be in the back, making last-minute calls and checking on catering and such." Lars pointed out the line of Sen's paintings against the front window. "We're agreed on how to position the pieces, and I assume you agree height as standard—sixty inches on center from the floor."

Sen nodded. "I can manage on my own, thanks." He tilted his head. "The wall is great. Bharti envisioned just the right element to set the tone and get the viewer primed."

"Isn't it just?" Lars called over to Otis, "We're admiring the wall." Then he clapped Sen's arm. "Okay, then, you know where to find me."

Otis made to get up as Lars left, but Sen waved him back. "Finish your lunch, take it easy. I've got this. Thanks."

Sen took his time. He tried several placement variations for each wall grouping and studied each. Then he decided on the look he wanted. He had the paintings up within an hour, and he took several pictures to document the process of his first solo show. Then he snapped pictures of the gallery from across the street, right outside, and endless vantage points and angles from inside.

The front windows were bare, save for his and his show's names in a sturdy, plain font. *Past Lives* was on the nose, yet open to interpretation. He liked the inside joke and couldn't wait to see Morgan's reaction.

"Lars?" he asked and knocked on the doorframe. "All set, if you want to have a look."

Lars stepped outside and looked around. "It's exactly right. I'm excited for everyone to experience this." Lars started to put the tools away. "You are welcome to stay and commune with the space until we open."

Sen considered it, but he wanted to go home for a bit. "Thanks, but I need to clean up and get changed, find my family, all that. I'll be back in plenty of time."

He finished a bit after three. That gave him a couple of hours to make it home, change, grab a bite to eat and some of Morgan before the opening at six.

Done! he texted. *See you soon.*

Morgan didn't immediately answer, and Sen told himself not to worry. They were attached on a transcendental level, but not quite at the hip. He would survive a delayed reply.

His apartment was empty. Not even Morgan's bags were there, which wasn't encouraging. Sen tried and discarded outfit options. He finally settled on what to wear, had a shower, and had begun to pace when his phone rang. His heart leapt and then fell when he saw the caller.

"Hey, Mom."

"Sweetheart, don't sound so pleased." She laughed. "We have the bus at a campsite, and we're on our way into the city. Should we meet you somewhere for early dinner before the show? Or do you need some alone time to charge up?"

Dinner with the family tempted him. He could afford to treat everyone, it would be a great distraction, and he just liked being with his parents. But his growing sense of unease about Morgan intruded, and he wouldn't be able to combat that and be sociable. Not even to fake it.

"I have to beg off and say the latter." Sen sighed. "I'm really glad you guys are here, though. And you're sticking around a few days, right? So we can visit and sightsee or whatever then."

"Yes. Your father wants to go on an eating tour, and Birch and I want to do cemetery ghost tours. I'm trying to determine if there are any combo tours— you know, a boo and chew or something."

"Mom." Sen snorfled. "Mom, that is terrible. Augh. I love it." He looked at the door when the stairs creaked, but it was only the wind. "I'll text you some restaurant recommendations. Then see you at the opening?"

"Wonderful, hon. We'll be there." She called past the phone and then everyone yelled, "Bye!"

Sen sent a short list to his mom and then sat on the ottoman in a huff. He should eat and change and get to the gallery, but he sat and stared at the wall devoid of portraits. He imagined their gazes and missed their company.

Dread and uncertainty started to weigh his belly, hot and leaden, and sweat beaded on his lip and forehead. Sen shivered. He had a fleeting thought it had all been a fever dream, and Morgan was as much a conjuring of his fantasy and imagination as the other portraits. He would get to the gallery and find the now-Morgan he'd painted the only one to exist, and he'd made up all the rest as he broke past his creative block.

"But that'd be crazy, ha-ha," he muttered and dropped his face into his hands. Crazy and terrifying, and he couldn't stay there anymore, chasing worries around.

Headed to the gallery, he texted Morgan. Then he pocketed his phone so he didn't just sit and stare at it.

Sen got to the gallery with ten minutes to spare, shook hands with the early guests Bharti and Lars had invited, and accepted congratulations on his show. But he didn't hear a word. Evening light, soft music, and his portraits hung with minimal fuss had transformed the gallery. But he didn't really appreciate any of it. Sen had an eye on the door and his phone in his hand. At quarter after six, he was ready to bolt.

The enjoyment of basking in his success and public appreciation for his paintings drained away. All he cared about was figuring out what had happened to Morgan.

Sen loitered off to the side. When movement caught his eye, wild hope surged through him. Adri and Dan came into the gallery, Phoebe cozy in a wrap against Adri's chest.

"Oh my God, Sen. This is so cool." Adri kissed his cheek and then gave him the stink eye. "I'm forgiving you for neglecting me completely, because I know you were working, and look at the result! But you don't have that excuse anymore." She waggled a finger at him and then peeked beyond the freestanding wall. "I'm so happy for you."

"Sen," Dan said and offered his hand. "I'm counting on you to explain all these to me, so I sound smart when I tell my friends about your stuff. And congrats, man."

"Thanks, you guys. It means a lot to me you came." Sen swallowed and smiled.

"Of course. Wouldn't miss it." Dan glanced around and grinned. "And I get to invite you to my opening. We signed a lease on The Place. Adri said you're about ready to skip town, but you have to come back for the grand opening."

"Of course I wouldn't miss it either," Sen echoed. He tried not to allow his distraction to take away from Dan's moment.

Phoebe did it for him as her unhappy cry cracked through the gallery.

"Awesome. And that's my cue." Dan winked and took Phoebe, almost swallowed by his huge hands, and he cradled her up under his chin. She yawned and fell back asleep. "Works every time. You guys chat. We'll have a walk around."

"Almost every," Adri said to Dan's smug expression. Then she melted as she watched them stroll the gallery.

Sen checked his phone. No messages. He rubbed his forehead and said, "Adri, Morgan—Mr. Ballard—he is real, isn't he? I realize the question is bizarre and inane, but just answer yes or no. Please."

He was overreacting. Even panicking. But he couldn't stop it.

"Yes. He definitely is. And I have e-mails and payments and all sorts of paper trail evidence supporting that." She squeezed Sen's arm. "Sweetie, what is it? You look so stressed. Did he screw you on that job you took?"

"No. It's nothing like that." Sen shook his head. "He was supposed to be here, and I haven't talked to him all day, but just last night we made plans. I can't explain it."

"Ahh." Adri chewed her lip. "So, you two got to be buds?"

"Something like that." Sen clenched his teeth and watched as someone who wasn't Morgan entered the gallery.

"You said that before." Adri's look spoke volumes. "And told me just as little then too."

Sen opened his hands. "I can't explain it. I mean that sincerely."

"Are you worried he's standing you up? After one day? That's...." Adri trailed off and then made a low noise. "I thought he wasn't your type."

"I thought he wasn't either." Sen rolled his eyes. "And we're not discussing it right now."

"It's awful that you're upset, but I'm kinda excited, not gonna lie. You like him."

Sen swallowed and couldn't look at her for a moment. "I do. A lot. And I can't stay here pretending to schmooze and care about the show while I obsess about it."

"Wow. You got it bad." She raised both fists in triumph. "Ahhh, I knew it was the perfect plan. Something just told me—beyond needing you to save my butt that day. I hope he likes you back even more, and has a nonjerk reason for not being here." She scanned the room. "How about I run interference and you go find him? I'll say you split your pants riding over on your bike, and you'll be back when you're decent again."

At Sen's blank look, Adri waved her arms. "What? It's a good, solid lie. It's too ridiculous to seem like an excuse, but embarrassing enough that people won't want to call you on it."

"Yeah, good point." Sen glanced around the freestanding wall at Lars and Bharti as they greeted people. He tapped his foot. "All right, I'm doing it. Adri, thank you. I'll be as fast as I can."

He wanted to run out the door, but he also didn't want to be completely unprofessional or disrespectful. Sen sidled next to Bharti and whispered the excuse Adri had come up with and that he was sorry and would be back as soon as he could.

Bharti's eyes twinkled with mirth as she wished him a speedy return and watched him leave—being careful not to turn his back from the wall.

Sen jumped on his bike and made a beeline for Greycote. He had no reason for doing so other than intuition, but intuition always guided him, so he didn't hesitate. That wasn't the plan. Tonight they were supposed to finally get it right. No storms—literal or figurative—no confusion or strangeness or upset. Just his paintings and knowing everything about each other and celebrating both.

"Dammit," Sen bit out. "Please be okay, and please be real." He repeated that several times as his brain churned though scenarios of what could have happened.

The ride took longer than forever, even though he sped as fast as he could pedal and disregarded almost every rule of the road. As he turned into the neighborhood, light rain began to fall. He laughed out loud in staccato beats of panic. Beams of bright red and blue light cut through the falling darkness from the direction of the house, and Sen's heart seized and shot into his throat. There were three police cars and a fire truck, and officers milling around the side entrance. The dorky Volvo was parked alongside the garage. Sen skidded to a halt and searched the house for signs of fire or damage, but he didn't see anything, so he raced to the portico.

"Morgan?" he called.

He thought he heard an answer, and he called again, but one of the officers approached and stopped him from riding to the door. Sen wobbled and tried to evade him, but the officer nabbed the handlebars.

"Whoa there, son. Let's get you off the bike and slowed down first." He steadied the bike and waited, and Sen, perforce, dismounted. "Now you just tell me who you are and what brings you here, and then we can get into the rest."

Sen glanced from the bike to the side door. "That does," he said and pointed at the figure he recognized as Morgan sitting on the ground. Then he darted away and pushed through the other officers.

"Hey," the officer yelled.

Sen ignored it, shouldered past everyone, and dropped down next to Morgan to scan for signs of trauma or some clue about what was happening.

"Morgan. Here you are." His voice shook as much as his hands when he reached out and took hold of Morgan's arm. "What happened?"

"Long story." Morgan smiled, weary but relieved. He twisted his arm in Sen's hold until Sen could grip his wrist. "Hi."

Sen concentrated on the *tha-thump* of their pulse and let out a long breath. Touching Morgan calmed him and cured the headache that had been building all day. Morgan's trembling eased under his hand.

"Are you in trouble?"

A car pulled up before Morgan could answer, and Sen shuffled around to see who had arrived. The officers talked to the man who exited the car, and he pointed at the house, then Morgan, then into a pocket. He pulled out a wallet.

The female officer on the scene walked over to them. "Well, it seems your story checks out, Mr. Ballard. You understand we had to make certain, of course."

Morgan grimaced but didn't balk. "Sure. Thank you, Officer Ngo."

Sen stood and helped Morgan, who hopped and staggered and then straightened onto one foot. Things were going faster than he could process, but Morgan was whole and there, which appeased him.

"And who are you?" she asked Sen.

"A very worried friend. I have a right to be here, and since you say his story checks out and he's cleared of whatever, it shouldn't be an issue." Sen looked at how Morgan favored his left leg. "Has he gotten any medical attention?"

"I'm fine," Morgan said. "It's okay."

The man from the car stepped over. "What a mess. I'm so sorry I couldn't get here any quicker, but at least you got a hold of me," he said to Morgan and then turned to Sen. "You must be Sen. I'm Antoine. My wife and I bought Greycote from Morgan."

Sen quit frowning at Officer Ngo to greet Antoine.

"No, no, thank you for coming. I'm sorry." Morgan held up a hand. "And please don't explain any more, or it'll ruin the kind of half surprise I still have."

"Can do, brother." Antoine chuckled. "You okay?"

"I am now." Morgan secured his arm over Sen's shoulders, and they shared a deep sigh.

Antoine looked at the house. "Did you even get in there for your phone?" At Morgan's head shake, he whistled. "Yikes. I'll be right back. Probably in the kitchen. You think?"

"Yeah."

Sen and Morgan kept silent. They waited patiently, because they were together. The rain was steady, and they watched the fire truck back up and two of the squad cars drive away. Officer Ngo and her partner stayed, talking on their radios and filling out paperwork that they eventually asked Morgan to review. He agreed with the summary and Antoine followed suit.

"Thanks for your cooperation, everyone. Have a safe rest of your evening." She nodded at each of them in turn and then joined her partner in the car, and they left.

Sen blinked away fuzzy dots as his eyes adjusted to the relative dark when all the police lights were gone. He noticed a few nosy neighbors twitching curtains or out on their porches, then dismissed them. They weren't his problem, and it wasn't like he'd ever run into them in church or anything.

Antoine walked up, carrying a large box. "Your phone, and I brought out that crate of beer you left behind. Thought you might need it." He grinned. "Let me get it in your car. Then you guys can get out of here."

Sen acted as Morgan's crutch, and they all went into the rain.

"Thanks again, Antoine. Please extend my apologies to the family for interrupting your dinner." Morgan shook hands with Antoine.

"I'm just glad it could be resolved so easily, and they let us off the hook without a lot of paperwork and red tape." He gestured to the house. "We're nearly settled in—you'll have to come for dinner before you leave town, see the place all overrun by toys and furniture and the havoc two pitties and four cats will wreak." Antoine turned his collar up. "Great to meet you, Sen. That invite goes for you too. Now I'm gonna get out of this rain. Talk soon." He dashed to his car. When he left, the driveway was quiet and dark.

"Can you drive a car?"

"Sure. I learned on a school bus, so I can probably drive a tank." Sen took the keys Morgan handed to him.

"Then you should probably drive." At Sen's look of alarm, he said, "I'm okay, but totally cramping from sitting in the damp and running around all day."

Sen got Morgan into the passenger seat, and when he stashed his bike, he saw Morgan's luggage and a few boxes. He stood for a moment next to the car, sketched a facetious wave at the neighbors, and eased down the driveway and drove without speed.

Morgan slipped his hand into Sen's and circled his thumb in Sen's palm. "Thank you for coming to find me, and I'm really glad you did, but you're missing your opening." He groaned. "This day has been the exact opposite of everything I wanted."

Sen lasted about a half second. "So what did you want? And why didn't I hear from you for hours? And why were you getting arrested—"

"Detained," Morgan corrected. "Not arrested."

"Fine. Detained. But why were you at the house at all?" Sweat and apprehension flushed across Sen's body. "I thought this whole thing wasn't about Greycote. I did research and dismissed the house or a haunting or whatever as the cause, and then there's the portraits and everything. Why would you go back there?"

"I am going to explain."

"Good." Sen pulled into a parking lot and picked a spot at the far end. "Then explain." He killed the engine and held on to the keys, because he'd started to shake.

Morgan leaned in and kissed his temple, then his cheek, then his lips.

"Sorry," Morgan whispered. "I'm sorry." He rummaged in the backseat and produced a gift box. "Something of an explanation and consolation in one."

The box fit in Sen's hand. He flashed back to the drawings Morgan had destroyed and kept, but it would be strange to be given such a thing, and the box rattled when it moved. Sen removed the lid. Nested in layers of multicolored tissue paper sat the rabbit with its sphinxlike smile he'd discovered hidden in the turret room. He gasped and tipped the rabbit into his palm, felt over the surface of its ears, its body, and the acorn, and looked to Morgan for more.

"Should we discuss this, or should I just info-dump?" Morgan rummaged in the back again and then took a drink from a travel mug.

Sen twisted in his seat so he could see Morgan. "Info-dump."

"Can do." Morgan pulled Sen's hand into his lap. "I wanted to get you something for the opening, and I've also been thinking about a memento to keep from the house—how we met and all of that. They go hand in hand, in my mind, and that's when I thought about this little guy and how perfect." He patted the rabbit with his finger and smiled ruefully. "Antoine was receptive when I asked if I could have it, especially when I explained it wasn't original to the house—it was added by a later owner on some whim. He met me at the house on his lunch hour so I could remove it. That all went fine.

"I was checked out of the B and B, and I was going to unload at your place, but you weren't there. I thought about going to the gallery, but I didn't want to interrupt, which made me realize I hadn't heard from you in a while, and that's when I noticed I didn't have my phone." Morgan massaged his brow. "I backtracked everywhere I'd been—searching for the phone, finally getting to the house—and I thought I could slip in and not bother anyone. But I tripped an alarm they just installed, and next thing I know, there's sirens and accusations. And I had to wait until Antoine could get over there to verify my story."

Morgan lifted Sen's hand and kissed it. "The cops only let me make one call. It was torture sitting there waiting, knowing you were worried and at the opening without me. I'm so sorry. But I was so glad to see you. You have no idea."

"I have some." Sen thought through Morgan's explanation and shook his head. "Wow. You have had one terrible day."

"Started amazing. Is amazing again." Morgan huffed and closed his eyes. "Oh, Sebastian. Damn."

Sen's shaking deepened, and he waved it off when Morgan apologized again. His laughter bubbled up and out, releasing the stress and anxiety from the day. Soon Morgan was laughing with him, and they continued past spontaneous humor and into tired giggles.

"After not hearing from you all day and getting to the house to find emergency lights…." Sen's hard swallow clicked. "Too many things raced through my mind I never want to think again. This is all so new and wonderful and already pretty much my everything, so it kinda got away from me. Even though I knew you were okay—you had to be—because you were still with me. In here." He tapped his heart.

"Next time I'll just find you and pester you, instead of making things easier for everyone." Morgan leaned in to rest his head on Sen's shoulder. "Happy opening?"

"Thanks." Sen held up the acorn and rabbit. "This is super, by the way. I love it, and it is perfect. Plus, A for effort."

Morgan snickered. "We'll have to make a pedestal or spindle for it to stand on. And we should really go, so you don't miss your whole opening to me being a doink." He pulled away and readjusted his seatbelt.

Sen nodded. He'd been away much longer than a change of pants should require. "Are you really okay? You don't need food or an ACE bandage or something?"

"I'm good. I feel awful and guilty and stupid, but I'm not much worse for wear." Morgan tightened his grip on Sen's hand. "Are you okay?"

"Yeah." Sen stashed the rabbit in the box and got them going again. "I care about the opening. I'm excited about it, and it's important, but it was the last thing on my mind all day with you gone. I'd give up the whole opening—the whole month—in trade for finding you."

"Good thing you already did." Morgan rubbed his face and then sighed. "Okay. I gotta say I'm sorry a last time. I'm sorry. And I can move on now. How did the start of the opening go?"

"Pretty good, I think, although I can't swear to that. I wasn't really paying attention." Sen turned into the gallery's neighborhood. "Start looking for parking."

They found a spot a few blocks away. Sen checked the time, relieved he hadn't been gone for hours and hours.

"You sure about your ankle?"

"I'm good to go under my own steam."

Sen nodded, pocketed the rabbit, and then jogged to the gallery in the rain. He burst inside, and Morgan pushed in behind him to a buzzing crowd.

Bharti came around the wall and started to clap. "The artiste himself," she said, and her clapping grew into applause.

Sen took a bow. The applause quieted, and he said, "My every apology for being delayed, and I'm so pleased you're all here. Thank you so much. I hope you appreciate the effort I went to ensuring you'd enjoy seeing the best, rather than too much, of me."

He played it just right. The ripped-pants excuse had obviously been spread, so his joke landed, and everyone greeted him with a general sense of amusement and celebration. He caught Adri's eye and gave a thumbs-up. She raised her glass of wine at him and winked.

Sen grabbed Morgan's elbow to keep him close as people started to introduce themselves and ask questions about his work. He squeezed and then let go, and Morgan nodded and stayed with him.

A familiar string bean emerged from the crowd, and Sen braced for a hug.

"Is this your boyfriend?" Birch asked. He gave Morgan a once-over. "You done good, if it is. I mean, I don't go for dudes but... whew." He whistled.

"Hey, Squirt. Nice to see you. How are you? When did you guys get in?" he rattled off.

Birch rolled his eyes. "Whatever. Good to see you too, loser. These are even pretty cool paintings. So?"

"So don't be a menace." Sen widened his eyes, and Birch made a yeah-yeah gesture.

Morgan leaned in and held out his hand. "So I'm Morgan, definitely his boyfriend. And thank you."

"Hi, good to meet you. I'm Birch, the youngest and best of his siblings. Just putting that out there, for reference." He grinned and then narrowed his eyes and said to Sen, "Suddenly I'm not believing the ripped-pants thing."

"How they got ripped doesn't make it less true," Morgan retorted without missing a beat.

Birch actually blushed a satisfying crimson from neck to scalp. "I brought this sudden need for brain bleach on myself, but that was still cruel." He made a pained sound. "I'm going to go drown this away with more fried dough." Birch got a step away and then said, "The paintings really are cool, Sen. I'm glad we got here."

"Me too. Ya brat," Sen said fondly. "He's the worst."

"I don't know. He's kinda cute." Morgan shrugged. "Gives me an idea of what you were like, and I'm here for that."

Sen tugged Morgan into the main gallery. "Let's find my parents."

The gallery wasn't big, and his parents were poised to pounce, so it didn't take long. They crowed at seeing him and embraced him.

"Mom, Dad, this is Morgan. Morgan, this is Gemma and Luke, my parents." Sen indicated everyone in order.

"Wonderful to meet you both," Morgan said and offered his hand.

She waved his hand away and pulled him into a hug. Sen's dad shook Morgan's hand.

"Look at you." His mom grabbed Sen's arms. "No more ennui. Completely cured, I'd say." She smiled. "As are your worries about the rest?" She meant Morgan.

"The rest proved to be amazing." Sen hugged her. "Oh, it's good to see you guys. Thanks for coming."

"Of course. We wouldn't miss it for anything. It's wonderful." She whispered, "He's a hunk. And I heard in the air he's rich—unimportant, of course, save for the glorious freedom that allows. New Orleans was kind."

Sen laughed. "Incredibly. Thanks, Mom." He pulled back. "What do you think of the paintings?"

His dad pointed at the stormy couple. "She has the exact same expression of defiant stubbornness you got as a kid when you were in trouble but thought yourself in the right." He grinned at Morgan. "They do say an artist puts a bit of themselves in every work, whether on purpose or not. Take that as proof."

Morgan grinned back. "Oh, I do. Trust me."

"Very funny, ha-ha." Sen looked at them and shook his head, but he joined their laughter soon enough. "Astute, Dad. Any other incisive observations?"

"I need to spend more time with each of them. Starting in reverse order." His dad pulled a mini composition book and pen from his lapel. "But I'll be ready then."

"Reverse order?" Sen was curious what he meant.

"Yeah. Start there and then back around to the front." Dad twirled a finger, indicating the back of the freestanding wall, then encompassing a counter-clockwise circle of the gallery to the front door.

Sen nodded.

His dad already saw and understood a lot about the portraits. "I look forward to talking about your time with them."

"How about over drinks and late dinner?" His mom eyed the reception area. "Munchies and a glass of white wine are nice, but I'm gonna need a bottomless hurricane and gumbo for this."

"Sounds good to me." Morgan got out his phone. "I'll even make a reservation at a great 'bottomless hurricane and gumbo' place I know."

She gave Sen an approving look and then took his dad's offered arm.

"Shall we?" His dad asked, and he walked them away.

"So, those are my parents," Sen said. "I should have warned you they were coming."

"Didn't you? I thought you had."

"Maybe I did? I can't remember. Also I already can't distinguish what I've actually told you out loud and what I just accept as being perfectly fine because of the whole 'sympatico in every way, soul mate' thing." Sen beamed. "Not to put too fine a point on it."

Morgan stroked his chin. "That seems rather broad to me." He squeezed Sen's shoulder. "Be right back."

Bharti and Lars appeared the moment Morgan was gone.

"You're a hit." Bharti pecked Sen's cheek. "After this show keep us in the loop of what you're working on. I'm sure we'd love to showcase more."

"I'm a hit? Thank goodness. And thank you for the opportunity. It's been a thrill and an honor. And we can certainly discuss my future work," Sen agreed.

The visions and inspiration for the portraits had come to an end—at least for a while—but ideas for new pieces swirled in him. He wanted to do some multimedia, some collage, and some found-object stuff, and a lot of those ideas were grounded in the illustrations he'd done and the single box of kept lifetime treasures he and Morgan shared.

"Excellent." Lars pulled in a breath and fanned his fingers. "And already a sale."

"Wow. Really?" Sen had forgotten that possibility as he prepared for the show and then was distracted by the day going sideways. "That's great." He hoped Morgan wouldn't mind their portraits going to a stranger's collection.

Bharti read his tone enough to say, "It's always tough to part with a piece, I know. But the joy in letting the pieces go to inspire and enrich someone else's life balances that out. Plus that whole paycheck thing."

Sen chuckled. "Yeah, doesn't hurt."

"There's a local museum with interest in the earthy couple." Lars frowned. "They're not sure they can meet the price."

"How neat. That'd be awesome, to have a piece there." Sen considered it. "I'm willing to negotiate or flat-out cut my rate for them. I'd rather that than have it go into storage or everything go to private collectors."

"Me too. We're agreed." Bharti nodded. "We'll get the best for everyone with it. Ah, here's the curator. Time to mingle."

Lars let her go ahead a step. "Good show, Sen. It's a pleasure to have our faith in that first glimpse of your series here so well rewarded."

"Likewise. Thanks again." Sen closed his eyes and felt Morgan approach and stand beside him.

"A toast." Morgan had two glasses of champagne. "To past lives." His eyes twinkled.

"And future ones," Sen added. He took a glass and clinked them together.

Morgan nodded in the direction of Lars and Bharti. "Are they happy with the outcome?"

"Yes. I'd say unequivocally yes. Which is a relief." Sen tugged Morgan into moving. "I want to see which one sold."

Morgan stayed silent and followed as Sen walked past the portrait of the pair with frills and pearls on the short wall, the stormy couple hung on the brick, the earthy couple and the star girls on the long wall, and their present day portraits on the backside of the freestanding wall. None of those were labeled sold, leaving other-Morgan and his young companion.

Sen should remember to insist that those two be labeled as not for sale. Being ready to share them with an audience and parting with them forever were very different things.

He regarded the portraits—the first two that had found him and started him on his journey—and reached for Morgan's hand as it moved to hold his.

There was a bright orange tag added to the title plate on the wall. "SOLD" was printed in bold lettering across the top, and under that Bharti had written *M. Ballard*.

"I don't mind you selling the rest, but these belong with us." Morgan tightened his grip on Sen's hand.

Sen shook his head. "I would have given you these."

"I know." Morgan stared at Sen in that particular way that had stolen into Sen's heart, as though they were on the verge of a kiss—or were already kissing, everywhere touching, and the only two people who had ever lived.

Sen shivered with his full body, and they did kiss. He saw all the portraits—the people he painted—in motion, in place, in time. Then Morgan pulled back and smiled.

"Thanks." Sen leaned against Morgan. "Where are we going to put them?"

Morgan snickered. "I have a little place. It's no luxury 'cabin' in Jackson Hole, but it's permanent and ours. They can go there?"

"Works for me. Where is your little place?"

"Just outside Santa Fe. It's an historic adobe." Morgan tilted the champagne flute back and forth. "I wrestled with there or someplace near the ocean, but that won out. Something about the light there just gets me."

Sen believed in the unbelievable when it came to Morgan. "You know, I've always wanted to live in New Mexico. I have since leaving home."

"How about that? Nice. We can go by there on our way out of town to wherever next." They stood in contented silence until Morgan hugged Sen to himself and moved away. "I'm monopolizing you. Go schmooze. I'm gonna eat some cheese and talk with your folks."

They stood a while longer, and then Sen let go of Morgan's hand. "Okay. Okay, I'm going."

He glanced over his shoulder to smile at Morgan, and then he went to Bharti to be introduced to the museum people.

CHAPTER EIGHTEEN

TAXIING, SO gotta go. Will text when landed.

Okay! Stay hydrated and stretch and enjoy.

Sen reread his mom's text and then turned off his phone. He sat back in the chair and peered out the window.

"Ready?"

"Yeah." Sen clenched his fists as the engines got louder and the plane started picking up speed on the runway.

Morgan ran his fingers along Sen's arm and tickled Sen's wrist. "And are you okay?" he said into Sen's ear above the screaming turbines.

"I'm super great." Sen licked his lips and watched the world turning into a blur outside the window. "Excited and a lot freaked by this whole flying thing, but still, super great."

"Imagine how many times you'd have flown by now if that bus had wings." Morgan grinned.

Sen managed a wan smile. "Oh, probably only a couple hundred." He chewed his lips. "Funny, isn't it? I've done nothing but travel my whole life, but I've never flown."

"You had to leave something for us to discover and explore together." Morgan took hold of his hand, leaned close, and kissed his neck. Sen tilted to give Morgan more access and watched the world drop away under them as Los Angeles rapidly turned into a sprawling mosaic.

The plane clanked and groaned, and Sen flinched, even though he knew the noises were normal landing gear and wing adjustments.

Morgan opened Sen's fist into his hand and stroked his thumb over Sen's palm. "I reserved a weekend at a campsite. The stars over the ocean are incredible."

Sen relaxed by increments and nodded. "That sounds good."

"It will be." Morgan kissed Sen's temple. "Just think about the last time we camped. That'll distract you."

It did.

After the close of his successful show they shipped their stuff ahead and then drove to Santa Fe. The dorky Volvo offered a surprisingly comfortable night's sleep—when filled with pillows and blankets and the two of them. They stretched an eighteen-hour drive into a week, hiked peak trails, stargazed and bird-watched, and stopped far too often to park somewhere hidden and make out and make love.

When they arrived in Santa Fe, they unpacked and intermingled their belongings. The portraits were a perfect fit in Morgan's home. Their home. Morgan hadn't ever lived there. He had bought it during a restoration project, and something about it made him unwilling to leave it behind.

The modestly sized house consisted of a floor and a half, with an open layout on the first floor and three large rooms above. Like Greycote, it was a perfectly restored and mostly empty shell. Sen looked forward to finally nesting somewhere and making it theirs, between jobs and adventures or whenever they decided to stop for a while.

Sen invited Morgan to snoop in his case of life treasures, and Morgan retrieved the old suitcase. Together they pored over their artifacts and keepsakes. Morgan laughed when he saw the *Aloha* keychain.

Sen packed it with them on this trip.

For three nights in Santa Fe, he and Morgan embraced in the desert and watched the sunsets. Sen soaked in its vibrations and colors, and listened to Morgan's heartbeat against his ear.

Morgan had proudly noted the room with awesome light, ready to become a studio, and that the five-acre property had plenty of room for the school bus. Sen gladly kissed Morgan senseless as a reward.

Then they hit the road and drove from Santa Fe to Los Angeles, although they detoured to see the Grand Canyon, Mojave, and Joshua Tree.

"We're nearly at altitude. Should be smooth sailing from here," the pilot said over the sound system. "The radar is showing clear skies for the duration. Our crew will be around to refresh you shortly, and my copilot and I will point out anything interesting down below along the way. Otherwise, sit back and enjoy your ride to the Aloha State."

The airplane banked and the last of visible land gave way to ocean and clouds. Sen's unease disappeared, replaced by awe and wonder at the sight.

"Wow. It looks like a Georgia O'Keeffe." Sen grinned at Morgan. He tracked Morgan's gaze from his eyes to his lips and shifted to lean over the armrest.

Morgan smiled and couldn't seem to resist kissing him, which worked out well, because Sen couldn't resist either.

"Hot towels?" Terrance—their cabin steward—politely interrupted. He gave them each one. "And here are menus for our in-flight meals. Now, what would you gentleman like to drink?"

Morgan cleared his throat. "More champagne, some water, and cranberry juice, please."

Terrance looked at Sen.

"Same," he said. "Thank you."

"You have about fifteen minutes until I return." Terrance took their towels, winked, and whisked them away.

Sen turned his attention to the menu. "This all actually sounds good. My first time flying, and it's first class to a tropical paradise. I feel like I'm starting from quite an unreasonably high bar."

"Eh, why mess around? You're the first person I've dated and fallen in love with. And if you think about it, you're my first kiss, first time…." Morgan trailed off meaningfully.

"First and last." Sen tingled all over. When he caught Morgan's warm expression, he leaned back against the window. "Okay. Conversational left turn, or it'll be another first I want no part of."

Morgan's grin turned predatory. "Maybe on the return flight."

"Or never. Never works too." Sen elbowed Morgan. "Stop giving me the business. You're not interested in that any more than I am."

"There are downsides to this whole connection-rapport-amazing thing." Morgan sounded put-upon. "So, back to that left turn. You were saying?"

"I know you said you told your father you're bringing me to meet him and everything, but are you sure he's okay with it? He's not too disappointed or shocked to want to deal with it already? I mean, I am the first person you're bringing to meet him, and you've never dated guys before or talked about liking guys, even. And I'm also just a bit nervous."

"Don't be." Morgan shook his head. "Wait. That's not really fair. How about, be nervous but also be reassured he's fine with it and really looking forward to seeing us."

Sen nodded. "I didn't give you any lead-in to meeting my folks, but they knew all about you, and I knew they'd be cool. And I knew you were cool with it—just by knowing, you know." He laughed. "Aha. And can I say *know* a few more times?"

"If you apply yourself, I bet so." Morgan snickered. "Your parents are great. Just to be clear on that."

"Good to know."

Morgan groaned. "And, contrary to assumption, the guys in the actual army doing actual soldiering don't give a damn about anything except if someone's a crap soldier. Dad's career predates openness in the military, but he's still seen everything. He's tough to shock."

"Is that in my favor?" Sen raised a brow.

"Duh. But yes, really." Morgan squeezed Sen's hand. "He's always respected my choices, and besides, I think he's going to be more relieved than anything. As you say, I've never talked about dating a guy—or anyone for that matter—much less being serious enough to bring anyone home. He's probably planning where to take you for a celebratory beer. I told him you're my heart's desire, and I'm spending the rest of eternity with you. He's happy for me."

Sen's insides fluttered. "Well. Put it that way."

Morgan kissed the back of Sen's hand. He nodded, let go, and then stood. He rooted for something in the overhead compartment and handed Sen a folder.

The plain front gave nothing away. Inside were building specs and histories of the land tucked behind a map of a neighborhood in Buffalo.

"That's an entire city block the Frosts just secured." Morgan pointed it out on the map. "All historic. There's a warehouse, a brewery, and storefronts with boarding rooms above. They've been derelict for decades."

"Sounds cool. Are you working this one?"

Morgan nodded. "Overseeing the whole thing—if I accept."

"Why wouldn't you?"

"No reason other than we haven't discussed it." Morgan smiled. "I guess I can alert Nina I'll take it when we land."

"You bet you can. My big successful soul mate, I'm so proud of you." Sen flipped through the pages and imagined the buildings and the setting based on the grainy, photocopied photos. He had to do it one-handed, because Morgan took hold of his other hand again. Sen didn't mind. "How long will it take?"

"We'll be there a year, maybe eighteen months." Morgan plucked an advance calendar from the papers. "This is the estimate. Could run long— likely will—but there's the off chance it could go short. After Hawaii we'll have time to stop in Santa Fe, if you want, then on to Buffalo."

"I've never been to Buffalo." Sen studied the map.

"Me either." Morgan tugged loose another map of the region that had Buffalo as a mere pinpoint. He ran his finger around from New York City, to Portland, and then back to Buffalo. "Where should we go after this?"

"Wherever the signs take us. And your job." Sen traced past the Great Lakes into Canada. "But if I wind up having to choose, then somewhere in Europe."

"Dad was stationed in Germany, so we were there a stint, but I haven't seen past that."

"Then Italy. I want to see Brunelleschi's dome." Sen followed the watercourse back into the States. "We have to go to Niagara Falls."

"In all seasons—see it mobbed by tourists and frozen over. Oh, and try ice fishing. And seeing that dome and all of Florence is on my bucket list, so. Sold." Morgan bumped him. "This means you can keep working with me, doing illustrations for the project."

"I had thought of that. And let's be honest, it's probably the only reason the Frosts offered you the job."

Morgan hummed. "Zero doubt."

"Should we buy something to restore too? Or rent? I'll need a studio space—I can't use the job site for my stuff." Sen paused. "Am I getting ahead of things?"

"Nope. You should hear my mind racing over the same." Morgan snickered. "Maybe you do. I thought after Hawaii we can investigate and decide on the best course."

"That is a good thought, and you're good for thinking it." Sen leaned on Morgan's shoulder and studied a picture of the warehouse taken from a distance. "These upper floors with all those windows wrapping around the corners would make awesome studio space."

"Ah. See? You *do* read my mind." Morgan ran his fingertip along Sen's hand, and Sen shivered. "I want a good section of the whole renovation to be used as community space—artists' spaces, outreach, affordable housing. We can offset that decision by making it mixed with luxury condos and primo office leasing."

Sen closed his eyes and imagined it as Morgan spoke. He could see it clearly.

"It's going to be wonderful." He couldn't wait to start drawing the illustrations and continuing his own work. He planned to paint a series of whimsical rabbits.

Morgan took the folder and laced their hands together.

"Everything is," Morgan whispered and kissed Sen's brow.

Sen sighed, suffused with contentment, and agreed.

ELLE BROWNLEE has always followed her creative, adventuring spirit.

Growing up she loved westerns and taking long hikes. On these explorations she'd craft miniature worlds with moss and rocks while making up stories about everything that happened there. This often included dashing cowboy heroes. As an adult, not a lot has changed. She still loves westerns, long hikes, and allowing her imagination to roam. She also loves spending time with family and friends, rooting for her baseball team, rainy days in autumn, and the perfect cup of tea (black, steeped extra strong, with milk—please!).

Her romances feature flawed but relatable characters in immersive settings, told with wit, tenderness, and a sly note of sarcasm. Though a cynic in many ways, Elle believes love can conquer all. Every story is a little bit naughty, a whole lot of nice, and will always end with happily ever after.

Elle currently lives in New York City, where she maintains her miniature worlds in terrariums and writing. She's so thankful to be able to share her work with a growing audience, and especially grateful to have you reading along.

Website: www.ellebrownlee.com/index.html
Facebook: www.facebook.com/elle.brownlee
Twitter: @ellebrownlee
E-mail: brownlee.elle@gmail.com

EMERGENCY
CONTACT

ELLE BROWNLEE

When Liam's best friend has to leave town on business, he asks for a favor—be an emergency contact for his cousin who is new in town. Liam doesn't think twice before he accepts. He's great with numbers and confidently plays the odds, because nobody ever uses those emergency contacts, right? Wrong. The very next Sunday, cousin Garrett shows up at Liam's apartment, fresh-faced, devastatingly gorgeous, and nothing like Liam had dismissively assumed.

Garrett arrived in New York City hoping to make it in the modeling world, and Liam isn't sure what to do with him. While he eventually warms to welcome the distraction, he's not prepared to have his steady, predictable world overturned. Liam is sure Garrett will soon tire of him and find someone closer in age and less eager for the quiet, settled life Liam prefers. But Garrett is too sweet-natured and naïve to recognize Liam's dismissal, and he's not as shallow as Liam presumes.

Although Garrett sees a future for the two of them, Liam manages to push him away. It is only then Liam sees the Garrett-shaped hole in his life.

www.dreamspinnerpress.com

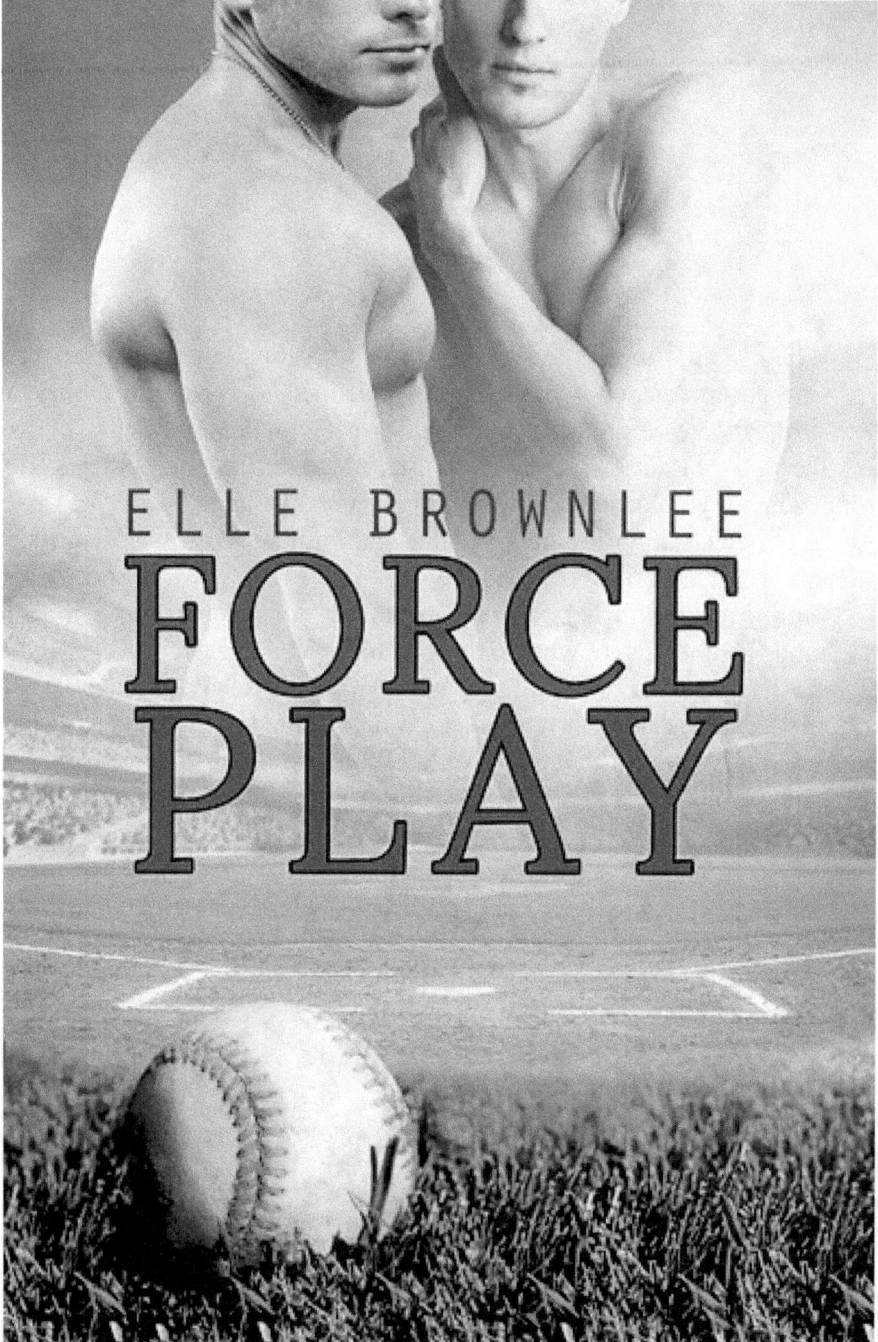

ELLE BROWNLEE

FORCE PLAY

Professional baseball player Harmon "Hawk" Kiel was a rookie sensation with dazzling talent and an arrogant attitude to match. But he's hit his sophomore slump, and his natural talent seems to have deserted him, along with the confidence of his team and the media's approval. During the All-Star Break, he hits rock bottom, gets careless, and sensational pictures of him at gay clubs go viral. All at once he's outed—and out of a job.

When he's dealt to the Loggerheads, a worse-than-terrible expansion team in Charleston, South Carolina, he can't imagine he'll get a warm reception—nor does he particularly want one. But it's the only chance at redemption he has.

There he meets Caleb Jackson, a former player who's part of the Loggerheads organization, someone who tries to be the friend Harmon so desperately needs. But Caleb has a secret too, one more gut-wrenching than anything Harmon can imagine. Together they try to put the past behind them, rediscover their love of the game, and maybe even find the love of their lives.

www.dreamspinnerpress.com

TERE MICHAELS
ELLE BROWNLEE
ELIZAH J. DAVIS

ONE NIGHT EVER AFTER

Just a Stranger by Elle Brownlee

The excitement of meeting a stranger in a club can't be beat. Loud bass sets the rhythm to Michael Wiercinski's primal urges as he flirts with Andrew, a cute guy offering the promise of a hot night with no strings, no complications. Still, when their night is done, Michael admits there was something about Andrew that left him wanting more. Months go by with no sign of Andrew until Michael moves back home to help after his father's heart attack. Once there, Michael is completely amazed to find Andrew Lucas living in his hometown. Despite surprising "complications" in Andrew's life, Michael vows to take advantage of this second chance to make Andrew more than just a stranger.

www.dreamspinnerpress.com